D1332179

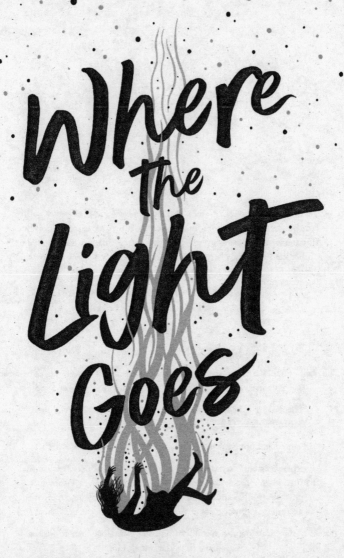

Where the Light Goes

SARA BARNARD

WALKER
BOOKS

First published in Great Britain 2023 by Walker Books Ltd
87 Vauxhall Walk, London SE11 5HJ

2 4 6 8 10 9 7 5 3 1

Text © 2023 Sara Barnard

The right of Sara Barnard to be identified as author of this work has been asserted in accordance with the Copyright, Designs and Patents Act 1988

This book has been typeset in Causten Round, Centaur MT Pro, Courier, Fairfield, Gilroy, Helvetica, Source Sans Pro and Wingdings

Printed and bound by CPI Group (UK) Ltd, Croydon CR0 4YY

British Library Cataloguing in Publication Data: a catalogue record for this book is available from the British Library

ISBN 978-1-5295-0913-7

www.walker.co.uk

MIX
Paper | Supporting
responsible forestry
FSC
www.fsc.org
FSC® C171272

A Note on Content

This book addresses the grief that arises from the loss of a loved one who has died by suicide.

Please be aware that the following pages therefore contain discussions of – and references to – suicide, grief and related issues throughout.

A list of further resources is available at the back of this book.

For Anna,
who lit the way.

Imagine you pick up the phone. The house phone, the one you don't usually bother picking up because why would anyone call you on the house phone, but it's weirdly early for anyone to be calling, and you're the only one up, standing in your kitchen, barefoot, eating toast, so when the phone rings you lean over and answer it.

Imagine you do that, just answer the phone. It's a Tuesday morning in June, days into what promises to be a long, lazy summer. Your exams are over, and so is the stress. You should have chosen a better breakfast in celebration; something with chocolate, or some kind of syrup. When you answer the phone, that is what you're thinking about.

Imagine that phone call is about to change your whole world, but you don't know it right up until it happens. Your whole life is about to stop making sense. Everything coherent and logical and linear is about to collapse.

Imagine you pick up the phone and your life and your world and everything you've ever known   s h a t t e r s
    into
        hundreds and thousands
          (of thousands of thousands)

              of

        p
              e
          i
                  c
                      e
                          s

GONE

The End — Tuesday

Andrew Saul @AndySaulJourno

BREAKING Lizzie Beck dead. More to come.

@frranchez Wtf???

@louise41stone No way

@rainbowm00n Fuck, no

@stanleylebulldog Um, SOURCE?

@wesleyfred4ever Got to be a hoax. She's 21. Verify or GTFO

[SEE MORE REPLIES]

12.46 pm

Breaking News UK @breakingnewsofficial

Lizzie Beck, member of British girl band The Jinks, has died at the age of 21, her family confirms.

@jonestim97 Shiiiiiit did she kill herself then?

@wiseoldferret Well she didn't die of old age, did she?

TRENDING IN UNITED KINGDOM

#1 Lizzie Beck

TRENDING WITH RIPLizzie, RIPLizzieBeck

849K TWEETS

@kerrysouthlee Shit this is so horrible, so sad. RIP Lizzie Beck.

@ninestopshome Fuck, it's true about Lizzie Beck? That poor girl. 21 is nothing at all.

@forthehijinks Can't even type. Devastated. Fuck this world. #RIPLizzie

> **@thisjinksygirl** What happened though?? Loads of people saying must be suicide but do we actually know that yet? #LizzieBeck

> > **@balebefore** Drugs, I reckon. Wasn't she in rehab like twice? #LizzieBeck

> > > **@lincolnlodger** Or murder. Wasn't her body found at Leo Peters' house?

> > > > **@balebefore** Er... are you accusing someone of murder, mate?

> > > > > **@lincolnlodger** Just asking a question. Mate.

@jonhawl33 Brass neck of the lot of you pretending you give a fuck about Lizzie Beck now she's dead

---

@backtoparris Can everyone just stop all the speculation? Think of her poor family. #RIPLizzie

TWEETS I DIDN'T SEND

(Even though I scrolled through Twitter for hours and read every single tweet I could find.)

Her name is Beth.
Her name is Beth.
Her name is Beth.

Her name   was   Beth.

WHAT I DO THE DAY
OF MY SISTER'S DEATH

- Scream
- Cry
- Scream and cry and scream and cry
- Lie on the floor in my mother's arms while we both wail
- Watch my father's feet as he puts his boots on and leaves the house to go and do things the father does when his daughter has been found dead
    - Words like "identify"
    - And "coroner"
    - And "inform"
- Brush my teeth
- Listen to my mum making call after call to everyone we love, frantic and calm at the same time – very weird – because this has to be done fast fast fast before someone who loved Beth – really loved Beth, not *Lizzie Beck* – finds out that she's dead from a tweet
    - She says, "It's Beth"
    - She says, "She's gone"
        - Or "She's passed"
        - Or "We've lost her"
        - Or "She's … yes…"
    - She doesn't say, "She's dead"
    - And she definitely doesn't say, "She killed herself"
    - But even though she doesn't say the words, she still tells them, somehow, and when she hangs up, I know they know
    - She turns and sees me
    - She says, "Oh, Emmy." Just that, nothing else

- Watch from my window as the journalists gather outside our house, knock on our door, stand in clusters on our driveway
- Hide in my room
- Open Twitter, wait for the storm to break
  - Watch the first tweet come in, the second, the third
  - Then 100, 1000, too many to count
- Scroll
- Scroll
- Scroll
- Ignore the WhatsApp notifications as they start filling my phone screen, the people I love, the people I should have told already but haven't, because to be honest I forgot that they exist, that there is anything but this shock, this grief, this pain
  - My best friend, my boyfriend
    - Who are still here, who love me
- Turn off my notifications
- Hear people in my house, more wailing (women) and talking (men)
- Go downstairs and see pizza boxes
  - Mum says I have to eat something so I
- Pick all the pepperoni slices off an entire pizza and eat them one by one
  - Then I am sick
  - And I cry some more
  - Ask who the man standing outside our door is *(a security guard)*
  - Ask who sent us a security guard *(the band's management)*
  - So quickly? *(it had to be quick, the journalists — if you can call them that — are ruthless)*
  - Why do we need a security guard? *(oh, Emmy, I can't — please, I can't deal with questions right now, I—)*
  - Security from what? *(from ... the noise)*
- Leave Mum in the kitchen so I don't have to see her break down again
- Watch the six o'clock news

- *"Good evening. Lizzie Beck, member of British girl band The Jinks, has died. She was twenty-one."*
- A clip of the first "Great British Sounds" audition, the sound fading as the colour turns to black and white
- A live reporter outside Leo Peters' house, telling the world that this is where her "body" was "found", as if this information is relevant or necessary
- A series of tributes from people all over the music industry, talking about how "devastating" it is, how "tragic", "what a loss", "what a talent", these people who never defended her when she was alive to hear it
- I can't bear it
- I can't bear it
- Cry
- Cry
- Cry

MY SISTER IN NUMBERS

Instagram followers: 5.1M
Twitter followers: 689,923
Years on this earth: 21
Years of celebrity: 5
"Last warnings" from management: 4
BRIT awards: 3
Stints in rehab: 2
Little sisters: 1

MY SISTER IN WORDS

Talentless

Embarrassing

Shameful

Spirited

Wild

Junkie

Talented

Sad

RIP

Bold

Slut

Troubled

Tragic

Beautiful

Shameless

Heartbreaking

Attention whore

I can hear my mother crying somewhere in the house.

My dad's low voice.

This is our family now. The three of us.

For as long as I can remember, our family was

Beth at the centre and us in her orbit.

Satellites to the star.

And now there's just …
darkness.

Except there's not. (I tell myself this.)

Because we're still alive, which means there's tomorrow.

For us, there's tomorrow.

1 DAY GONE

Tomorrow (morning)

Official statement from
The Jinks

We are utterly <u>devastated</u> at the loss of <u>our friend,</u> bandmate and <u>sister,</u> Lizzie Beck. We are focusing on supporting each other and <u>Lizzie's family</u> during this dreadful time. We are so thankful for the support and love that is being shown to all of us by our fans – we love you all so much and we're so grateful. As we're sure you can understand, we as a band are going to take some time to grieve, comfort each other and try to come to terms with this tragedy. We ask that the press and the public respect our privacy – and especially the privacy of Lizzie's family – at this time. We are <u>heartbroken.</u>

Lizzie, <u>we love you,</u> and we will miss you every day.

Jodie, Aiya and Tam
THE JINKS

LIES. ALL LIES.

Official joint statement from Electric Records, Skyscape Management, and NorthWest Entertainment

The death of Lizzie Beck has come as a tremendous shock to everyone who has worked with, <u>nurtured</u> and <u>supported Lizzie</u> and The Jinks over the past five years. Our deepest condolences and thoughts are with her family and friends. We are focused now on supporting Lizzie's bandmates, Jodie Soto-Hahn, Aiyana Mehta and Tamryn Lord, and <u>providing whatever assistance we can to her family</u> during this unimaginable time. The planned relaunch of the band has been postponed indefinitely, and all booked engagements, including interviews of any kind, have been cancelled.

For all press enquiries, please contact Melissa Sandford, publicist, at *melsandford@electricrecords.co.uk*

SELF. SERVING. LIES.

They're all LYING.

Talking like they loved Beth
    worried about her
        cared about her

FUCK THAT.

They wanted her out. They wanted her gone.

They
        kicked
                her
                        out
                                of
                                        the
                                              band.

The band she STARTED.

The band that wouldn't exist if it weren't for her.

"The relaunch is postponed." I BET IT FUCKING IS. The relaunch that was going to go ahead WITHOUT BETH. The Jinks with three members instead of four.

I bet they're glad they hadn't announced it yet. Bet they're glad that people didn't know that those RUTHLESS UNGRATEFUL HEARTLESS BITCHES had ganged up on my sister and KICKED HER OUT OF HER OWN BAND and now

She's   Fucking   DEAD

It wasn't official yet, oh no. Because Beth FOUGHT. She wasn't going to roll over and let them steal her band from her, kick her to the kerb like a dog.

It had been all negotiation and ultimatums and promises. She would have won them round, I know it.

Now they've got what they wanted, haven't they? And even better, they got what they wanted without any nasty headlines about them, no trolling on social media about how pathetic they are, no chink in their armour of being THE GOOD ONES in the band while Beth soaked up all the hate, all the abuse.

Now she's gone and they get to be sad.

They get to say they're "sorry" but not for what they should be sorry for.

They get to say they loved her.

They get to call her their sister.

She wasn't your sister.
She was mine.

I say to Dad, "Can they do that?"

"Do what?"

"Pretend none of it happened? Them trying to get rid of Beth?"

A look on his face like he'd swallowed pain. "Not now, Emmy."

"It's not right."

"It's business. It's the music industry."

"You think it's OK?"

"I don't think they should start sharing their dirty secrets with the world, no. I don't see what that would achieve."

"But Beth—"

"There's no need to taint the band," he says. "There's still a chance they could carry on without her. Why deny them that?"

Me, speechless. My head going, *Carry on without her. Carry on without her. Carry on without her.*

Unthinkable. Monstrous.

Dad is still talking. "Do you really want the world to know that Beth had been thrown out of the band? Do you think that would make her look good?"

"It's the truth."

"Em." Gritted teeth, eyes closing for too long. Breath in through his flared nostrils, like a horse. He says quietly, "There's a lot you don't understand."

And isn't that the truth.

His eyes open and he looks at me, sudden and piercing. "You haven't posted about this, have you?"

"What do you mean, 'posted'? *Online?* Of course not!"

"Good. Don't."

"I know that!" How can he think I need to be told this? The number one rule in the world of the famous is "no comment". Literally, don't comment. Don't say it in a phone call, don't post it on the internet. Don't risk exposing secrets, don't tell anyone your feelings, just don't say a word.

I was eleven when Beth got famous, and sometimes my parents act like I'm still that young. Like I'm not sixteen, like I'm not literally a student at Shona Lee School for the Performing Arts, where learning things like this is basically part of the curriculum.

Beth did it too. Coddled me.

"Have you posted *anything*?" Dad asks.

"*No*, Dad!" And what would it matter if I did, anyway? All my accounts are private.

"Good," he says again. He hesitates, then shakes his head, sighing. "Thank you," he adds, quietly. "I know I don't have to worry about you. You're a smart girl."

Maybe this should feel good, but it doesn't. It just makes me think of how Beth used to pour seemingly every innermost thought onto the internet for the world at large to feed on, how she was a lot of things but never smart in the way Dad wanted her to be, how he did have to worry about her, all the time, and how there will never be a post from her ever again. Her last post already exists, and I know what it is, but when I think about it my entire heart convulses with pain.

"Thank you," Dad says again.

Dad is part of The Jinks' management team.

Before, he was an IT consultant for a water company. Before that, before Mum and then Beth and then me, he was in a band called Owlface. They played weddings and corporate gigs and never had a record deal. He became the unofficial manager for The Jinks before their "Great British Sounds" audition. When they won and got big, they also got a team of managers, and Dad, now official, got a salary.

A big one.

(Bigger than the band got.)

He was part of the reason they couldn't just get rid of Beth from the band without a fight. Dad fought for her. (And his job.)

Now I don't know what there is left to fight for, but he's still fighting.

Obituary
Lizzie Beck

Lizzie Beck, founding member of "Great British Sounds"-winning girl band The Jinks, has died aged twenty-one after taking her own life.

A young star of the British music industry, Beck co-founded The Jinks aged just fifteen with best friend Jodie Soto-Hahn and their two friends Aiyana Mehta and Tamryn Lord. The band won the hearts of viewers and topped the popular vote in the high-profile BBC1 talent show less than a year later. The Jinks' subsequent string of hit singles cemented Beck's fame, while her straight-talking attitude earned her infamy in numerous tabloids.

From the outset, Beck attracted the most press and social media attention of all the bandmates, quickly forming a reputation for being outspoken and, occasionally, outrageous. Her response to "Great British Sounds" judge and industry legend Ricardo Patmore – who criticized the band during the show's semi-final for wearing "distractingly revealing clothes" – "Dude, we're sixteen, that's on you" was one of the show's most memorable moments, and remains a favourite meme in certain feminist circles five years on.

The Jinks secured their win despite resistance from within the competition and the wider music industry, and amid calls to drop the group entirely in favour of a performer deemed more suitable for "The BBC Proms", where the show's winners were scheduled to perform as part of the prize. Unbowed by this pressure and perhaps boosted by the ensuing controversy, The Jinks' fame only grew after winning the show, bucking the trend of talent show winners fading into obscurity, with three number one singles and a number one album in just eighteen months. They also won three BRIT awards, two of which were in recognition of their third and most successful single "Daylights", co-written by Beck and Soto-Hahn.

Despite the success of her musical career, Beck frequently garnered more headlines for her personal life, in particular for her relationship with TV personality Leo Peters, and also the reported frictions between members of The Jinks. Beck regularly addressed these stories on her own social media accounts, attracting millions of followers who enjoyed her candour. Despite being the source of frequent tabloid controversy, Beck was supported and beloved by loyal young fans, to whom she was known for being warm and responsive.

Off-screen, Beck struggled with her mental health, about which she spoke openly and frankly, most notably in the podcast "Mind & Soul", where she revealed she had been battling an eating disorder for several years, in addition to anxiety and depression. Beck also spent time in recovery for addiction and, after a second admittance to rehab last year, the band was placed on an indefinite hiatus. Recent reports in the press suggested that the band had reunited and were beginning to record new material.

She is survived by her parents, Ellen and Malcolm Beckwith, and sister.

Elizabeth Jane Beckwith, known as Lizzie Beck, singer, BORN 21st September 1996; DIED 12th June 2018.

And sister.

It smarts. It stings. It aches.

But it's true.

I want to be more than that – I've always wanted to be more than that – but it's the truest thing about me.

And sister.

I don't even get a name.

But why should I?

Every trace of me is a trace of her.

And now she's

1 DAY GONE
Tomorrow (afternoon)

We've been assigned a Family Liaison Officer.

(Which until today I didn't know was a thing.)

Her name is DC Dhanji, but – she says – we can call her Sufiya.

Actually, what she says is, "Please, call me Sufiya."

Just like that – "Please".

Sufiya's job is to look after us, basically.

Explain difficult police stuff to us.

Be the *liaison* between us and the police while they investigate.

(Even though she is also a police officer, which is confusing.)

"Investigate what?" I ask.

I blurt it out, really. It comes out while she's mid-sentence, but she doesn't even flinch, just smiles kindly at me and explains – so gently – that in circumstances like these it's customary to have *an inquest*.

"What circumstances?" I ask.

Because my heart has started racing, because maybe this means it wasn't suicide, that everyone's got it all wrong, that Beth didn't do this to herself, that someone else, maybe, someone—

"When someone takes their own life," Sufiya clarifies. "This kind of inquest isn't about . . . finding fault. Or assigning blame, necessarily."

While she speaks, my heart is slowing, sinking, aching.

"We want to try to understand," she says.

"Didn't the obituary kind of sum it up?" I ask, and I can hear how my voice has turned cold and sarcastic, the way it's never been before.

Dad says, "Emmy."

Mum says, "Emmy."

Sufiya says, "Do you think it did?"

I don't say anything. Of course it didn't. It wasn't even close. It was like it was written by someone who'd read about Lizzie Beck on Wikipedia. Someone who didn't even know her actual name was Beth and, even if they'd been told, wouldn't care.

After a silence, Mum says, "Please, carry on, Sufiya."

Sufiya does. She tells us how an inquest works, how long it will take, what to expect. I try to listen, but I keep realizing that I haven't taken in anything she's said. Maybe she can tell, or maybe she's just been doing this a long time, because after she's finished explaining coroner's court she turns back to me and says, "Emmeline. This is an incredibly difficult time for you. Please know that I'm here for you too."

She pronounces it "Emma-*line*" instead of how everyone else says it – Emm-ah-lynn – which shouldn't matter at all, but somehow does.

But then she says, "Is it OK if I call you Emmy?"

(And I'm distracted by a realization, which is:

Sufiya is the first person I've met in this new world where Beth is dead.

The first person who will only ever know me without her.

For the rest of my life, all the new people I meet will know not Beth, but the fact of her being dead.)

I almost want to say no, because how can I still be that person, Emmy, in this new life? How can that still be my name?

Maybe I should become an *Emma-line*. Someone new. Someone unfamiliar.

But I just say, "Sure."

I slip away and no one stops me.

Go into the bathroom and stare at myself in the mirror.

I still look the same. I don't even look as sad as I expected.

I look normal.

Beth and I never really looked the same, which used to bother me, because all I wanted in the world was to be her.

Now, I see her in my cheeks and my eyes and the way my chin curves.

I used to say, "I wish I was as pretty as you." And she'd say, "Oh, shut up, you're gorgeous."

I reach out to touch the mirror. My fingertips leave smudges on the glass.

When we were kids, Beth and I used to play the alphabet game constantly. We'd pick any topic — animals, songs, celebrities, food — but whatever it was, she always won.

Now she's gone and I've started playing the game by myself, in my own head, with her as a theme, like an obsessive intrusive thought sequence I can't shake off.

Like right now.

When I walk into Beth's room, it's like my head won't let me deal with the mindfuck that is *standing in my sister's room when my sister is dead so therefore is it still her room or is it just a room and oh god oh god she's dead she's dead* so instead it trips a switch and I almost *hear* the lilting pattern of the opener to the game in my head—

I walk into Beth's room and in it I find

A armchair (inherited from Gran, a weird rusty orange colour, still with a Beth-shaped slouch in the cushions)

B books (the same books she had when she was fourteen, none added or removed)

C corkboard collage (of photos, mostly her and Jodie, some with Tam and Aiya too, all of them frozen in time as smiling fifteen-year-olds, lucky them)

D dressing table (housing a haphazard collection of make-up and products, too many for her to keep track of, surely)

E envelopes (stacks of, all addressed to her and unopened, piled up by her bed, Mum used to leave them there ready for when she next came home, which will now be never)

F flowers (dried, pre-dating her death, a corsage from an awards ceremony she went to with Leo during one of their happy times)

G guitar (her favourite thing, a present from Dad when she first formed the band, because — he said — *I know you're going to make it and you should have the best guitar*)

H headphones (metallic red, noise-cancelling, the kind of expensive that made her say to me when they arrived, *Em, I totally bought these just to prove to myself that I could*)

I iPod (extremely old, like *years* old, she was so proud of the fact that she still had it, that it still worked, she called it her time capsule of music)

J jewellery tree (my gift to her on her birthday when she turned sixteen — it was hard to get presents for her because she could get anything she wanted herself)

K keys (the keys to our house that she kept losing, so eventually Dad told her to stop taking them with her because of that time we got burgled and he was sick of having to change the locks, this was a big fight, one of their biggest, and I wonder if the keys abandoned on the desk have moved since then)

L lanyards (too many to count, she used to collect them at the start of everything, I guess she stopped but I don't know when, didn't notice at the time until the time was already over)

M moisturiser (the expensive kind that I didn't realize was expensive until I used it the whole time she was away once and she came home to find it empty and yelled at me that I was an annoying little freeloader, *get your own fame, get your own money, get your own sodding moisturiser*)

N notebook (her lyric book, plain a4, night-sky-navy-blue front and back, unlined, I want to read it but can't even let myself touch it because what if all the answers are in there, what if they aren't)

O Ormaie bottle (her perfume, if I pick the bottle up I can spray it and I'll smell her, right here, like she's in the room with me)

P poster of The Jinks (that she put up on her wardrobe door as a joke when she was seventeen)

Q quilt cover (bright yellow; a pure, rich, sunshine yellow)

R rug (thick fake sheepskin, fluffy and cosy, where I used to sit or lie when Beth was home, watching her walk around the room in her underwear, face mask on, as she talked to me about the band, the road, Leo, everything)

S Sebastien (cat, a pure white Norwegian Forest, Beth's Christmas present for the whole family the year after she got famous, but who was only ever her cat really, who loves to snuggle with her and purr whenever she's home, who is now sleeping on her bed, oblivious)

T tiara (plastic with pink fake gems, a joke present from Jodie when they were thirteen that she wore that whole day at Thorpe Park and kept all the eight years since)

U umbrella (gold, a prop from the first video The Jinks ever shot, an elaborate dance sequence in the rain)

V Vans (collectible edition, Jinks-branded, from the Kaleidoscope era, bright colours inside jagged black lines, the word LIZZIE on the back of one, BECK on the other)

W wardrobe (huge, walk-in, full of clothes that she will never wear again)

X x...

I can't find an X, not anywhere in the room, and it feels like I've failed. Failed at some kind of superstitious checklist I was making, failed *her*. I cry over this missing X like it's actually a real thing instead of something I've invented that doesn't even matter. I sit down, heavy, on the bed, and Sebastien starts awake with a chirp of alarm.

I tell him, "Beth died."

He blinks, yawns, stretches.

"You'll never see her again," I say.

He arches his back, gives himself a shake, pads over to the end of the bed, away from me.

"It's not because she didn't love you," I say.

He looks back at me.

"I'm still here," I say.

Sebastien jumps off the bed with a graceful *whump*, leaves.

Silence.

"I'm still here," I say.

The other thing I don't find in that room.

Is a goodbye.

I know it's not there because I looked everywhere. Through the B for Books and E for Envelopes and W for Wardrobe and in the missing X that marks the lack of a spot where she thought of me, thought of us, thought to say goodbye before she left the world and me and us behind.

I think a part of me really thought it would be there, somewhere. That she would have left a message for me, something only I would be able to decipher, like what always happens in films after someone dies. A secret code. A treasure hunt. Just something. Anything.

But there's nothing.

A NOTE ON OUR HOUSE

(Which is to say, why we have our house,
   which is to say, because of Dad's salary,
      which is to say, because of Beth,
         which is to say, because of *Lizzie*,
            which is to say, the good things we have are because of her.)

After "Great British Sounds" and Beth's fame and Dad's salary, one
of the first things my parents did was buy our house. This house.
   We moved to a town in Surrey called Hethersett.
   The kind of town that gets described as "leafy".
   It's nice.

The house is big. You could fit our old house in it twice.
Four bedrooms, a sun room, a massive garden.
A study for Dad, a music room to fill with instruments.
   (And a loft, airy and spacious, that we called Lizzie's room,
      because we filled it full of Lizzie stuff.

                        So proudly. We were so proud.
      I will not ever set foot in there again.)

We moved for the house, sure, but also for me.
   So I could go to my new school.
      Shona Lee.
         (The performing arts school of my dreams.
           Of *our* dreams, mine and Beth's, in the before-land.)

I left my whole life behind and didn't look back.
   I think we all did that.

(Though maybe not as dramatically as Beth, suddenly famous.)

Beth was away most of the time and so
    when we moved
        we just packed up her room in the old house
           and put it back together again in the new one.

She and Mum were planning to do it up properly.
    Make it her perfect safe haven, Mum said.
    But Beth dithered and procrastinated over paint colours and furniture
        and then she started saying how
           actually
                she liked it that way.
    Like a piece of her old life, she said.
    It's already a haven, she said.

It became a relic, that room.
    Partly because it was like a living snapshot of the past,
        but also because she was hardly ever in it.
           Beth was away all the time,
                even though our home was still her home,
                    officially.

And it still is. (Was?)
    Jodie, Aiya and Tam all own property of some kind,
        all have their own flats.
    It was just Beth who never got her act together.
    Was never quite stable enough to make the leap.
    Even though she always planned to move out,
        get her own place somewhere in London.
    ("And, Em, you can come and stay all the time, yeah?")
    There were always flats she was "planning" to "check out".
    But it just ... never happened.

So, in a way,
   even though she travelled the world,
      she never really *left home*,
         and now she never will.

That's kind of tragic, in a way.

But the most tragic thing –
   at least for me –
      is that even though this was her home, her haven, her safety,
         this wasn't the last place she slept.
   She died in Leo's bedroom.
   Away from all of us.

Alone.

Grief is a scream you're living inside.

Relentless. So fucking loud.

But it's like no one else can hear it because they carry on talking like words still matter, making cups of tea, telling me to wash my hair, brush my teeth, eat some toast, how are you Emmy, how *are* you?

Those sympathy eyes.

And I want to say,

Can't you hear it?
    It's so loud.

2 DAYS GONE
Other people

There is a shrine for Lizzie Beck outside Leo's house. Sprung up as if from nowhere, a sea of flowers and teddy bears. Cards, even letters.

It's fucking weird.

I mean, maybe the flowers I could understand, because that's what people do when someone dies – send flowers. (Or put them in a makeshift shrine on the side of the street, I guess.) (Even though, when you think about it, it's a bit obscene that we've made flowers a cultural thing to send or leave after someone's died. Like, sorry about that death you experienced. Here, have something beautiful to watch wither and die.)

But teddy bears? Beth was twenty-one.

And cards? Letters? To someone you didn't know? Who is literally dead?

Bizarre.

"Why is it there?" I ask Dad, because I can't say Leo's name. "Why not here, where she actually lived?"

Dad grinds his teeth so hard, his whole jaw judders. He says, quiet and tight, "It's where she died."

I look at pictures of the shrine online. I wonder what will happen to it when the news cycle moves on and people forget. What's going to happen to all those flowers? What if it rains?

I want to go and look at it, but my parents won't let me. Won't even consider it.

Some people – people who actually know us – have sent flowers too, but mostly it's cards ("Please let me know if there's anything I can do," they all say) and casserole dishes left with the security guard (still stationed outside our door during the day). Sometimes the dishes are still warm.

"I don't get it," I say, and Mum sighs.

"People want to be kind," she says, which is not the same as, *People are kind.*

There's not enough space in the fridge for all the casserole dishes. They pile up on the counter. I take one at random and go and sit in the living room with it on my lap. I eat cold macaroni cheese with a spoon while I watch BBC Parliament, which I choose because it's so boring, and so distant from my own life, that I find it soothing.

The politicians keep calling each other "my honourable friend", even when they're on opposite sides and clearly loathe each other. It's the most British thing ever, and I find it weirdly fascinating. Like nothing in the world matters more than decorum.

It's how we are about death, isn't it? No one says what they really think — "I want to claw out my own heart to stop it hurting this much" — or does what they want to do (scream in the middle of the street). And everyone else turns away from it until they have no choice. They don't look you in the eye. They send delicious casseroles and cute teddy bears and beautiful flowers, because they need to believe that delicious and cute and beautiful still matter.

I used to believe those things mattered too.

But now Beth is dead, and I eat the macaroni cold.

It's been two days, and there are still so many articles.

So. Many. They just keep coming.

- *Lizzie Beck: British pop's latest tragedy*
- *TIMELINE: Lizzie Beck's final hours*
- *REVEALED: Drugs at home of Leo Peters where Lizzie Beck was found dead*
- *From reality TV to tabloid favourite: Lizzie Beck, a life in pictures*
- *What can we learn from Lizzie Beck's death?*
- *Lizzie Beck's death exposes the rot at the heart of our obsession with celebrity*
- *One thing is clear: we let Lizzie Beck down*
- *Lizzie Beck: a reckoning for reality TV*

(And always with that "*we*". Who is "*we*"?)

The same facts, over and over again. The same opinions too.

And so much detail, about everything. Details no one in the world needs to know, not even me. Especially not me.

It's grotesque.

And among the news articles there are the interviews and the features, the comments, the columns.

There's a feature on fans of The Jinks, how they feel. (Like it matters.)

There's a quote from one of them, saying,

"We've lost such a light."

And I think, no you haven't. You haven't lost anything.

And if you have lost a light, maybe you've lost a torch. A candle.

In a world with a thousand other torches. A million candles.

But there was only one Beth.

And that is who we've lost.

You didn't even know her name.

Subject: Love and condolences
From: Marianne Keane m.keane@shonalee.sch.uk
To: Emmeline Beckwith e.g.beckwith@shonalee.sch.uk
CC: Ellen Beckwith ellenbeckwith@outlook.com

Dear Emmeline,

I and everyone at Shona Lee was so very sorry to hear the news of your sister's passing. Please know that the love and best wishes of the entire student body – and staff – are with you and your family. If there is any way we can be of assistance, please do let us know.

Your audition to continue your time at Shona Lee and join the sixth form centre was scheduled for July 17th. Please be reassured that this requirement has been waived as per Shona Lee policy for students experiencing periods of bereavement or trauma. You are a much-valued member of the student body, as well as being an extraordinarily talented, conscientious and skilled performer. We will be delighted to welcome you back in September. If you could confirm your acceptance by the end of this month, I would be appreciative.

My sincere condolences to you and your family. We are thinking of you, Emmy.

With very best wishes,

Marianne Keane
Headmistress
Shona Lee School for the Performing Arts – *Exprimere ad somnia*
Rated "Outstanding"

I've never had an email from my school with the word "love" in it.

(It's weird.)

If Beth hadn't been famous, would I still have got an email like that?

It's really nice and everything, but is it also a bit … much?

I've never lost a sibling before, so I've got nothing to compare it to.

But it sort of feels like it's because Beth was Lizzie Beck, not because she was Beth.

And I hate that.

(So much.)

Which is probably ungrateful of me. It was a nice email. It's nice that they care about me.

And it's good that I don't have to audition for next year.

Because the thought of singing feels as suddenly alien to me as sprouting wings and flying away.

I haven't sung a note since Beth died,

and even though that's only three days, which maybe doesn't sound like much,

I used to sing constantly.

At school, with my friends, in the shower, in the garden, in my bedroom.

And with Beth, always with Beth.

(Sometimes, when she was bored, she'd send me a voice note of her singing the first line of a song we both loved, and I'd reply with me singing the next line, and we'd carry on until one of us got summoned; me to class, her to an interview or the microphone or somewhere else cool.)

Now, there's just silence.

The kind of silence with no room for music or joy or the planning of a life built on both.

*　*　*

But,

I love my school. I love my teachers. I love my friends.

Knowing I'll be going back to Shona Lee in September regardless – even though Beth will still be gone, even though my voice might have gone with her – makes something inside me calm a little.

Like maybe there's still a part of me that cares about my own life, and not just the fact that Beth isn't in it any more.

Like maybe this black hole of grief has an edge I'll reach one day,
    and when I get there I'll be able to put my hand up,
        and there'll be someone to
           reach in,
              take a hold,
                pull me up.

My whole life, it's been music.

Every memory I have of my childhood has a soundtrack.

- Dad playing his guitar for Beth and me when we were tiny, Mum singing with her eyes closed, smiling
- Listening to the songs he played us on his record player with its crackly needle, how alight with happiness Dad's face was when we liked them too
- Sitting on the piano stool next to Beth, watching her hands move, trying to mimic her, the way Mum laughed when I got frustrated, how she said, "Be patient, Emmy! Your hands will grow!"
- Long car rides with the music playing — always playing — taking turns to choose the tape, then the CD, then the playlist
- Dancing to ABBA songs with Beth in the bedroom we once shared in our old house, wild and free, laughing, bouncing, jumping
- Singing "Top of the World" at my Auntie Char's wedding with Beth, her with a guitar in her twelve-year-old hands, feeling so grown up, so proud when everyone clapped for us, when one of the guests said to our parents, "They're very talented, aren't they?"
- How Dad said, "Oh yes, they're going to be stars, our girls."

Music is how I've always understood the world.

There was no happiness that couldn't be brought to life by a happy song.

No sadness that wasn't comforted by a sad song.

Not just listening to them, but playing them, singing them.

Music has always been what lifted me if I needed lifting,
carried me if I needed to sink.

The music has always been there — just like Beth was always there — in me, and around me.

But now … it's just *gone*, like it's been drained out of me.

Like it was never mine really, but hers,
and she took it with her when she went.

And now I'll have to live my life without a soundtrack
without a big sister leading the way
without anything it was meant to have.

Who *am* I now?

I try to sing, but nothing comes out.
I try to play my guitar, but my hands won't move.
I try to listen to music, but I have to turn it off.

The instruments in our music room lie still.
The piano lid closed.
No music comes drifting from the kitchen, the study.

Everything is silence.

3 DAYS GONE
My people

Suddenly it's Friday and Mum knocks on my door and says that Scottie's here to see me and I swear for one long goddamn moment I actually think, *Who?*

And then I remember he's my boyfriend.

Scottie Wilde. My lovely warm hug of a boyfriend, come to see me like a good boyfriend would. Flowers for my mother and a doughnut in a bag for me (because in my former life I liked doughnuts) and he is somehow both smiling and not smiling in a way that is respectful of the situation while also still loving me.

I hate him.

A good boyfriend would get it wrong so I could blame him for getting it wrong. But I have to say thanks for the doughnut and Mum has to say *how lovely, Scottie, you brought flowers* as if our entire fucking house isn't full to the fucking brim with fucking fucking fucking flowers.

Scottie is a certified *softboi*. Kind, cute, reliable. He has long mousy blonde hair, dimples, green eyes. A smile you remember. He's the sort of guy everyone likes: friends, parents, even Beth, though she called him "cute" in the way you'd call a puppy cute one too many times for my liking. We've been friends for two years and together for six months, since he first kissed me on my sixteenth birthday, his eyes bright with hope, our smiles wide.

I know him better than almost anyone.

He is a total stranger.

He's talking; has been talking for a while. We're in my room – not sure how that happened – and I should be listening to him because

"—know I can't begin to imagine what you're going through—"

he's my boyfriend and it's basic politeness to listen when someone's talking but also I cannot summon even the tiniest jolt of caring and it's so tedious to have to explain that – out loud, with words – why can't he just *know*. It's so exhausting having to *be*, having to exist in this world with other people.

You know who doesn't exist in this world any more?

Beth.

"Emmy?"

"Huh?"

"Did you hear me?"

"Yeah."

"Are you sure? It's OK if you didn't."

"You're sorry. I get it. I heard."

What kind of a stupid boy name is Scottie? It's a name you give a dog. Or at the very least a name you outgrow by the time you're sixteen.

I don't like hating him like this. I've never been a bitch. I don't know how to wear it. I'm too big for my skin.

He moves to hug me, saying, "I'm here, Em, I'm here."

And I physically shove him away from me, properly hard. I don't even say anything, just push.

"Woah," he says. "OK. That's OK. I'm sorry."

I don't know how to tell him that I don't want him here. That I don't want his kindness or his understanding. That his sweetness, his softness – the part of him I used to love most – leaves me cold.

"Can you go?" I ask.

He looks at me, confusion and uncertainty radiating out of him. "Can I... I mean, yeah. I can, of course. If that's what you ... if that's what you need."

We stare at each other. I wonder if I seem as much a stranger to him as he does to me.

"It is."

Scottie is a cinnamon roll. But I don't want a cinnamon roll.

I don't want soft and sweet and wholesome. I want chilli flakes on my tongue. Peppercorns crunching between my teeth. The wince of wasabi.

It's not his fault. I know it's not his fault. It's not mine, either.

It just is.

The thing about Scottie turning up at my door (uninvited) is that it reminds me about life carrying on outside of this house and the fact that I actually still have one – a life. Which is weird.

I decide to take a look at WhatsApp, which I muted in the first few minutes of my grief explosion and haven't checked since.

WhatsApp unread messages: 247

(Fuck me, I've never been so popular.)

There are messages from friends, acquaintances, friends of acquaintances, teachers, cousins, friends from school, non-friends from school.

A huge variety, all these people connected purely by me and this horror.

And they all say some version of:

I'm so sorry. Please let me know if there's anything I can do.

(Messages from my sister, my favourite person in the world, my idol, my best friend, sent before she wilfully and deliberately and permanently left this plane of existence and our sistership for ever: 0)

Delete.

(Are you sure you want to delete all?)

(Yes.)

(Actually, no.)

The ones I don't delete: three message chains, stretching way back into the before time. One with Scottie – which I don't read but also don't delete – one with my best friend group and one with my best friend,

Grey. I open hers first, knowing – because I know Grey – that there will be just one message, simple and sincere, the kind that could have come from an adult, not a sixteen-year-old. I'm right.

I love you so much and I'm so, so sorry xxx

I reply with a single heart, then open the group chat.

Emmy: I love you all too. Thanks for your messages. Not OK, obvs, but here, I guess?

Ella: EMMY!!!

Trix: EMMY!!!! ❤❤❤❤❤❤

Grey: I'm so sorry, Em. We're all so sorry.

Trix: SO SORRY!

Emmy: Yeah. Thanks.

Grey: What can we do?

Emmy: Literally nothing but thanks. Just wanted to let you know I'm OK. Going to go quiet again now.

Grey: That's totally OK. Whatever you need. We're here.

Trix: 100%

Ella: Always

Grey: xxxxxx

Ella: xxxxxx

Trix: xxxxxxxx

Emmy: xx

It doesn't make me feel better.

I thought it would, but it didn't.

Every !

Every x

(in excess)

Prickles up my spine, to the back of my throat

a kind of fierce, fizzing rage I don't even understand.

I know I can't expect them to know what to say

I wouldn't know, would I? If it were them this was happening to?

But it's not them.

It's me.

Sebastien has changed, just over the last couple of days. He's started following us around the house, keeping us in sight. Mewing outside our doors at night.

Mum and I are sitting in the kitchen, letting cups of tea go cold. Mum has a support pack in front of her, one made for parents bereaved by suicide. She has a pen in her hand and she's going through some kind of checklist, because apparently there are a lot of logistics involved in death. I didn't know that, three days ago.

At first, I was asking Mum what was on the list, but she kept flinching and crying, so I stopped.

Now, after an extended silence where I'd watched Mum's face as she looked down at that terrible checklist no parent should ever see, Sebastien has come into the room, mewing.

"Do you want more food, bud?" I ask. He leaps up onto the table, knocking some of the papers to the ground.

Mum says, "He knows."

She reaches out a hand to him and he rubs the side of his furry little face against her fingers. This cat, who would barely go near anyone who wasn't Beth.

"How?" I ask.

"He can feel that she's gone," Mum says. "Gone from the world."

"How?" I say again, and it comes out annoyed, belligerent.

Mum doesn't say anything. Sebastien leaps gracefully onto her lap. He pushes against her chest, her neck. I hear him purr.

"Thank you," Mum whispers. Her eyes close. "Oh, thank you, sweet boy."

I sit there and watch.

I think about how, if he really does know, he must feel so lonely in the world. So left behind. Abandoned, with this family of people who are not Beth.

Beth didn't say goodbye to him, either.

Beth, nineteen, home for Christmas. Holding Sebastien in her arms, swaying by the Christmas tree as she sang to him, *"Oh Sebastien, oh Sebastien, how furry are your trousers."* Me, watching from the doorway, giving myself away by laughing. How she'd turned her head, seen me, how her face had lit up in the automatic grin of someone who loves you, who is happy to see you. How she'd shifted on the spot, lifting Sebastien, so he could see me too. "It's Emmy!" she said to him. "Hiiiii, Emmy!"

Of course he knows. Beth is gone, and he knows.

That night, I dream of her. I walk into the garden – unnaturally sunlit – and there she is, waiting for me, on a bench that doesn't actually exist. Her sunglasses are on but still her arm is crooked over her head, her hand shielding her eyes. She's grinning.

"Hey!" she says as I approach. I want to run, but I'm strolling. "I've been waiting for you!"

I say, "Beth."

She holds out a hand to me.

I wake before I reach her.

4 DAYS GONE

Hell is other people

Someone has tweeted the video of Beth covering Amy Winehouse's "You Know I'm No Good" from three years ago. The tweet says: No words, just tears. #RIPLizzie

Beth recorded the cover in our bathroom at home, just her and a guitar, with me sitting by the sink to watch, out of shot. Beth was fresh out of her first stint in rehab, when she was newly clean and hopeful. She'd come into my room with her guitar – hair in a carefully casual ponytail, subtle make-up on to make it look like she wasn't made up, smiling – asking if I wanted to sit in and watch.

(Actually, no. That's not what she said, was it? It wasn't "if you want, Em". She said, "please, Em?". It wasn't a treat for me; it was support for her. Did I realize that then? I'm really not sure I did.)

(Or am I just imagining that now? Adding in another word, an extra plea, that wasn't there?)

(It feels like my head is being crushed in on itself, realizing that I can never know. Who can I ask? It was just me and her there. There's no one else left to remember. And now I'm scared that I don't.)

I watch the video, blurry through my tears. Beth's voice, so raw as it was then, raspy at the edges. Her eyes closed for most of the song, the way her whole face moved through the emotions of the lyrics, the emphasis there in the tightening of her jaw on *trouble*, the slight shake of her head when she sang that she was no good.

No one could watch a video like that and not see the real person, Beth, in all her vulnerability, trying so hard, and love her for it.

But.

This wasn't a real person, was it?

Social media ripped Lizzie Beck apart for that video. *Embarrassing*, they'd said. *Pathetic*.

Who does she think she is?

Oh my God, someone tell Lizzie Beck she's a fucking skank. She can't even sing!

> Is this Lizzie Beck being SERIOUS now? God fucking save us all.

> Holy shit, was there ever anything so desperate in British music?
> You're not Amy Winehouse, love, you're just a junkie whore.

> LOLOLOL she thinks she's Amy Winehouse??

Beth cried a lot of tears over those comments. She read every single one, and there was no convincing her that they were wrong (they were), and she sounded amazing (she did), and she was beautiful and talented and brave (she was). She took every toxic comment inside her heart and left them there to rot. All those anonymous people who probably don't even remember they ever said anything.

In fact, they're probably the same people reposting it now with comments like,

> **@karlo201** Fuck, this is so tragic.

> **@un_luckyseven** God, she really could sing, couldn't she?

> **@borderfollie** This breaks my heart. Almost can't bear to watch this. RIP Lizzie.

And, worst of all:

> **@sighwrensong** Lizzie Beck and Amy Winehouse are duetting in heaven now.

I mean, seriously. S E R I O U S L Y.

I shouldn't read all these comments, just like Beth shouldn't have read them the first time around, but there's no one to stop me, so I do.

I scroll

and read

and cry

and rage.

Don't pretend you cared about Lizzie Beck

By Douglas Ruthie

Remember when the words "Lizzie Beck" were a punchline to a joke? I do, being that it was less than a week ago. Lizzie Beck was the pinnacle of trashy celebrity, favourite of tabloid journalists and gossip columns, by all accounts pretty dim. So here's my question to all you wailing mourners: why are you pretending you care?

Of course it's sad when anyone dies, especially someone young, but it should also be a private sadness. My deepest sympathies are for this poor girl's family, who in this time of unimaginable pain are having to deal with the rest of the country acting as though they've lost their best friend, as if the past several years of judgement never happened. Nothing rewrites history like death, does it?

But Douglas (you are already saying), aren't you also getting a headline out of this girl's death? Aren't you just the same? Well, far be it from me to pass up an opportunity to point out liberal hypocrisy. Lizzie Beck clearly needed support when she was alive, but in death she'll get your sympathy. Slow clap for you, friends. Try not to feel too pleased with yourselves as you hashtag the tweets of your tears.

Lizzie Beck is the inevitable casualty of an age that favours clicks over substance, personality over intelligence, attention over sanity. The truth is that no one cared about Lizzie Beck when she was alive, least of all those for whom her existence was a form of entertainment measured in tweets and headlines and Instagram captions. Have a little integrity: stop the crocodile tears and just leave Lizzie Beck alone.

Raised voices are the first sign that Dad is home.

(He's been out all day doing Death Things. Words like "coroner" and "inquest".)

I'm in my room, sitting on my bed, doing nothing except thinking about my sister, which is something that used to be nothing at all, and now is everything.

And then – "... *by all accounts pretty dim?*"

"Keep your voice down. Emmy's home."

A muffled quiet for a few seconds, rising and falling in volume so I hear snippets like

"What kind of a sociopath..."

and

"It was COMMISSIONED—"

and

"Monster!"

and

"Callous BASTARD."

"Mal, Mal, shh. Emmy."

Mum's soothing, unintelligible voice. I imagine her hand on his arm, anxious eyes on his face.

"I'll fucking sue the bastard. Sue the entire magazine. Sue fucking everyone who ... who..."

"Mal."

I go downstairs and into the kitchen, which, from the look on Mum's face, is a mistake. But I don't care. That "Keep your voice down. Emmy's home" has set my head on fire. Why is she trying to keep all of this from me? How can she think that's possible? Or that it *ever* was?

When Dad sees me, he jerks in surprise, wiping at his face as if he's been crying, but that can't be right, because Dad doesn't cry, not ever. He starts to say something – I will realize later, once the ambient rage has gone from my head and let my thoughts clear, that it was going to be something soft and nice – but I don't hear what it was meant to be, because I've already started.

"At least it was honest!"

He blinks in bewilderment. "What?"

"That article. (Yes, Mum, I read it. I can read. I'm sixteen.) No one else is being honest! Everyone talking about Beth like she was *theirs*, and they're so sorry now, it's all..." I flounder for the appropriate awful word. Nothing is awful enough. I go with, "Bullshit! It's fucking bullshit!"

This doesn't get the reaction I expect. My parents, who have always coddled me

> (*yes*, I've *known* they've always coddled me, because I was always *the good one, the youngest, the baby*, instead of *the only*)

are just staring at me, and suddenly they don't look like my parents; they just look like two ordinary people. Two sad, confused, tired, ordinary people.

I want my parents back. I want Beth back. I want it all back.

"I'm *glad* he wrote it! It's better than all those features about how brilliant they think she was. The same people who called her pathetic! Why are you letting it happen? Why aren't you fighting for her?"

Embarrassingly, I'm crying now. Ugly, pathetic crying. Heaving sobs.

And the worst thing?

Dad is crying too.

And Mum is crying.

I wait for Dad to yell at me, to tell me how wrong I am. For his face to go that puce colour it used to go when he was yelling at Beth, all those hundreds of times they fought right here in this kitchen, when she screamed at him and threw things and he said worse things to her than anything Douglas Ruthie wrote in that stupid, horrible article.

But he just walks out of the kitchen.

I'm left standing there, hearing my own ragged breathing in my ears, my fists still clenched. I look at Mum, waiting for her to *be my mum*, but she has buried her face in her hands, shutting herself away, closing herself off from me.

I wait. I say, "Mum."

But she just shakes her head.

5 DAYS GONE
Leo (part one)

That Sunday is the first morning I wake up remembering that Beth is dead. No moment of blissful forgetting. I open my eyes and her death is the first thought my head holds.

I lie there and let the intrusive thoughts crawl all over me.

Dead.

Dead.

Dead forever.

No more smiles on greeting. No more hugs. No more arguing about nothing like it's everything. No more closing my eyes under her fingers as she sweeps eyeshadow over my lids. No more posing as she takes pictures and calls me "fucking spectacular". No more holding her hand while she cries. No more saying, "Love you" as carelessly as if there is no death. No more phone calls. No more blue ticks.

Tears slide down the sides of my face, into my hair. I stare at the ceiling as it blurs and unblurs. I taste salt and snot.

I used to think grief was about absence, but it's not. It's so physical.

I never thought it would be something I could taste.

Eventually, I get up, because that's what you do.

When you are alive you have to get up.

I wash my face. Brush my teeth. Cry about Beth never brushing her teeth again. Imagine the rest of her rotting away while the teeth remain *what the fuck Emmy why are you thinking about rotting flesh fuck fuck fucking fuck.* Cry some more. Wash my face again.

I get dressed before I go downstairs. I want to stay in my pyjamas all day, but people seem to always be around, grown-up strangers who go bug-eyed with discomfort when a grieving teenager tramps across the kitchen in Snorlax pyjamas.

So now I wear clothes.

I'm expecting there to be someone in the kitchen, because I hear voices as I come down the stairs. I expect it to be one of the management team — they've been around a lot — or one of my uncles come to help out, or really anyone except who it is, because who it is is

Leo.

Leo "The Trainwreck" Peters.

Leo the fuck-up.

Leo, my sister's on-and-off-and-on-and-oh-look-they're-off-again boyfriend.

Leo, sobbing into Dad's shoulder as Dad … *hugs* him. What the —

"WHAT THE FUCK???"

Leo jerks out of Dad's arms (like a startled cat), rubbing at his wet face, gasping as if for breath.

Because he can still cry, gasp, breathe.

Because he is still alive.

Still alive and in my kitchen.

Mum says, "Emmy." Soft and gentle. All wrong.

"WHAT   THE   FUCK???"

"Emmy," Leo says, his voice all cracked and broken.

I haven't been thinking about Leo. This whole time, these hellish days, I have not thought about him, because I can't.

But now here he is.

THINGS LEO PETERS DID TO MY SISTER, AN INCOMPLETE LIST:

- Cheated on her
- Twice
- Gave her drugs
- Lots of drugs
- After she'd stopped taking drugs
- More drugs
- Lied. A lot.
- Loved her
- Made her love him
- Broke her heart
- Slept in the next room while she was dying on the other side of the wall

I ask, "Why are you hugging him?"

(I don't really *ask* it. I scream it, right across the kitchen.)

Mum is suddenly standing in front of me, her hands on my shoulders, eyes trying to meet mine. She's saying my name.

Leo is the only person who was there before, during and after Beth died. The only person. They were together, and then she was dead.

Everything we know about what happened that night is through the filter of Leo. What he remembers and what he's told us and the truth – some combination of the three.

She was crying a lot, mostly incoherent, he says.

She yelled at him a lot, he says.

She threw things, he says.

He yelled back, he says.

Maybe it got a bit physical, he says.

He didn't hurt her, he says.

She made him sleep in the other room, he says.

He didn't know she'd done what she'd done, he says.

If he had, he would have stopped her, oh God, he would have stopped her, he loved her, oh God, why did he sleep, he could have—

"Shh," Dad says. "It's OK. You don't have to go over it again."

Leo says, "I've lost everything."

Over and over.

And over and over again.

While Dad hugs him like a son. Cupping his head into his shoulder. Clapping his back.

Leo doesn't say, "Sorry."

Which is probably a good thing, because I think if he did, I would kill him.

I think about Leo.

Waking up.

Thinking it was going to be an ordinary day.

Ready to apologize, maybe.

Stretching, taking his time.

Going into the bedroom to wake my sister.

Thinking she was sleeping, maybe.

And then

And then my mind goes blank, won't let me imagine it.

Protecting me.

Keeping any sympathy at bay, so I can hate him in peace.

Mum takes me away from the house. (Tries to act like she'd been planning it all morning, as if they're not all clearly extremely worried that I'm going to launch myself at Leo and rip his eyes out.)

We go to a coffee shop. Mum gets a latte, I have a white hot chocolate.

Neither of us drinks them.

We don't talk, either.

Just sit there.

I'm thinking about Leo and Dad at home, what Dad is saying, why Leo is in my house and I am here and Beth is dead.

Mum is watching a young mum two tables over, bouncing a chubby baby on her lap.

"Oh, Ellen," comes a woman's voice. Mum turns.

I don't know her name, but I recognize her, very vaguely, from my mum's fortieth birthday party. A teacher from the school where Mum works.

Really, it doesn't matter what her name is, because she could be anyone, with her sympathy face, her empathy eyes, the earnest way she looks at Mum before she says, "I'm so sorry about Beth. I'm so very sorry."

At least she calls her Beth. It makes me love her.

Mum doesn't say anything. Very quickly, it's awkward.

"Thank you," I say.

The woman looks at me like she might start crying, but – thank God – she doesn't. She just nods, chin all wobbly, says goodbye and leaves.

I was never the one who had to speak up. If Mum couldn't, Beth did, because she was the older one. The first child, the elder.

Now I am
    the elder,
        the first,
            the only.

That night, I'm woken by the motion of someone climbing under the covers beside me. The room is pitch black, the air still, and I swear, for one heart-stopping moment,

      every   single   cell   in   me
thinks it's Beth.

It's not even half a second of blinding emotion (not one, but all of them at once) before sense catches up with me and I realize that it's Mum,

but it's enough to set my heart on fire.

It takes all my energy to keep my breathing steady so she doesn't realize she's just given me an emotional heart attack. I manage a whispered, "Hi."

"I'm sorry, darling, go back to sleep," she whispers back, and yes, it's definitely Mum. The last wisps of subconscious hope dissipate. "I just wanted a cuddle with my girl."

It's more of a squeeze than a cuddle; she hugs me too tight. But I let her, of course. I lie still until her arms slacken and she's asleep, her breath loud in the dark. Falling asleep myself feels impossible as I stare at the shadow of the ceiling with her body wrapped around mine, but then

suddenly it's morning,
Mum is gone,
the bed is empty
and I'm alone.

6 DAYS GONE
Message from the dead

There is a voice note on Beth's phone.

There is a voice note on Beth's phone.

There is a voice note on Beth's phone.

There is a voice note on Beth's phone.

She recorded it the night she died.

She recorded it for us.

She did leave a message.

She did think of us.

She did.

Sufiya, our family liaison officer, came round this morning to talk to us.

(All of us, even me, not just Mum and Dad.)

She said, "I have something to share with you that you may find difficult to hear."

(Mum immediately started crying, even though she couldn't have known what it was going to be.)

Sufiya didn't drag it out or anything, didn't try to build up the suspense. She just told us straight out that the police had found a voice note when they were searching through Beth's phone, one that was meant for us, and now they were ready to share it.

(That line snagged for me, because what does that mean, why weren't they "ready to share it" before, what else might they be keeping from us? But Mum or Dad didn't stop her talking to ask about it, so I didn't say anything, and now the moment is gone forever.)

She seemed to talk about the voice note for a long time before she actually played it, but it was probably only a minute or two.

(Before she played it, she said, "Would you like me to leave the room?" Which I thought was really nice of her, to think of us like that.)

(Mum said, "No, no. I'd like you here. Please.")

(Dad didn't say anything.)

(And neither did I. Obviously.)

Sufiya played the voice note for us right there at the kitchen table where we all used to eat dinner together, which actually wasn't all that often because Beth was always away being Lizzie Beck. But she still had her seat, the one not Mum nor Dad nor me would ever dream of sitting in. The seat that was at that very moment occupied by Sufiya, kind and oblivious, who probably sits at a lot of kitchen tables delivering gut punches to devastated people.

(Because that voice note *was* a gut punch. As physical as emotion gets, right into the deepest part of me, a heartache so unbearable I couldn't even cry.)

The voice note was twenty-three seconds long.

(Which really isn't very long.)

But it turns out that, at the end, there isn't all that much to say except

      I'm sorry,

         I love you,

            goodbye.

Sufiya explained that the police have a copy of the file and a transcript. Apparently, something like this is important for the inquest.

It hurts me to think of those words meant just for us being included in a death file. I wanted them to be kept secret. Ours. No one else's.

"It doesn't work that way," Dad said. And then he looked at me, and something happened to his face, and he said, "I wish it did, though, Emmeline." And his chin wobbled and he shook his head and walked away quickly.

Since that moment Mum started crying when Sufiya said the words, "I have something to share with you", I don't think she's stopped. I check in on her every hour or so, bringing tea that she doesn't drink and snacks she ignores. She just wants to hug me, close to her like I'm still six years old. Too close. I think it would be nice if I believed it were me she was hugging, and not Beth by proxy.

I let her do it anyway, and I don't tell her to stop.

I won't say what Beth actually said in those twenty-three seconds, because it was just for us.

It was despair and pain and guilt and love.

It was my sister, saying goodbye to her family.

Private.

7 DAYS GONE
Jodie (part one)

[Image description: A photo in black and white. Two young teenagers, fourteen or so. Jodie and Beth, looking at each other instead of the camera, mouths wide open in laughter. Faces so close, the kind of close that only comes with being best friends.]

Caption: I miss you so fucking much I can't breathe.

When I see it, five minutes after it was posted, it has 7,594 likes. When I look again, half an hour later, it has almost 100,000.

The post is a lie.
A lie.
A LIE.

If I try to be generous, I can think that it's a lie Jodie is telling herself. But I don't feel very generous.

Jodie is just playing a part. The Jodie the world expects her to be; the Jodie who loves and grieves for her best friend, not the one who betrayed her.

I click through to her profile. Click message. My hands are shaking as I type and delete, type and delete.

Fuck you, you lying bitch.

Send.

I swallow. The words are so bare and savage, waiting there on the screen for Jodie to see. I've never spoken to anyone like this, and especially not someone like Jodie. Now, I can't take it back. (I don't want to take it back.)

As I watch, four letters appear beneath my words, tiny, greyscale: SEEN.

I wait. My heart is pounding as if I actually care. Jodie used to give me piggybacks across the garden, neighing like a horse. She thumb-wrestled with me while Beth straightened her hair. She called me Emster.

So long ago.

She doesn't reply.

Once, Jodie was the mousy friend.

The shy kid.

She and Beth were *best friends for ever* friends.

I used to hear them singing together in Beth's bedroom, practising, when they were younger than I am now. Not famous, not yet, just kids sharing a guitar and a dream. Bursts of laughter between the perfect harmony of their voices.

God, I *idolized* them. Both of them.

I'd creep along the hall and poke my head around the door, hopeful.

"Come in!" Beth would say, spotting me. "Come watch!" Or, "Come sing!" Or, "Em! Isn't Jo-Jo amazing? Isn't she going to set the world on fire?"

Jodie's face, pink and beaming, shoving Beth, telling her to "Oh my God, stop!" Sweeping her hair back from her face, laughing.

They let me sing with them, sometimes. They'd play games with me in the garden, even when they were old enough to be too cool to play with a kid. Do my hair for me, teach me how to apply mascara, even — treasure of treasures — let me help them with their make-up.

Jodie's an only child and she used to say to me,

Emmy!

I'm basically your sister, right?

You've got two big sisters.

I loved that.

I'd say, *Yes!*

And Beth would say,

Hands off! Emmy's mine.

It's late when Dad gets home. I don't know where he's been. I hear his footsteps on the stairs, and then the surprise of his knuckles against my door.

He says, "Em?"

I say, "OK."

He dawdles in the doorway before coming to sit on the bed beside me. There's a long pause, then he finally speaks.

"That message you sent Jodie was

   unfair

   cruel

   not like you at all.

You have to understand that she

   is in pain

   lost Beth too

   loved Beth.

There's a lot

   you don't understand.

Please

   don't make this harder.

For any of us."

What *us*? The *us* should be him and Mum and me.

Why is he making an "us" that has anyone else in it but us?

He's right. There's a lot I don't understand.

The Jodie from before would have replied to me. I don't know what she would have said, but she — *"I'm basically your sister, right?"* — wouldn't have gone to my dad, told on me, showed him the message, made him talk to me.

Now I am someone so unimportant, so irrelevant, that she doesn't even reply. Just makes me someone else's problem.

I want to roll my eyes and sneer, say that I meant every word, that Jodie deserves all of it and more. Tell him that Jodie isn't his daughter, I am, Beth was. That the only thing he should care about is us. *That* us.

But when I try to speak all that comes out is tears, and I hear myself apologizing, and he's patting my shoulder and telling me it's OK, they all understand, this is hard for me, they love me.

Maybe it should help, but it doesn't.

"What's going to happen?" I ask.

I mean to Jodie, to the band. The band that surely can't exist any more, not now Beth has died. But if they don't exist any more, why is Dad still their manager? What is he doing, going to work, when there's nothing left to work for? Why is he talking to Jodie enough that he knows about my message, but not telling me what they talk about? That Instagram post is the first time she's said a word publicly since Beth died. What is she saying in private? Does she feel any guilt for what she did to Beth before she died? Is she *sorry*?

What is going to happen to her? To all of us?

But Dad misunderstands me. Maybe on purpose, maybe not. I guess I was quite vague.

He says, "Nothing, Emmy, don't worry. We all understand you're hurting."

I don't correct him. I nod, let him leave.

8 DAYS GONE

Penguins

Auntie Char is here.

Her name is actually Charlotte but she's always been Auntie Char. She's younger than Mum but acts older.

Mum and Auntie Char are a two, like Beth and I were.

Mum used to say, *two sisters is special.*

I know she would have said that whatever the combination
   but still
      I liked that.

It *is* special.

Anyway.

Auntie Char is here because
   she and Mum are planning Beth's funeral.

Mum keeps crying but Auntie Char is very calm.

When I sit on the stairs to eavesdrop I hear Mum say, in a voice all cracked and broken, "I don't know how to do this."

And Auntie Char says,

"I'm here.

The next day Auntie Char says,

"Let's have a day out, Emmy. Just you and me."

Like it's not really obvious that Mum has asked her to get me out of the way while the police come to the house to talk about the investigation.

I don't mind.

We go to the aquarium.

I don't know why.

(But it's kind of nice?)

It's a Thursday morning so it's very quiet, just Auntie Char and me, walking from tank to tank.

We talk about yoga

and jellyfish

and how she's looking forward to Wimbledon

and if she should keep her Netflix subscription or not

and sharks.

There's a colony of Humboldt penguins in their own special exhibit and I spend way too long there, watching them waddle.

Auntie Char reads out some of the facts about Humboldt penguins from a display board, leaning with her arms crossed over the fencing. She stumbles over the word "piscivore", then laughs. She says, "Their average litter size is two! That's good, two is sp—"

She stops abruptly. Coughs awkwardly.

Two is special.

After a long, long pause, she says, her voice a little shaky, "Which is your favourite, Emmy?"

"All of them," I say.

When we get home, we both sit in the car, quiet. She doesn't move to open her door, so neither do I. There's no music playing. That would have been the strangest thing, once.

She says, "Emmy." Then nothing.

The quiet goes on.

"I wanted to talk," she says. "Today, with you. But I just waffled on, didn't I? I'm sorry."

I don't say anything.   (What is there to say?)

After a long pause, she adds, "I can't imagine how hard this is for you."

"Probably best not to try," I say.

She touches my hand. "Don't let this make you cold."

I shake my head, look away.

"Emmy? Talk to me."

But I don't want to talk. I want to scream, that's what I want to do. Beat my fists against the dashboard. I feel like I'm fizzing all over, in the worst way. Like I could explode.

"I'm trying to help, Emmy," Auntie Char says in a voice that is very soft, very calm. "I want to help you."

"Not help *me*," I say. The words come out before I've even realized it's what I'm thinking. "You're here to help *Mum*. Helping me is a way of helping *her*. That's your job, isn't it? As her sister? Isn't that what sisters do?"

Her face has creased. "Oh, Emmy, no—"

She carries on talking, but I'm not listening. I'm thinking of the two of them being kids together, her and Mum. Growing up together, becoming adults together. Building their own lives that are separate but forever connected. Regular phone calls and daily messages and laughing over glasses of wine and reminiscing over their unique shared childhood and being aunts to each other's daughters and commiserating over their first grey hairs and everything and everything and everything I will never have with my sister.

Auntie Char is here for Mum in a time of crisis. That's what sisters do.

Who will do that for me, in my future?

Who can do that now?

Auntie Char is still talking to me. I know, without listening to the words, that she is saying all the right things. All the things an aunt who loves her niece would say to her when she's in pain. Comforting, kind words. I dimly realize that her hand is resting gently on my arm.

"What would you have done?" I say abruptly, talking right over her. She stops, confused. "If Mum had died when you were sixteen?"

Her whole face transforms. Her mouth opens in a hopeless little 'O'. I wait, but I've silenced her.

I know why, too. It's because she can't answer with the truth, which is that it would have broken her, that she doesn't know if she could have survived it, that she would be a different person if that had happened. She can't tell me that. But she can't lie, either, because she knows I won't let her.

So she just stares at me, helpless, and I look back. Her hand is still on my arm.

Finally, I say, "Everyone thinks they know what to say."

Slowly, she nods.

"But it's not..." I try to find a way to finish the sentence, but I don't know how. "It's not about the words. There aren't any."

"OK," she says, nodding again, like she's concentrating hard.

I bite down on my lip. I give up on trying to find a way to explain. "I liked the penguins."

This makes a smile break on her face. Just a small one, a mix of sadness and relief and love. "I'm glad."

"I'll remember the penguins," I say.

10 DAYS GONE
Prom

THE NIGHT THAT SHOULD HAVE BEEN

It's the night you've talked about together for years. The legendary Shona Lee Year 11 Leavers' Ball. You get dressed with your best friends at Grey's house, drinking real Prosecco out of real flutes, singing along to Beyoncé together. You're all wearing prom dresses worthy of a national awards ceremony.

(Yours, a gift from your famous older sister, a sequinned mermaid dress in midnight blue, one she'd worn to an actual awards ceremony four months before and kept for you, especially for you, even after your mother said, "She can't wear that to a school prom! It won't even fit!" and your sister said, "Yes, she can! I got it tailored for her," and when you got tearful she laughed and hugged you close and kissed the side of your face and whispered, "You're going to look gorgeous.")

You take so many photos before you've even left Grey's house that your jaw hurts, but you carry on beaming anyway. Grey's mum says, "Oh girls, you look fabulous," as you beam for yet another camera before you walk out the door, all four of you arm in arm, to the waiting limo.

When you get to the school the hall is transformed. You feel like you actually are at a ball, a real one, like you've stepped into a Disney film. You shriek and hug everyone you know. You all laugh with relief about exams being over, the summer stretching ahead. You compare notes on what summer programmes you'll be doing. Olivia Valero is filming a Netflix pilot; everyone acts cool about this, and not at all jealous.

Your boyfriend arrives late wearing a suit that fits him perfectly. You've never seen him in a suit before. He looks incredible. You hug him, giddy, and he kisses you even though all your friends are right there. You think, I *am so happy*. Your boyfriend hugs your friends, who are also his friends. These people you love and have survived all these years at Shona Lee with are here and happy and free, dancing together like kids at a birthday party, even Olivia.

When a Jinks song comes on, everyone cheers, and your friends point at you, and you pose, grinning, like it's your band instead of your sister's. You all sing along, every word.

At the end of the night your feet are sore, you're holding your heels by the ankle strap. You're wearing your boyfriend's suit jacket and you feel more grown up than you've ever felt in your life. Everyone is drunk, even though the official beverages were strictly — strictly! — non-alcoholic, clustered outside in the cooling June evening. Trix is kissing Renee Bern, and you will shriek about this with her at length the next day. Ella is dancing barefoot on the grass, arms in the air. Grey is on the phone to her boyfriend, who is on his way to pick her up, and even though you've never liked him, you smile at how happy her voice is when she says, "Hurry up, I love you."

The crowd disperses slowly. You and your boyfriend are two of the last to leave. You get a taxi back to his house, which is quiet and dark, his parents asleep. You both try to be quiet, but you're giggly and silly as you scurry up the stairs together, to his room, to his bed, where you kiss and kiss and kiss and kiss until the promise of six months of *boyfriend* and *girlfriend* meets its climax under sheets that smell like him.

After, before you fall asleep, you message your sister. You say, "I, Emmeline Grace Beckwith, am no longer a virgin, just thought you should know", which is what you've always planned to say when it finally happens. She will reply, "Virginity is a social construct YOU SLUT lol how was it tell me everything SPARE NO DETAILS fuuuck I love you! I'm so proud! Get some sleep though, it's late xxxx HEY HOW WAS PROM????"

You are smiling as you write that you'll tell her everything tomorrow, and she replies with more kisses, your brilliant sister who you love beyond words and is alive to share your highs and your joys.

The night is over, and you sleep.

THE NIGHT THAT WAS

I sit on my bed in my pyjamas.

> (The mermaid dress, still in its garment
> bag, buried in the back of the wardrobe,
> hanging quiet and cold in the dark.)

Watch the night unfold on Instagram stories.
  Loud and bright and giddy.

All my friends in beautiful clothes
  having the night of their lives.
  A night they will always remember,
    without me.
  I will always have not been there
    because ten days ago my sister died.

And they are celebrating being one step closer
  to the kind of life that killed her.

The world didn't stop because Beth died.
  The prom wasn't cancelled because Beth died.
  My friends didn't not go because Beth died.
  I understand why. (Really.)

But it still hurts to watch, from my quiet, empty room,
    the glitz
    the laughter
    the music
    the dancing
    the joy.

The world isn't just *carrying on*.

The world is having a party.

11 DAYS GONE
I still have friends

The very next day, my best friends turn up on my doorstep. It's the first time I've seen them since the last time I saw them, which was two days before my sister died, after our last exam. Grey and I had walked across the Shona Lee car park with our arms around each other's necks, practically breathing each other's breath, laughing with each step. Ella and Trix were just ahead of us, dancing rather than walking, singing the George Michael song "Freedom".

That memory should have been long forgotten by now, buried by the mountain of what has come since. But it's vivid in my head, and it rises up like a pain when I see their anxious, hopeful faces staring at me from my doorstep. I had been so happy in that moment. I don't think I even knew it at the time. But, God, I know it now. My stupid, oblivious, happy past self.

"You can tell us to leave, if you want to," Grey says. Even she is anxious, I realize, taking in her calm, familiar face. It isn't as obvious as it is on Trix and Ella, both practically radiating with anxiety, but I know Grey, my unflappable best friend, and I can see it in her eyes.

I wish she'd come alone.

I step aside to let them in. Grey touches my wrist on the way past, but Ella goes in for a hug. I stand there and take it, and then of course Trix has to do the same.

We go upstairs together. I'm in the lead, and I've turned to go towards my bedroom before I realize that they're already on their way towards the stairs that lead to the loft.

"Not that way," I say, and it comes out far too sharp, like I've shouted at them. I don't think I've ever even raised my voice at my friends, not ever, and they turn to each other in instinctive bewilderment.

"But we always—" Ella begins, then stops. She lets out a shaky laugh. "Cool, of course, let's go to your bedroom."

"Where's Sebastien?" Trix asks.

"Somewhere," I say. I should have told them to leave. It's too soon. I need more time to figure out how to at least pretend to be Emmy again.

Grey is looking steadily at me, not smiling or frowning. When I catch her eye, she mouths, *OK?*

I shake my head.

She taps her chest with her right hand, which is our signal for *Hug?* Grey gives excellent hugs.

I shake my head.

In my room, I sit on my bed and they cluster awkwardly around me. I think about how last night was probably one of the best nights of their lives, and now they have to sit in grief-land with me. Poor them. Maybe they thought this would at least be easy; that I'd be sad, and that would be it. I'd cry, and they'd comfort me. Simple.

"Sorry about the mess," I say.

Ella's forehead crinkles in confusion. "It's not messy, Em." The tag on her wrist is purple. It says SHONA LEE LEAVERS' BALL 2018 in black letters.

"We brought you something," Trix says. There are flecks of glitter still on her face from last night; I see them when they catch the light. "It's a care package. We put it together, all of us." She hands over the gift bag I'd been steadfastly ignoring this whole time. It's bright, pink, glitzy. Very inappropriate. I imagine Ella saying, confidently, *Everyone around her will be all solemn and sad; we should bring her something bright and happy.* If this had been happening to her and I'd been the impossibly lucky one, I would have made the same suggestion.

The bag contains:
- A teddy bear with soft fur
- Chocolate
- A card that I don't read
- A book of poetry
- A make-up palette
- A bag of marshmallows
- My Shona Lee Leaver's hoodie; purple with white lettering

"Thank you," I say. "This means a lot to me. Thanks."

I actually just feel cold.

I can see their relief in their smiles, like I've followed the script for the first time. I open the bag of marshmallows and eat one, then pass the bag to Grey.

"How was prom?" I ask.

They tell me at length, and I honestly try to listen, even as their voices fade in and out like an old radio losing signal. The kisses, the dances, a break-up, a fight. I would have cared about all this *so* much. I wish I cared now. I *want* to care.

"We missed you," Ella says. "It wasn't the same. Without you."

"Did they play any Jinks songs?" I ask.

They all go silent. Trix smiles nervously. She's picking at the skin around her fingers, the way she isn't meant to do.

Grey says, "No. No, they didn't, Em."

"Were people talking about it?" I ask.

"No," Ella says, soothing.

"Yes," Grey says. "Don't lie, Ell. Of course they were. I'm sorry, Em."

I shrug, looking down at my hands.

Grey says, "Do you want to talk about Beth?"

The question is ridiculous. Absurd. Ludicrous.

As if I have a choice.

As if there's anything else in my brain.

As if "want" has anything to do with it. (With anything.)

It is a question with only a yes or no answer.

But yes is wrong, and no is wrong.

So what am I supposed to say?

I say, "They think she'd been dead a couple of hours before Leo found her body."

All three of their faces jerk with horror, even Grey's. Ella recoils slightly; Trix bites down on the side of her thumb. I watch them wordlessly try to decide how to react, even as they're already reacting.

No one says a word.

It is very, very uncomfortable, and I'm glad.

After a long, long silence, Grey reaches out a hand and touches my knee, like an adult would. Softly, she says, "We're so sorry, Emmy."

"So sorry," Ella and Trix repeat, in perfect unison.

I look down at the teddy bear in my lap.

"You can go now," I say.

One of the very best things about my friends: they always understood.

I think that's the most important thing in any friendship. It's why people who don't seem to have anything in common can be such good friends. It's more than liking the same things, watching the same films, eating the same food.

The best thing we can say to each other is, *You get me.*

Or, *You get it.*

Grey is the kid of famous parents.

Ella was one of the first Matildas on the West End stage.

Trix's brother, Hiro, is a principal dancer with the Royal Ballet.

They knew the world I was in because of Beth. They always understood all of it. I never had to explain. They got that Beth was always just Beth to me, when Lizzie Beck was soaring and when she was falling. They never went starry-eyed at the highs, or judgemental at the lows. They never thought I was just copying my sister.

It's like an anchor in the world, being understood.

And now they don't. The understanding is gone, the anchor lifted along with every other anchor I ever took for granted. How can they understand? They've never lost anyone.

They *want* to understand, I know that. I can see it on their faces and in their eyes. The need to care, to help, to get it right.

But you can't will understanding into existence. It's either there or it isn't.

And it isn't.

12 DAYS GONE
Questions

The inquest into Beth's death is still going on. The police have gone through Beth's phone — which is how they found the voice note — and her Macbook. They've gone through the room she died in, and her room at home, for anything that might be somehow relevant.

("Relevant to what?" I asked Mum.

"Her mental state. Her life. Oh, Emmy, I don't know. Everything.")

The police are also interviewing people.

("Will that include The Jinks?" I asked Dad.

"Of course it will, Emmeline."

"But they'll just lie."

"What do you mean?"

"Like they did in their statement. And on Jodie's Instagram. Pretend they cared."

"They did care. And they won't lie. But remember that an inquest isn't about assigning blame, OK? It's about understanding."

Like I'm ever going to be able to understand any of this.)

Anyway, today it's me being interviewed.

There are two of them, plus Sufiya, our FLO.

They tell me their names, but I forget them immediately.

In my head they are One and Two.

They ask me about Beth, and they let me ramble as I tell them story after story about the two of us as kids, how she'd give me piggybacks on family walks, what shampoo she used, how she taught me to harmonize, the size of her feet, the way her voice changed when she was high, that when she wanted to annoy me she'd call me "Emmbop."

* * *

They are very patient with me.

They even make notes, which they probably don't need to. Two says, "Were there any warning signs that you can remember? Anything beforehand – any amount of time beforehand, it could be weeks or even months before she died – that you can think of?"

One says, "Anything you could tell us, even if you're not sure it's significant, may be helpful."

Two says, "But if you can't think of anything, or if there were no signs at all, that really is OK, Emmy. You can tell us that too."

Were there any warning signs?

Watching *A Star Is Born* together on the sofa, the Judy Garland version. Beth recently back from her second stint in rehab, curled under a blanket. Her breaking down in sobs at the end that were so guttural, so terrifying, that I ran to get Mum.

The interviewer on that late-night TV show. *Does it bother you that you're the one no one likes?* That second of naked pain on Beth's face, the mortification, before she covered it up and made a joke. The way the audience laughed. The way her face dropped when the moment was over and she thought the camera had gone. How tired and sad she looked.

The sound of her and Dad yelling at each other. Glass smashing against the wall.

Beth, aged twelve. *I think I might die young.* Me, horrified, seven years old. *Why?* Her. *I don't know. I just have this feeling.*

The slump in her shoulders the last time I saw her. The way she couldn't smile.

The way she said, *Do you love me, Em?* before I left, the need in her voice that felt shameful in a way I didn't understand. How she didn't look happy when I said yes, just relieved.

I could pick one. Any one of the six that rose, immediate, in my head. Or one of the hundred more that followed them. I could say, yes, this, this, this.

But for what? How can you say they were warning signs when you're only looking backwards? You don't know the red herrings from the clues until you've finished the book, but by then you already know how it ends, so what does it matter?

What are these two police officers, who have listened so patiently to my memories of my sister just so they can get to the dirty truth they think I am keeping, asking of me? *Tell us all the reasons you should have known what was coming.* Or, worse, the possibility that I might not have seen any signs at all, which is really just asking, *Did you know your sister?*

Anyone who spent any time with Beth would have their own list of "warning signs". Haven't they realized that yet? What are they actually asking me to look back into the past and see?

Hindsight is a weapon.

Hindsight is a gift.

Hindsight is a lie.

I say,
"She was just Beth."

QUESTIONS I CAN NEVER ASK BETH AND WILL HAVE TO CARRY INSIDE ME FOR THE REST OF MY LIFE, UNANSWERED, UNANSWERABLE

- Why?

- Were you scared?

- Did you change your mind? Even for a second?

- What was the last thing you thought?

- Could I have done something?

- Could I have saved you?

- Did you not give me the chance because you knew I couldn't have?

- Or because I could have?

13 DAYS GONE

I still have a boyfriend

Scottie keeps messaging me. Nice messages, supportive messages.

I'm here whenever you're ready.

I love you.

You'll get through this xx

Each one makes me want to punch him.

Scottie
What time is the funeral?
Should I meet you there?

Emmy
What?

Beth's funeral?

Fucks sake Scottie I KNOW
THAT.

Sorry.

You're not coming to the
funeral.

??? Why not?

Why would you?

Emmy. Look, I know this is hard,
but it's me here. I love you.
I want to support you.

You didn't know Beth.

Not very well, maybe. But
I want to support you.

The funeral isn't about me. It's
about Beth.

Don't you want me there?

No.

Why not?

Why not?

Because if you are there I will need to think about you.

Because I have no space in my head for you.

Because when I cry you will try to comfort me and I will want to hurt you.

Because you are so annoying in every way right now.

Because I hurt.

Because you don't.

And I hate you for that.

Because I hate you.

                    Look, can we just not do
                    this please.

Do what??

                    Can you please leave me
                    alone for a while.

I can give you space, of
course I can. But I'm worried
about you.

                    This isn't about you. Will you
                    just go away please.

Emmy, I want to help.

                    THEN HELP. GO. AWAY.

Grief has made me mean.

It's not Scottie's fault. I know that. None of this is his fault. He is the same warm cuddle of a boy that he was before. He hasn't changed at all.

Which is (*o b v i o u s l y*) the problem.

We were so perfectly matched, before. We shared the same goofy sense of humour that we were too cool to reveal within the corridors of Shona Lee, so it only came out when it was just the two of us.

We were affectionate. Cuddly, even. Hand holders, snugglers. Cringey in all the right ways.

The thought of being that way again, ever, is unfathomable to me. Like trying to wear shoes you've long outgrown.

But, God, I loved those shoes. I did. I remember how comfortable they felt. How wearing them made me feel most like myself.

I message him again.

> I'm sorry. I do love you.

I love you too, Em.
It will be OK again,
I promise.

It's the wrong thing to say. Not the I love you, not the "OK", not the promise he can't keep.

The "again".

There is no going back. There is no "again". Just a new life I should never have had to live that I now can't escape.

I throw the phone against the wall.

I can't message anyone and complain that my boyfriend is annoying me by being too nice while I'm grieving. All my friends are his friends too, which used to be a nice thing and now isn't.

I would have messaged Beth. She would have got it. She would have understood and said something to make me laugh, and she would have been on my side, because she was always on my side, even when I was in the wrong. Just like I was with her.

I would have said:

Emmy
> Omg Scottie is being so annoying.

Beth
UGH, what a DICK! (what did he do)

> He's being so nice to me, trying to do the right thing for me while I'm grieving.

UGH, the WORST. Being NICE to you? How DARE he. Want me to be a bitch to make up for it?

Like you need an excuse?

OMG, you're a bitch too! The BECKWITH BITCHES. You got it from me. I'm super proud.

❤❤

Scottie looks like a puppy dog with his long hair. It makes me want to pet him.

I like his long hair!

There, you like him again now. You're welcome!

Omg, you got me.

Woof! 😉

LASTS

Last WhatsApp to her sister: *LOL it's cute tho*

Last WhatsApp to her family: *Miss you guys*

Last tweet: *Look I'm doing the best I fucking can ok*

Last Instagram post: *A black and white photo of a rubbish bin.*
Caption: If I climb inside this will you say you always knew/Or would you pull me out and say, there, my darling, good as new.

Last hug: *Brief one-armed, leaning down into the car, cheek to cheek for half a second.*

Last piece of advice: *Don't wear your hair like that, Em. Christ, it's not 2007.*

14 DAYS GONE

Exclusive (part one)

Exclusive:
HEARTBREAKING LAST WORDS OF TRAGIC LIZZIE BECK

- **"I'm sorry, I just can't be here any more."**

- **Troubled star left voice recording for family before taking her own life**

- **Apologized to parents and younger sister**

- **No mention of boyfriend Leo Peters**

SEE PAGE 5 FOR FULL TRANSCRIPT OF TEARFUL LAST STATEMENT

There are people in this world
who make money out of pain.
Who leak confidential information about dead girls to the press.
Who get that information and print it in huge block letters on the covers of national newspapers.
And there are people
who buy that paper and drink their morning coffee while they read it,
talk about the tragic dead girl with their friends,
what she said in the last message to her family.

Beth left that message for us.

It was just for us.

There are things that the media aren't supposed to do when it comes to reporting suicides, especially famous-people suicides.

I know because Dad was yelling about it, and also I looked it up.

They're not supposed to say what method was used.

They're not supposed to say, or even imply, that one single thing caused it.

They're not supposed to glamourize their death or them being dead.

They're not supposed to overly memorialize, make it seem like attention is a favourable outcome.

They're not supposed to print suicide notes or letters or anything like that.

They're not supposed to do these things because they can all be triggers to other people. People who might hurt themselves, or worse, because they've read them. So the experts, the people who *know*, do all they can to try and protect them, by making guidelines, based on research and compassion and humanity, to send to the press.

Who ignore them.

I read the list of guidelines on my phone and make a mental *check* by every one the media has broken since Beth's death.

I check every single one.

We get an apology from the police for the leak.

(Like it means anything now.)

This happens, they say,
    with high-profile cases.

We're very sorry, they say.
    But it happens.

I think about that word: *leak*.

I imagine a bucket, holes punctured into it, all the journalists standing under it to catch what falls.

All Beth's secrets leaking out.

As I think it, the image transforms and it is Beth that is punctured,
    her body they're standing around,
    her blood leaking out into their waiting hands.

They are laughing.

They say, *This will sell so many copies.*

The next morning, Dad explains to me that the leak was from someone on the investigating team. He assures me that they've lost their job because of it, as if this will make me feel better in some way, as if he thinks I won't understand just how much money they would have made from the utter betrayal of a grieving family and a dead girl.

"When will it stop?" I ask.

"When will what stop?" Dad asks. He's been very gentle with me since the story broke; unusually attentive. I think it's because Mum didn't leave their bedroom all day yesterday, and hasn't yet emerged today, though neither of us has acknowledged this.

"Why can't they just leave her alone? She's dead. Isn't that enough?"

Dad goes very quiet. "None of this... I know it's hard to understand, Emmy, but none of this is ... personal. It's not about Beth. They don't see her as Beth. I know to us she's our Beth ... but to them, she's just..." He bites his lips together, shakes his head. "She's just another headline."

JUST ANOTHER HEADLINE

A couple of years ago, Beth took me out for afternoon tea for my birthday, which fell on a cold, crisp Wednesday in early December. It was during one of the times when things weren't going all that well for her: she'd broken up with Leo (again) and the story was all over the headlines; she'd ranted on Twitter while she was high and that had made it even worse; she was at home more and arguing with our parents almost every day.

But she made time for me on my birthday. Smiled for me. Made it seem like turning fourteen was something special. Tried, like she did, to redirect the perks of fame onto me.

A trip to London. My hair done by The Jinks' personal stylist. Browsing the kind of boutiques I could never have dreamed of. Fortnum & Mason for afternoon tea.

"Posh as fuck," Beth announced when we sat down.

"Beth," I whispered. Her voice was always loud, but in the moneyed quiet of Fortnum & Mason it was gratingly loud. Embarrassingly loud.

She wilted – I see this in retrospect, but I don't know if I noticed it at the time – and shrugged, smiling at me. She mouthed, *Sorry*.

She kept up a stage whisper for the next five minutes, until I finally laughed and told her to stop, and she grinned, tossing back her hair, reaching out and squeezing my hand. "It's your birthday," she said, not whispering but this time using her inside voice. "Whatever you want, OK?"

We ate cake and tiny sandwiches. Scones with cream. Talked about the song she was writing, Shona Lee, how amazing it would be when I was a singer too, and we could do stuff together. Beth was great at articulating elaborate daydreams for the two of us, down to the dresses we'd both wear to the Grammy Awards. (There was no limit to Beth's imagination when it came to our mutual success.) She was convincing; she'd always been convincing, it was a big part of what had got The Jinks through their first shaky audition for "Great British Sounds". And I believed her. I saw us sitting side by side at the Grammys, our dresses complementary shades of blue.

"Maybe we'll be a duo," she said. "I'll ditch The Jinks and we'll tour together."

"The Becks," I said, and she laughed, delighted.

"Exactly!" She was beaming. "God, wouldn't that be great? You and me, up in lights. Together."

"You wouldn't ever leave The Jinks, would you?" I said, and the shine left her eyes, her smile dimming.

She looked away from me, shrugging. "Maybe it would be better for everyone."

"No way," I said. "What's The Jinks without Lizzie Beck?"

"God," she said. "It's so weird when you call me that. Anyway. I don't care. I'd give that up for you."

I smiled so wide I felt it in my ears. "You would?"

"Gladly."

(I thought that was about me, but maybe it wasn't.)

When Beth paid, the waiter asked us how everything was, jovial but distant, and I said it was all quite lovely, words that made Beth raise an eyebrow at me like, *Who are you?* As he handed her card back he said, "Lizzie Beck. I'm a big fan," but he didn't say it like it was true, more like it was a joke. Almost sarcastic, but not quite. I saw her flinch. I expected her to snap back, say something loud and savage, and I could tell by the twitch in his mouth that he was expecting this too. A scene at Fortnum & Mason. A story for the tabloids. An anecdote for his friends.

Beth's eyes flickered towards me, then back to him. She smiled. "Thanks. That means a lot."

I took her hand when we got up to leave, and she squeezed it tight.

When we walked outside onto Piccadilly, the press materialized as if from nowhere. Six or seven men in jackets with cameras.

"Hey, Lizzie!"

"Lizzie!"

"That your sister, Lizzie?"

"How's Leo, Lizzie? You seen him lately?"

Beth put her arm around me, pulling me close, ignoring them all. She took off the cap she'd put on before we'd even left the table, and put it onto my head, pulling it down low so no one could see my face.

"Hey, Lizzie's sister! Hey, Little Beck!" This got a laugh from the others. Beth's grip on me tightened.

The call went up. "Little Beck! Hey, Little Beck!"

"Are you like your sister, Little Beck?"

"You going to join the band, Little Beck?"

"You a whore like your sister, Little Beck?"

You think, when you're not in this world of cameras and shouting men, that people wouldn't say something as disgusting as that, out loud, to you, a minor, about your sister, who is right there beside you, and is actually still a teenager herself. But they do. Let me tell you, they do. And it wasn't for me, that's what you have to understand. They didn't care about me. They wanted Beth. *Lizzie.*

But whether it was for me or not, I heard it. I whipped around, still in Beth's tight grip, to see who had said it, and stumbled into a bollard. I was too disorientated to save myself, so I fell onto my knees on the London concrete, right in the middle of the scrum.

"Fuck!" Beth leaned down to right me, pulling me up beside her. "Fuck, just get up, Em. Come on. Don't look at them."

Her face was such a vivid, fierce blank. Maybe that's weird to say, but that's what it was. Just ... blankness. Like she'd turned something off.

"You OK, Little Beck?"

"Are you drunk, Little Beck?"

"Did you get your sister drunk, Lizzie?"

"Look, just fuck off, OK?" Beth snapped, whirling around, suddenly blazing. "Leave my sister alone. What the hell is wrong with you?"

That's the picture they got: Lizzie Beck yelling at reporters. Lizzie Beck swearing at reporters. Except they didn't say that was who she was yelling at, let alone why. They just said she was swearing in the street. No mention of me, of course. They cropped me right out of the pictures, as well.

It was a lie, all of it, but no one cared. Not the people talking about it on social media, not the columnists (*"I'm worried that my daughter is a fan of Lizzie Beck"*), certainly not everyone who made money out of the photos and the papers they sold. My parents didn't care about the lies, either. They were just angry at Beth for "exposing" me to the press, for "risking" my "safety".

"But it's not her fault," I said, over and over. I really didn't understand. It was so obvious to me that Beth was the victim in the whole thing, that anyone would have reacted like she did, having someone shout at them like that. Why didn't anyone care about that? "Can't I make a statement or something?"

"Don't be ridiculous, Emmy," Dad said. "And for God's sake, don't make it worse."

"Listen," Beth said to me later, the two of us in her room. "I love you to death and everything, but literally no one will care if you say anything. So just don't. OK? It's not worth it. They're just headlines."

"But—"

"Hey, look – look at me. Don't get upset. Look, am I upset?" She grinned at me, fanning out her hands to the sides, posing. She looked ridiculous, and I let myself laugh, like I knew she wanted. "Nope, I'm totally fine. Let them have their headlines. Sad little press men." She shook her head, sighing. "So sad."

I wanted to say, but you *were* upset. Remember how you cried once we were safely in the taxi? Remember how tightly you held my hand, like it was the only thing keeping you in place?

"Right, Em?" she prompted. She reached out and poked me.

"Right," I said. "So sad."

Her grin relaxed into a smile. "Next time we'll go out the back entrance, OK?"

There never was a next time. Not for just the two of us, anyway. There was always a chaperone of some kind after that day if Beth ever wanted to take me anywhere. Mum or Dad, her publicist, an assistant or two or even three. Beth's fame was meant to make everything bigger, but instead our world shrank and shrank and shrank, until it was this house, her bedroom, the two of us; the only places that were safe.

No cameras, no headlines.

I'm sorry, I just can't be here any more.

They're just headlines.

Sad little press men.

So sad.

And now tomorrow there's going to be a funeral.

16 DAYS GONE
Funeral

Have you ever thought about a funeral in the summertime?

I mean the height of summer. Thirty-two degrees of summer. In England.

You can't wear black tights to that kind of funeral. Can't wear a cardigan. Can't wear black trousers.

Can't wear any normal funeral clothes. You'd sweat through them before the first eulogy.

I wear a plain black dress and the silver heart pendant Beth bought me for my sixteenth birthday. Black mules that I hate.

I wanted it to be raining.

But it's thirty-two degrees and sunshine.
Too hot.
Too bright.

Thirty-two degrees is for weddings.

I start crying before we've even left the house.

Walking out my own front door and seeing the funeral car waiting for us.

A funeral car. Black and sombre. Too big for the kind of street where normal life happens.

The driver is standing beside it. He is holding his hat, and that is what makes me start to cry.

I think about how he does this probably every day.

Goes home to his family, eats beans on toast, watches TV with his feet up.

Has good days and bad days.

Complains about colleagues.

Keeps his shoes by the door.

I wonder where he keeps his hat.

In the car Mum holds my hand very tight and doesn't cry.

Dad keeps clearing his throat. Over and over. It's very annoying.

I don't know how I'm going to get through today.

But I do.
    It happens.
    And then it's over.
    And it will never happen again.

16 DAYS GONE
Wake

The wake is at our house. Private; family and close friends only. No band members, no management, no one band-related at all, which I guess is why they thought that our house was the best place for it. Private, familiar, our home. The most comfortable place in the world.

Except now it is, and always will be, the place we had Beth's wake.

Also, people know the address (so even though it's meant to be totally private and no one is allowed in without permission, there are still people – excuse me, *strangers* – hanging around on the street, which, I'm sorry, is fucking weird).

Anyway. We're here, it's happening, and it's too late for a change of plan. Too late for a lot of things.

The sun is still shining, so most people go into the garden.

Someone says, "It really is such a beautiful day."

At the wake for my nan, it was actually pretty nice. We ate sandwiches and talked about her, shared stories, even laughed over old memories.

No one laughs at Beth's wake, even though I reckon it's what she would have wanted. She would have wanted us to dance. Sing. Jump around on a bouncy castle. Wrestle in Sumo costumes. Get drunk.

But she can't tell us that for sure because she's fucking dead, so we just sit around and try to talk about Beth without actually talking about Beth, because we can't talk about anything negative – suicide, drugs, her general trainwreckness – and it's pretty hard to talk about Beth in any real way while ignoring those things. Especially at her wake.

Wake. What a stupid joke of a word. The thing Beth will literally never do again, meaning she will literally never do literally anything literally ever again.

Wake. Go fuck yourself, English language.

I message Scottie and ask him if he can still come over.

He turns up within ten minutes, already dressed in a smart black suit. He must have been waiting for my message, just in case, all ready to go.

There's something about that gesture that is so nice, I have to look away from it.

I tell him he needs to get a haircut.

And then I kiss him, right on the doorstep.

He doesn't say, *Woah, mixed messages*, because it's Beth's wake and so I can apparently get away with anything, which is a very dangerous message to send. I *feel* dangerous.

"How was it?" Scottie's voice is soft and gentle. I want him to yell.

"Let's go upstairs," I say.

No one is meant to go upstairs, even me. Mum thinks if anyone sees one of us go upstairs they'll think it's OK to do that too, and then someone might try and look in Beth's room, and that is Not Allowed, because—

"I'm glad you messaged," Scottie says. He follows me, one step behind, because he doesn't know it's not allowed. If he knew, he wouldn't follow, because he's Scottie, and Scottie is good.

I don't say anything. I pause to look out the hall window at the garden. Clusters of black against bright green grass, blue skies.

Beth would hate this so much.

"Woah, Em." Scottie's nervous voice as I push open her bedroom door. "Is this OK?"

I'm still holding his hand, knowing he won't let go, and I tug him in behind me. I close Beth's door and we are standing in her room together.

Beth would like this. "Look at you, rulebreaker," she'd tease. "*Upstairs* when you're meant to be *downstairs*. Hardcore."

"Kiss me," I say to Scottie, and his eyes widen.

"H–here?" he says.

"No one will look for us here," I say, as if anyone was going to look for us anyway.

He glances around the room, like he's spooked, like he thinks Beth might be hiding somewhere, ready to jump out and yell at him. (He was always a bit scared of Beth, even when she was alive.)

I kiss him. He kisses me back, sort of, though I can feel the uncertainty in his posture, his lips. I imagine what his head is doing right now.

This is wrong. This is right. Be there for Emmy. Don't kiss in a dead girl's room. Dead Beth. Don't think about dead Beth. Alive Emmy. Emmy kissing.

Beth's voice in my head. *What are you doing, Em?*

I kiss him harder, digging my fingers into the cotton of his shirt, waiting for his body to respond like boys' bodies are supposed to respond when girls kiss them like this.

"Woah." He breaks away from me. Laughs a little, half-strangled by it. "Are you OK?"

For fuck's sake.

"Yes." Trying to make my voice breathless and sexy, like ... like—

I kiss him again, my mind galloping ahead, imagining bare skin and hands and lying underneath him—

"Emmy." This time he steps back slightly, taking my hands. "Talk to me."

"I don't want to talk to you." It comes out like a snap, and I'm sorry, but I don't want to talk. *I obviously don't want to talk.* I try to kiss him again and he jerks away, harder this time.

"No," he says. "I can't do this."

"Why not?"

"Because it's not right."

"Not right? For God's sake, Scottie – can't you just... I want something nice instead of ... instead. With you. You're nice."

A cautious, nervous smile twitches. "I want to help you."

"I know."

I touch his waist and he leaps away from me. "No, Em, I can't. Not today, not ... not here. Fuck."

The *fuck* slips out. He's really stressed, but he's trying to hide it, to be nice, to be boyfriendly. To be kind.

I'm being a monster. I know I should stop. But there's this feeling inside me that I can't explain, something dark and twisted, like

140

a scream contained. The black clothes, the burning sunshine. The tears. The headache from the tears. Jodie's face. Leo's wracking sobs echoing. The coffin. The way people try to shake off death when they walk out of a crematorium; you can see them do it. How I instantly regretted choosing "Halo" to play during the ceremony, because I have ruined it for ever, for me and for every single person there. I should have chosen a song I would never hear again, not ever. I should have worn different shoes.

Beth is dead. Beth is ashes.

Scottie touches my arm and I smack him away, shrieking, "Don't touch me!" like a cliché from a TV show.

There's a very long silence. He says, "I think I should get your mum."

I let him leave. I climb onto Beth's bed, curl up on top of the covers, bury my face into the sheets, and I let the scream out. I scream into the sheets that still smell like her, but less like her than they did yesterday, but more than they will tomorrow. I scream as every molecule of her left on Earth fades. I scream and the world doesn't end. The world just keeps on going.

OK, so.

Objectively,

I know it would have been a bad thing to lose my virginity on my dead sister's bed during her literal wake.

Like, I know that.

Objectively.

But also, it would have been absolutely the right thing.

(Beth would have got such a kick out of it.)

It was what I wanted. For all the wrong reasons, maybe. None that would make me feel proud of myself. But still – it was what I wanted.

I know that's an ugly, confusing, uncomfortable truth, one I can't explain. Scottie would never understand it. No one would.

But I hate him for not understanding. For trying to save me from a moment of darkness instead of seeing that I needed it.

For thinking that the good thing is always the right thing, that the right thing is always the good thing.

What kind of monster does this make me?

He has done nothing wrong. He's trying to take care of me. He is doing everything right.

But I am wrong.

We had a perfect, gentle happiness in our relationship. Warm and safe. I appreciated that before—

Before.

My

world has

changed

shape

And his is the same.

We don't fit any more.

So what do we do?

I thought I'd feel better when the funeral was over.

I thought it would feel like I'd been holding my breath, and I could finally let it out.

It doesn't.

And I don't.

Stars out in force for Lizzie Beck Funeral

Dozens of celebs packed the funeral of beloved popstar Lizzie Beck, who died last month aged just 21.

Beck's former bandmates in British pop sensation The Jinks were, of course, all in attendance. Jodie Soto-Han looked mournful yet meticulous in an all-black Versace suit with a matching black and silver-clasped Chanel bag, while Aiya Mehta and Tam Lord wore matching dresses by Givenchy.

Perhaps surprisingly, none of the girls spoke – or sang – during the short ceremony, and no music by The Jinks was played at any point, though a written tribute from the band was read by the celebrant on their behalf.

Also noticeably silent at the funeral was TV star Leo Peters, Beck's troubled boyfriend at the time of her death, who could be seen after the ceremony being comforted by Malcolm Beckwith, Beck's father and manager of The Jinks, who gave a moving eulogy to his daughter.

CLICK THROUGH THE GALLERY BELOW FOR OTHER FAMOUS FACES IN ATTENDANCE: [GALLERY: 24 IMAGES]

Mum and I were there too.

Just for the record.

sad
is a small word
to carry so much pain

17 DAYS GONE
After

Scottie and I
        break up.

We meet at the park to talk about the wake. He'd asked me to come to his house, and I'd said no because even thinking about how kind his mother would be made me want to shrink into myself and disappear.

So we met at the park, which is why our break-up happens on a bench. I'm vaguely aware that our relationship deserved better than this, that he definitely does, but still, it happens.

He cries, and I want to cry too, but I just sit there, staring at him.
    He tells me he loves me and I want to say, "So?" but I don't.
        (So maybe there's part of me that is still me, Emmy, and not
        a terrible person.)

When I get home, Mum is sitting at the kitchen table, staring into space. She's wearing her dressing gown, her hair isn't brushed.
    I say, "I broke up with Scottie."
    She looks at me, brow crinkling into a slow furrow, like she's hearing the words from somewhere far away. A conversation she's overhearing, instead of one she's meant to be in.
    Finally, she asks, "Why?"
    I shrug.
    She breathes in a long sigh, eyes closing, then opening.
    "I'm sorry, Emmy."
    I wait for more, but more doesn't come.

Obviously, I know that me breaking up with my boyfriend is
    in the grand scheme of things
        (or even the mundane scheme of things)
    pretty minor.

People break up all the time. And we just had Beth's funeral.

But still.

I thought she would care more. (Just a little more.)

Mum always loved Scottie. She always smiled and hugged him when he came round, told him to call her Ellen. (She never did that with any of Beth's boyfriends.) (Especially not Leo.)

In the before time, she would have been horrified for me, demanded to know what happened, why, how I feel.

But today she doesn't even say,

"Are you OK?"

Then again, I guess – to be fair –

I am OK.

How can I blame her for not caring when I barely care?

I know I should care, but I don't.

It's just … blank. Not even numb, just empty.

It's a relief to know I won't have to deal with the ambivalence about things that should be nice any more, like

kisses

hugs

his smile.

I don't have to worry about cringing away from his warmth.

I can just be cold.

NOT THE SPAGHETTI, FERNANDO!

Ella: EM! You broke up with Scottie????

Emmy: What?

Trix: !?

Grey: …?

Emmy: How do you all know? I haven't told you yet

Grey: So you were going to tell us?

Emmy: Doesn't matter now, does it?

Grey: Emmy ffs. What happened?

Emmy: I mean, you obviously already know what happened.

Trix: We don't, just that you're broken up

Emmy: HOW

Ella: OK just like don't be mad but Scottie told us in the WhatsApp group.

Emmy: What group?

Emmy: Oh wait I get it. One I'm not in because I'm boring now?

Ella: No!

Ella: I mean like yes it is another group but like

Ella: Oh god I don't know what to say

Trix: You're not boring!!

Emmy: Oh good.

Grey: You know we love you, you don't have to be a bitch about this

Emmy: OK

Grey: You get why we might need one, right? It's not because we don't love you, we just still need to be stupid and silly and you don't need to see that, you know?

Emmy: OK

Grey: The world doesn't stop, that's all.

Emmy: Thank you for that clarification.

Grey: And none of this is our fault.

Emmy: Do you think you're helping right now

Grey: Why are you being shitty? You should have told us about Scottie yourself

Emmy: Who gives a shit about fucking Scottie for fucks sake

Grey: Em

Emmy: I don't want to talk right now and that's OK. I'm allowed this.

Trix: Of course it's OK, Em xxxx

Ella: We understand xxxxx

Grey: It's actually not OK? If you've broken up with

Scottie and you're not talking to us, who are you talking to? Don't bottle it all up.

Emmy: I'm sorry, when did you turn into my mother?

Grey: When you started acting like a totally different person?

Emmy: I'm fucking grieving OK

Grey: I know. I really know, Em, OK? Look, we're made of stronger stuff than Scottie Wilde. You're going to have to get a whole lot bitchier than this to push us away. xxx

Emmy: Fuck you.

Grey: Fuck you too, gorgeous. I love you xxx

Emmy: You're the worst x

Emmy: I love you xxx

21 DAYS GONE
"No loss"

Ricardo Patmore: Death of Lizzie Beck is "no loss"

By Meg Morris

- **Record executive under fire for "insensitive" comment on Lizzie Beck death**

Ricardo Patmore has received widespread criticism after being caught on camera commenting on the death of The Jinks member Lizzie Beck. In an impromptu exchange outside his London office, Patmore was asked by a member of the public if he felt "sadness" following Beck's suicide, to which he replied: "Well, it's no loss to music, is it?" When asked to elaborate, he is seen laughing and shaking his head before walking away.

The animosity between The Jinks and Ricardo Patmore, particularly with the outspoken Beck, has been common knowledge since the band's stint on "Great British Sounds" in 2012, but the insensitivity and timing of the comment may still come as a surprise to those who respect Patmore and his role in the industry, and consider him an important player in the original success of The Jinks.

Patmore's ex-wife Julianne Russo, who created "Great British Sounds" with him, has distanced herself from his comments, stating publicly that "Lizzie Beck's death is an utter tragedy, and any other commentary is irrelevant, not to mention breathtakingly insensitive. I dedicate my thoughts and sympathy solely to her family and send them nothing but love."

When contacted for further comment, Patmore apologized for any offence caused, but stated that his comments were "taken out of context".

Aiya Mehta @aiyamehta

@aiyamehta Apparently I'm meant to be a good little girl and not say anything about this but fuck that. I'm so fucking angry I've been crying all morning. Ricardo Patmore, you are a fucking monster. We JUST BURIED HER. FUCK YOU, YOU SOCIOPATHIC SHIT.

@forthehighjinks 🔥

@thisjinksygirl GO AIYA WE LOVE YOU

@waitingfordaylights YES. THIS.

[SEE MORE REPLIES]

@jodieso I love you.

>@aiyamehta I'm channelling my inner Lizzie. Think she'd be proud?

>>@jodieso DAMN PROUD.

This, they talk about.

    This, they comment on.

    They get flame emojis and love.

I write my own reply to Aiya.

We didn't bury her.

We literally burned her.

At least get it right if you want points for being mad about it.

I stare at the words on the screen. Imagine sending them, all permanent and public. Imagine the people who will look at my name and think, *Who is this? Who is "we"?*

Because I'm nobody, aren't I?

    I delete the words one letter at a time.

Mum doesn't talk about the article. Not Ricardo Patmore's words, not Aiya's tweet, nothing. This is how she was when Beth was alive; pretending none of it mattered, or was even happening. At least, that's how she always was with me. Sometimes, I'd hear conversations drifting up the stairs between her and Dad, either with or about Beth. It never bothered me that they didn't include me in them. In fact, I used to put my headphones on, didn't I?

It bothers me now, though. It really, really bothers me.

I wait for Dad to get home, ready for the by-proxy cathartic release of his inevitable fury, like how he shouted and raged after the Douglas Ruthie article. This time, I'll be there with him, in it. I'll say, "I know. It's awful. How dare he?" Like I should have done last time, instead of yelling at him. (I still feel guilty when I think about that.)

But when Dad comes home, he's quiet. There's no rage, no shouting. Just his stooped shoulders and tired frown. He's in the kitchen when I go down to see him, peeling the lids off takeaway containers, calling for Mum to come down for dinner.

I wait for him to say something about the video, but he doesn't. Eventually, after Mum has joined us at the table, I say, "I watched the video."

"So did the whole world," Dad says shortly. "I wish you hadn't. You know better."

"Mal," Mum says.

They've already talked about it, I realize. Just from that one syllable and the way they look at each other. At some point today, they shared this.

I wait for one of them to ask me what I think about Ricardo Patmore and the whole thing. How it felt for me to watch that video, with that old familiar smirk-sneer on his face as he spoke those awful words. I already know what I will say; that it hurt more than any of those other articles that have been and gone, anything he said when Beth was still alive. How I always knew he didn't like Beth, and she hated him, but this is different. This is cruel.

But neither one of my parents asks me anything about what this horrible man said about my dead sister in a viral video that has been watched by millions of people.

Eventually, I say, "So what's going to happen?"

"Happen?" Mum repeats, after a moment too long.

"To Ricardo Patmore," I say, impatiently. "Like, consequences."

Another silence. Mum and Dad look at each other.

"That's not really how it works," Dad says finally.

"Why not?"

"Ricardo is a very powerful man."

"So?"

I want to say, *I thought* you *were a powerful man.*

"There's no point," he says.

"*Aiya* said something. Aiya was *raging.*" *Like you should be.*

"Yes, she was, but she shouldn't have sent that tweet. She knows better. She's been talked to." He lets out a long sigh. "It's better to just let it be forgotten."

"Better for who?" I ask, frustrated. "How can you just let him talk about Beth like that?"

"Emmeline," Dad says. "Ricardo has said all that and far worse about Beth, and so have a lot of people. This was just caught on tape, and you know what? I'm glad it was. At least the world has finally got a glimpse of what I've had to listen to for *fucking* years."

"Mal," Mum says.

"What do you mean, a lot of people?" I ask. "Who?"

"Stop it, Mal," Mum says. "Emmy doesn't need to hear this."

"Yes, she does," Dad says, and now his voice is raised, now he's angry. "How are you still surprised, Emmy? Why is this news to you? The music industry is not a kind place. It is ruthless and cruel. I don't know why I..." He falters, and for a horrible moment I think he's about to start crying. Mum reaches out to take a hold of his hand, but he flinches away, shaking his head.

I try to not ask. I really do. But, after another few minutes have passed in silence, I say, "What other people say stuff about Beth? You mean … industry people? Like Ricardo Patmore?"

"Forget I said anything," Dad says. "It doesn't matter."

"I thought people were all saying nice things about her now," I say. "Because she's…" I swallow. I think about the coffin at the funeral. So still and quiet. "Because she's dead."

"Publicly, they are," Dad says. "And that's a good thing. Focus on that. It will be better for you."

All those people at the funeral. All those industry people. Is it any of them?

"Your dad is just upset, Emmy," Mum says, softly. "Focus on the people who loved Beth, like we did. They're the only ones who matter."

But that doesn't help at all. I thought Jodie loved Beth, but she betrayed her. Leo loved Beth, but he destroyed her. Beth loved us, but she left us. So what does *love* even mean? How can I count on it?

I feel like I'm falling apart. It sounds melodramatic — if there's such a thing as melodrama after a real tragedy — but that's really what it feels like. Like I might crumble from the inside, with none of my old certainties left to hold me together.

Mum reaches out to touch my hand. "OK?" she says.

I swallow it all down, down, down. "OK," I say.

The next day, the biggest bouquet of flowers I've ever seen arrives on our doorstep. There's a card, and it says:

Dear Malcolm and family,
I deeply regret that my callous words about the passing of your daughter were caught on camera, and that this may have caused you greater pain at this time. I have made a donation to the Samaritans. It will not be made public.

Sincerely,
R. Patmore

The flowers are beautiful. There are sunflowers, roses, freesias. Yellows, greens, pinks, purples. The bouquet is wrapped in an elaborate white ribbon. It towers over the kitchen table.

Mum, who has come into the kitchen behind me after Dad called about the flowers, is shaking her head. She smiles a smile that is not a smile at all, though it's still the closest thing to one I've seen on her face for twenty-two days.

"Orla?" she says.

"Oh, I expect so," Dad says. "She's a kind woman."

Orla is Ricardo Patmore's personal assistant. When I visited the "Great British Sounds" set while the show was filming, she was always nice to me, bringing me cans of Coke, asking how school was going. (Ricardo himself never spoke to me.) "Your sister is very talented," she said to me then. "Very, very talented."

The three of us stand there, staring at the flowers.

"*The Morning Show* have invited us on tomorrow," Dad says. "To talk about Beth and how we're feeling."

Mum's expression is completely unreadable, her eyes still on the beautiful, dishonest flowers. "Because of what Ricardo said?"

"That's the prompt, yes, but they've assured me they won't mention it, if we don't want them to. We can agree all the questions beforehand."

She turns to look at him. "Have you lost your mind?"

"I think it would be a good thing," he says. "For Beth's reputation. To talk about the daughter we loved."

"Yesterday," Mum says. "*Yesterday*, you acknowledged how 'ruthless and cruel' the industry is. The industry that *destroyed* our daughter."

"Ellen—"

"And now you want us to perform our grief for it? I have never done a single public thing, not since 'Great British Sounds', and you know how I hated that, Malcolm. And you want me to start again *now*?"

"For Beth," Dad says, standing firm. "Yes, I do. For Beth."

"You mean *Lizzie*," she says. "And for *you*. Not for my Bethie." Her voice breaks, and so does my heart. "No, Malcolm. No."

I wait for Dad to fill the silence, but he doesn't. Finally, I say, "I'll do it. I'll come on the show with you, Dad."

His head jerks towards me, surprise on his face. "Oh, Emmy, that's—"

"Absolutely not," Mum interrupts, before I'd been able to read the tone of his voice to figure out if a yes or a no was coming. "Not a chance."

"I want to talk about Beth," I say. I already know all the things I'd say, the stories I'd tell. No one would ever talk about Beth like Ricardo Patmore did after they'd seen her through my eyes. This, finally. My way to save her. In a way.

"No, Emmy," Mum says.

"Maybe we—" Dad begins.

"No." Mum cuts him off, short but sharp, all at the same time. "You're a minor, Emmeline. This isn't your fight. I don't want you hurt by it. And that's the end of it."

I think about that word, "minor".

I can't do anything because I am a *minor*.
    Can't talk to the press.
    Can't give interviews.
    Can't do anything.

I *am* minor. A minor.
    A minor character.
    A minor consideration.
    A minor; secondary to the former, Beth.

A minor is a chord.
    A triad of notes.
        A, C and E.
            Three fingers, three notes, one sound.
                The sound: a melancholic hope.

A minor is a scale.
        Based on *A*
            with the pitches A, B, C, D, E, F and G
                the key signature has no flats, no sharps
                    relative major is C major, parallel major is A major.

My key signature has no flats and no sharps, no troughs and no peaks.

My relative major is Beth. My parallel major is Beth.

That's me, isn't it? Emmy in *A minor*.

Lost in the melancholy, waiting for the hope.

25 DAYS GONE

Loss

Dad comes home with an urn. It's been nine days since the funeral, which is apparently how long it takes. (I try not to think too hard about this gap, and why it exists, and what happens in it, especially not in the middle of the night, when I can't sleep.)

"Beth's in there?" I say, pointing at the urn.

I want him to say, "No."

And if he can't say that, because I know he can't say that, I want him to say something stupid and comforting, something like, "Beth is in the air and the sunlight and in your smile. She's in your heart."

He says, "Yes."

I ask if I can hold it, and he hands it over. "Heavy," I say.

"That's one word for it," Dad says.

"Can I look inside?"

"Why would you want to look inside?"

"Just to ... I don't know. Check."

He looks at me like he doesn't know whether to be annoyed, amused or sad. "If you want to, I suppose you can."

I open the lid carefully and peer inside. I'm not sure what I expected, but it just looks like ... dust. Dirt, even.

"What are we going to do with it?" I ask. "It" doesn't feel like the right word, but "her" would be even worse. "Her" would be obscene. "Scatter it?"

"To be honest, I don't know," he says. "That's something we'll need to decide together."

"OK," I say. I put the lid back on the urn that contains my sister and hand it back to my dad.

And then I start sobbing. Wild, uncontrollable, animal sobs exploding out of me, completely from nowhere. Dad looks utterly horrified, standing in front of me with an urn in his hands. Maybe he doesn't hug me because he's holding the urn, which would get in the way, I don't know. But he doesn't hug me, and I stand there basically *wailing*, until Mum is there, taking hold of me, hugging me. I hear something that sounds like, "For God's sake, Malcolm."

I don't hear anything in return. When I finally get a hold of myself and look up, he and the urn are gone.

Beth wa.
blood and nerve
and skin and ha.
and fingerprints an
song and tears an
toenails and bruises ar
oxygen and tissue and fibre a.
iron and love and muscle and smiles a
memory and ears and ink and marrow a
bones and thoughts and plans and calcium
cartilage and hope and tattoos and laughter and t
and muscles and fists and nitrogen and veins and sister and
and sneezes and eyelids and smirks and dark and dreams and hydrogen and
and fire and fight and winks and cartwheels and plans and carbon and daughter and
and lips and heart heart heart and scars and healing and loss and ad
and poison and mistakes and regret and hugs and warm and cold an
and hunger and passion and pain and two eyes one nose one mouth one

Now she is

ash

Beth

Beth said,

"I think we're the wrong way round."

"What do you mean?"

"You should have been the older one."

I laughed. "Why?"

"I just think things would have been better," she said. "If you'd gone first instead."

She liked sleeping in my bed when she was home, sometimes sliding in beside me in the middle of the night, burrowing in, whispering *"no, don't wake up!"* in a hushed burst when I stirred, then squeezing me close.

She liked to hug me, burying her nose against the back of my neck, telling me my hair smelled nice.

Once, I muttered – grumpy and groggy with sleep – "What are you doing?"

And she said, "This is the safest place in the whole world."

And I said, "Less safe if you don't shut up and let me sleep."

And then she tickled me until I shrieked.

Sometimes, she'd ask questions right into my ear, whether I was awake or not. As if my life was the interesting one instead of hers.

"How's Scottie? Is Grey still with that boyfriend? Do you still hate him? How's school? What are you reading for English? You know what I miss? Maths. I was good at Maths, did you know that? Ask me a question. Go on, test me. Did you fall asleep? Are you awake? Em?"

Sister is the start of a sentence.

Sister means *I am* and *I have*. Sister is a verb and a noun. Sister says *I belong to*. Sister says *I love* and *I am loved*.

You say *I have* a *sister* and you mean, *I'm not alone.* Not in your family, not in the world.

But what happens when one sentence   stops?

(And the other carries on?)

And sister means *I was* and *I had.*

And there is no present tense for what is passed.

And *we* and *us* and *our* and *two* becomes

   me.

      And   only.

Here's something I'm grateful for:

WhatsApp.

Thank *God* for WhatsApp. Quietly saving slices of life we don't even think about at the time until suddenly they are all that's left. A part of Beth and me, something that belongs to no one else, that I can hold in my hand and look at whenever I want.

All those hundreds upon hundreds of messages, those hours of conversations, mine to lose myself in again. That last message from her, LOL it's cute tho, the one now burned into my brain. She'd been responding to a screenshot I'd sent her of a message Scottie had sent me. You're my moon and stars even in the daylight, he'd written. To Beth, I'd said, Omg look at my cringey boyfriend xxx

Messages from a different life. How incredible it seems now, already, that I was able to send thoughtless, silly messages like that to my sister, confident there would be more to come, that there was time, always more time, to be serious.

If I sent her a message now, where would it go?

I scroll back in determined swipes of my thumb, reading our messages in reverse, watching my sister come back to life through the screen. Her playfulness, her silliness, dulled over her last few months but reappearing the further back I go. There are selfies of her in make-up chairs, her hair foiled, eyes crossed, tongue out. There's bitching about her bandmates, complaining about Dad. Voice notes of her saying my name in a Kermit voice and nothing else. Short videos of her getting celebrities she knew I liked to say hello to me. All of our messages, back and forth, peppered with pictures and videos of Sebastien, growing in reverse as I scroll back until he is a kitten again, tiny in Beth's gentle hands.

I find myself near the end again, or the beginning, depending on your point of view. I see the date — two days before she died. I'd asked a casual, How are you? And she replied, Peachy! I stare at the words, both hers and mine. I knew at the time that the meetings between her, The Jinks and management were going on. Why didn't

I ask how they were going? Was I scared to, did I just not realize, or was that the real question I was asking? I can't remember. I really can't. Everything is so completely clouded by how it ended, and now that's all I can see.

Did I really believe she was "peachy"? I'd replied, I love you, and she told me I love you too. Obviously. I cling to this; this evidence that I had said it so close to the end, even though the truth is we said it all the time, especially over WhatsApp, and this probably wasn't special. At least, not at the time.

But it's there.

Beth said,

"You know what I'm looking forward to? Being, like, *thirty*."

"Why?" I asked. Where were we? The kitchen? I remember her being slightly above me, so maybe she was sitting on the kitchen counter, me at the table.

"Because then no one will care if I record a load of folk songs with a ukulele," she said. "They'll be like, fuck her, she's old, let her do what she wants. And I'll be so free."

"To make folk music?"

"Hell yeah!"

"Oh my God, I thought you were cool."

"Fuck you, I am cool!"

No, we weren't in the kitchen, we were in the bathroom. I was in the bath and she was propped up between the taps and the wall, shaving her legs. I remember, because at this point in the conversation, she flicked some hairy foam at me, and I shrieked louder than the offence required and splashed her.

"And they'll stop wanting me," she added. "I'll be able to wear what I want. Do what I want."

"Who's 'they'?"

She made a face. "*Them.* You know. When I don't have a young body any more, they'll leave me alone, and it'll all be so much easier. I can just, like, be."

"It'll still be your body," I said. "You'll still be hot."

I thought I was helping, but she laughed the kind of laugh I didn't understand. It irritated me, that laugh, because it meant she thought I was young and naive, little more than a baby, really. Her tiny innocent little sister.

She was so right. I was a child.

"Oh my God," she said. She jerked her head so her fringe – it was too long at the time, I remember that too – moved away from her eyes. "If I have one wish for you, Em, it'll be that you never understand what I mean by that."

I try and bring the memory into focus, squinting at it. When did this happen, exactly? At what point was Beth in her career? Was it early, when her eyes were still shiny all the time and she smiled properly? Or later, when her face was sunken and it seemed to take a lot of effort simply to move in the world?

It doesn't matter, does it? *When* it was. Just *that* it was.

That wasn't the end of it. I reach into the past, pulling more of the memory out of the dark.

"When you're famous," she said. "You'll handle all of this better than me."

"Better how?" I asked. I loved when she'd talked like that, like my being famous one day was a certainty.

"Just *better*," she said, reaching for the lotion and squeezing some out onto her smooth legs. "Promise me you'll learn from your fuck-up sister, OK? Promise?"

"Promise," I said. It felt good how she smiled at me. "But you'll be there too, so … no need to worry. We'll both be fine."

"Promise?" she asked, half teasing, half serious, and I laughed because it seemed funny then.

"Promise."

Beth yelled,

"What was the best day of your life?"

I shouted, "What?"

"Trick question!" Beth yelled back. "The answer is *today*."

My thirteenth birthday, which happened to fall on the same day that The Jinks were performing at the O2. My present had been to go along before the show and watch them do their soundcheck, explore the whole backstage area, let them dress me up, even do vocal warm-ups with the band. Everyone, even the crew, was treating me like a mini superstar, and I loved every second of it.

I was watching the show from the side of the stage, dancing along, cheering, my whole body buzzing with joy and music and light. The band was midway through the set, which meant it was Jodie's solo, and so Aiya, Tam and Beth were doing a lightning-fast costume change.

And it was this moment, them on their way back to the stage, that Beth grabbed my hand and yelled – she had to yell, because it was all so loud – that question, about the best day of my life. And how it was today. Because—

"It's right now!" Beth was holding an extra microphone. She was sweeping my hair back from my face, dabbing glitter on my cheeks. My heart started beating very, very fast. "The best moment of your life. You ready?"

I managed, "Beth?!"

"Happy birthday, Emmbop," she shouted, and then she pulled me onto the stage with her.

Lights. Noise. The cacophony of a crowd of 20,000 people. Jodie saying something into the microphone, a wide smile on her face, gesturing to me. When I glanced behind us, I saw my face filling the screens.

The Jinks started singing "Happy Birthday" to me, and all those thousands of people joined in. Beth's arm around me the whole time, tight and steady.

When they were finished, Beth said, "Now, it's only fair, Emmy, since we've all sung to you, that you do a bit of singing for us too. What do you think, Jo-Jo?"

"Definitely," Jodie said. "Are you up for it, Emmy?"

"Hell yeah," I said, and they all laughed.

Out of nowhere, two stools appeared beside us, and then I was on one, Beth sitting on the other, and somehow she was holding a guitar, and the rest of The Jinks had left the stage. (They would appear, three minutes later, make-up retouched, water bottles refilled, Jodie in an entirely new outfit.)

"This is a Beck special," Beth told the audience. "For one night only." She smiled at me. Mouthed, *Ready?*

We sang "Emmylou", which we'd been singing together for years at that point. Beth said it was our song, that it had been written for us. So many times, we'd sung it together in her bedroom, in my bedroom, in the car.

Now, together, on stage at the O2. The best moment of my life.

Afterwards, my ears rang for hours and my smile shone for twice as long. Aiya said, pouring me a glass of champagne when the show was over, "Damn, I thought that was going to be cute, but you're actually really good?! You're better than the big Beck. You hear that, Lizzie B? She's better than you."

"I told you she was!" Beth said. "She can be our back-up member. A little mini-me."

"God, don't go that far," Aiya said. "One of you is enough."

"Those harmonies, though," Tam said. She smiled at me. "Really beautiful."

Tam hardly ever seemed to speak when I was around, so this particular compliment hit me twice as hard. I smiled back and tried to make myself stand as tall as possible. "Thank you."

"Stardom awaits," Beth announced, pulling me in close for another hug. Into my ear, she said, "So damn proud of you, Em. That was incredible."

For months after that, she would randomly send me YouTube videos that fans had recorded of that moment at the O2. She particularly favoured those with video titles like, "Lizzie Beck's Little Sister Is SO Talented!" and "LIZZIE AND EMMY BECK LIVE AT THE O2". She messaged I've seen the future and it is BECK SHAPED and Remember when we rocked the O2? and THOSE HARMONIES, THOUGH.

"It's so amazing she did that for you," Ella said at the time. She's the middle of three sisters, and she's always said that they argue constantly, that the very last thing they'd ever want to do is share a stage.

It was, but it also wasn't. Because — and I remember how I said this, with such pride and confidence, such utter obliviousness, at thirteen, of everything that was going to happen to her and to us and to me —

"That's Beth," I said.

There's a thing I would say
   if I was being honest
               (Which is a hard thing to be when someone is dead.)
    and that is that I'm being selective
      with the memories I'm choosing,
        not just to tell, but to remember.
   I know I am.

She wasn't always soft and warm and loving.
   She was hard and cold and wild.
   Out of control, even.
   Not in a cool way, not in a fun way.

                       (In a frightening way.)
   She did things that didn't make sense to me.
   Made choices that didn't make sense to anyone.

                           (Even her.)

But she loved me.
   That's what you have to understand.
   Why my memory is selective, why the softness is at the surface.
   Because she loved me,
     and I loved her,
       and that's the truth.
   It's what matters.
   The only thing that matters.

29 DAYS GONE

Away

We – our family of three – go away.

Mostly because of my minor meltdown over the urn,

but also because, "Enough is enough," Mum says. "Enough of
this circus."

(I assume Sebastien is going to come with us, but Auntie Char arrives
the night before we leave to take him away with her.

"But he won't understand," I say, through tears.

"I'll tell him," Auntie Char says. "Every day, I'll tell him that
you're coming back.")

We go to a cottage in the Scottish Highlands. It's right on the edge
of a loch.

"Beautiful," Mum says. She says it over and over. That first
morning she tells me about the trip, and while we're packing, and
when we arrive two days later. Like the word is an incantation, but
summoning what, I don't know.

The cottage is ours for three weeks, which is the longest holiday we've
ever had. (Not that this is a holiday. Mum calls it "convalescence".
Dad calls it "running away".)

I don't know what they expect to happen in twenty-one days.

(One day for every year of Beth's life.)

Whether they think it's certified Grief Time, and when we get
home it'll be

over.   Back to normal.   Done.

Maybe that the three of us will figure out how our family of three
will work.

Talk.   Cry.   Bond.

But the only thing that really happens in Scotland is that time
passes. Each of those twenty-one days starts and ends, and though
the three of us cry – even Dad, I hear him in the bathroom sometimes
– we barely talk, and we certainly don't bond. I watch a lot of TV.

I don't sing, or play the guitar I brought with me. Dad spends most of his time in the office he sets up for himself in one of the rooms, though I don't understand what he could be doing in there, what work there is when there's no Jinks left to manage. Most likely, it's just an excuse to hide from us, to not face what's left of our family.

Mum and I go for walks, but they're mostly silent. When she does talk, it's about birds or stags or lochs. If I bring up Beth, I see the way her face tenses, like she's bracing against an approaching storm, and I can't bear it, so I stop trying and I ask her instead to tell me more about birds and stags and lochs.

And then the days are gone, and it's our last week in Scotland, and Dad gets a phone call to tell him that Leo has overdosed.

Not on purpose. Not a death wish.

The drug addict kind.

He's in hospital. Stable; he'll be fine.

"OK," I say, when Dad comes into my room to tell me, like he thinks I will care.

He waits, as if for more. I say nothing.

"Emmy," he says.

"What?"

Another silence. "I'm going to London," he says.

"Why?"

"He needs someone there for him."

Leo doesn't have much in the way of parents. I know that in a vague way; no details.

"OK, but why are you going?"

Dad shuts the door without answering me.

He's gone by the time I get downstairs.

Dad doesn't come back. He says — Mum tells me — that there's no point, because we're due to leave in a few days anyway.

It's up to Mum and me to pack up the cottage and get ourselves home.

"Could we just stay?" I ask. I don't think I really mean the cottage, or even Scotland. I think I mean this stasis, this limbo, where there is no life, no forward motion, just being.

Mum doesn't reply to this. She just smiles, the sad kind, like she understands. She doesn't say what I know, which is that we have to go home, back to our lives, because that's what you have to do. I appreciate that.

But that's also what hurts. I know that the expectation will shift to *moving on* when we get home. It won't be like it was before, when I was allowed to just wallow in grief and that was OK. Now, Beth's death will become something that *happened* to me, instead of something that *is happening* to me.

Moving on. What does that even really mean? Carrying on, I guess. Moving on with my life without Beth. Figuring out who I am now, what my life is. It just seems so … impossible.

The truth is I still don't know how I can live my life without her, even after these three weeks of quiet, when I was probably meant to start figuring it out. I don't just mean that in any kind of dramatic way; I mean it in a literal way. I really don't know *how*. What will my life look like without her in it? When this period of grief is over — and I do know it will be over one day — and my life has found some kind of new normal, what is that going to be? Will I ever truly think of myself as an only child? *Am* I an only child?

For the rest of my life new people I meet will say, do you have any siblings? And I'll have to decide whether to kill the chilled vibe by saying *I had a sister who died* and *yes, it's awful, isn't it, well actually it was suicide* or save the chilled vibe by telling a lie that will be exposed as a lie later if me and this imagined stranger become friends and then I'll look weird for having lied.

God, and not just a sister who died by suicide either. A *famous* sister who died by suicide. 99% of people I tell in my imagined future will know, instantly, who Lizzie Beck was, and how she died. And I'll say, *she was always Beth to me*, and they'll nod as if they understand. Maybe, as I get older and further away from her, the Beth and the Lizzie will merge until I stop thinking of them as separate people. Or maybe they'll get further apart, and I'll be left with Beth.

My whole life, the five years between Beth and me has been the marker of growing up. At every one of Beth's birthdays, I've thought, *in five years' time that will be me*. It always felt impossible, but also something entirely dependable. By the time I got there, I would have learned how to be that age, because I was following her. Always, following her.

Every year from now, that gap will shrink, until it disappears entirely. One unfathomable day I will be older than she ever got to be. One day I will turn twenty-two. Will I still think of her as my older sister, that day when she is long gone, and, impossibly, younger than me?

How do people deal with people they love dying? *How?* It's happening to me and I don't even know.

I miss Beth so much I think I might die with it.

I am the only child of two grieving parents and it's going to wreck me.

I don't know how to live in this life any more.

I don't know how to be.

50 DAYS GONE

Home, again

I hate being back home.

Hate it.

Hate it.

Being in Scotland felt like taking a break from my life to grieve,
which was nice.

But the thing with taking a break is that the break ends
and then you have to carry on with the thing you needed to
take a break from in the first place.

And when you take a break from life to grieve, then you come back,
you find out
that life has just carried right on.

No one is talking about Lizzie Beck any more.

When I check, her name isn't trending.

Or in the headlines.

And I should probably be glad about that
but I'm not.

Because she died, and how can they just stop caring about that?

It has only been fifty days.

She should be on the front pages for the next fifty years.

Our first night back home, the three of us — Mum and Dad and me, reunited — eat fish and chips at the kitchen table, which feels too big now after the small table I'd got used to in the cottage in Scotland. It felt like a manageable space, up in the Highlands. Now, our familiar house seems strange and huge; ballooned in all the wrong ways.

When I walked over the threshold earlier, dragging my suitcase behind me, I thought, *I'm home again*, followed by the inevitable, *Beth will never be home again*, and then I went into her bedroom and lay on her bed and cried. I only re-emerged when Auntie Char came round to return Sebastien to us. He rubbed against my legs, purring, which made me cry again.

To me, Auntie Char said, "He missed you!" and to Mum she said, "How was it? Do you feel … any better?"

And Mum said, "Thank you for looking after Sebastien."

Now, Auntie Char has gone and Dad is talking about Leo. His "state of mind", his "trajectory of recovery", the rehab centre he's going to go to. The same one Beth was in.

"What's the point?" I say.

Dad looks at me. "What do you mean?" he asks, but so tiredly, like talking to me is such an effort.

"It doesn't work, clearly," I say. "What with Beth being dead, and everything."

There's a silence. So I carry on.

"And who gives a fuck, anyway? Why do you even care about him?"

Mum starts to say my name, but Dad's already talking over her. "I don't know what's got into you, but it has to stop. We didn't raise you to be so utterly selfish and cruel."

There are so many things I could say back, but he doesn't give me a chance. He stands up before he's even finished speaking and leaves the room.

Mum sighs. She closes her eyes for a moment, then says, "Leo needs kindness. He loved Beth."

"So? What difference does that make now?"

She could explain, but she doesn't. She could actually talk to me, but she won't. She just says, "Oh, Emmy," and it makes me want to throw my plate across the room. Maybe even *at* her.

Instead, I say, "I wish he'd died."

"You don't, Emmy."

"I do!"

She's staring at me like she's never seen me before.

"What?" *Yell at me. Please. Scream at me. Do something.*

"This isn't like you," she says.

"What does that even *mean*?"

"You've always been compassionate," she says, face pinched. "Empathetic. Leo is hurting, Emmy. He's—"

"Fuck Leo," I say, and the words are so satisfying, and her face so shocked, I say it again, louder. "*Fuck* Leo."

She closes her eyes again. Sighs again. "Maybe you should talk to someone."

You. I want to talk to you. I want you to talk to me.

"You're angry. That's ... that's understandable. Maybe you'd benefit from some sort of support group."

"You think there are support groups for the siblings of dead celebrities?"

Mum's eyes open as her face tightens. I expect her to say, *Don't use that tone with me, Emmeline.* But instead, she says, "Don't call her a dead celebrity."

"Why not? It's what she is."

"She's your sister. She's Beth."

"And Lizzie Beck. And dead."

"Stop it, Emmy."

"Are we pretending none of that happened now?"

"Emmeline."

"You can't just forget about the Lizzie Beck bit. That's basically the reason she's dead."

"What is the matter with you?"

"*Me?* What's the matter with *you?* Maybe you're the one who needs a support group."

"For God's sake, Emmeline!" She shouts this, right at me, out of nowhere, and I shrink back, despite myself, in surprise. "Why are you being like this with me? Don't you think I've got enough to deal with?"

I want to yell back at her, to force her to see me and to actually *talk* to me, even if that's at a particularly high volume. But there are tears coming, the unstoppable kind, even though I'm so sick of crying, so *fucking sick* of crying, and instead of yelling I crumple right there at the kitchen table, and she hugs me, and cries a little too.

We still don't talk. We just stay there, all crumpled together, crying. At one point, I glance up to see that Sebastien has made his way onto the table — a certified no-Sebastien zone — and is fully buried in the remains of Dad's fish. There's batter on his ear. Fish flakes in his whiskers.

"Sebastien!" I say, sharp and automatic.

He barely flinches, just carries on eating.

"Oh, leave him," Mum says, so tiredly. "I'm glad at least one of us is happy." She runs a hand over her face, squeezing her fingertips against her eyes. "I'm sorry I shouted, Emmy."

"That's OK."

"No, it isn't. You've obviously got a lot of … a lot of feelings."

A lot of feelings. Seriously. Seriously?

I don't say this. I don't say anything.

"I think you should talk to someone," she continues. "I've been thinking that for a while, but I kept forgetting. I'm sorry. There's just so much…" She shakes her head. "Last month, Sufiya recommended a therapist who is good with this kind of thing."

This kind of thing.

Death?

Suicide?

Fame?

Shouty teenagers?

"What do you think?" Mum says. I wonder if she notices that I haven't spoken.

I nod and shrug at the same time.

"Good," she says, standing. She sweeps up Sebastien with one arm – he yowls his outrage – and moves towards the kitchen door, all without quite looking at me. "I'll book in some sessions for you."

51 DAYS GONE

Summer

Summer is happening all around me. I'd kind of forgotten it even *was* summer, up in the Highlands. But now I'm back in Surrey, and it's so hot outside, and with the window open I can hear *life* happening somewhere out there, where normal still is. I stay inside, sometimes in my room, sometimes in Beth's, sitting with the cat for as long as he'll tolerate, or with my guitar, not playing it. My friends message me, alternating between overly cautious, loving messages, asking how I am, and trying too hard to be normal. Except Grey, who is just herself.

Grey
Anderson Jay is having a party.
Come?

Emmy
You don't even like Anderson Jay.

So? Party's a party. We're all going. Please come? You can leave if you hate it.

I'll think about it.

Please, Em. I miss you. Like, SERIOUSLY MISS YOU. You know I love Ell and Trix but they are NOT YOU. I need my girl.

Grey, it's just hard.

I know. I'm sorry. But I promise you it will be less hard with your friends, OK? In the sunshine?

Maybe she's right. Wouldn't it be nice if she was right? The sun on my face and my friends by my side. Totally all I'd need to forget that my sister is ashes.

I close my eyes and breathe in and out in a long sigh. I wish I could just will myself into *being* myself again. That I could simply decide to go out and have the summer my friends and I had planned, months ago.

Because in the alternative universe version of my life? This summer would have been *everything*. I'd have been focused on my audition for Shona Lee, on worrying for myself and my friends and our futures – because, I thought, there was no future without Shona Lee – practising constantly, probably driving my parents crazy by singing around the house at all hours. Scottie and I would have had sex by now, or at the very least been getting closer and closer to it, which I would have obsessed over, in between all the singing and worrying. Trix, Ella, Grey and I would have spent long hours at each other's houses, out at the rec, trips to the West End, going out to parties closer to home, just *being sixteen* together. The summer between Year 11 and sixth form is meant to be Shona Lee gold, and I've already missed so much. Can't I at least *try* to be there for some of it?

Anyway, so I say yes to Grey about Anderson Jay's party, and she's thrilled. So thrilled, in fact, that I almost change my mind.

Come and get ready at mine! Grey commands. Like old times. Swiftly, she deletes this last bit. It'll be fun! she writes instead, clearly hoping I won't have seen the original.

I'm trying to be the old Emmy, the fun-time Emmy, so I agree and send a smiling emoji. I decide this is progress, not snapping at her. Maybe I'm getting better. Maybe.

Getting ready with my friends used to be one of my very favourite things to do.

A dance playlist on Spotify.

Perfume spritzed in the air between us.

The four of us tripping over each other, we were that close.

Buttons and zips and straps and hair grips between teeth.

Giddy with laughter and Prosecco and anticipation.

The getting ready bit was always better than whatever happened wherever we were going.

(That and the coming back at the end of it,
   ready to fall asleep on Grey's gigantic bed, pyjamaed and
   scrubbed clean, after debriefing the night with toothpaste
   breath and the alcohol afterglow.)

I think a part of me thought it would all still be there, waiting for me. That safety and that giddy joy. It was separate from Beth, I thought. Something that was entirely mine; part of the reason I cherished it so much.

But I step over the threshold and I know immediately that it's gone, like everything has gone. Something else sacred that disappeared with Beth.

It's just a bedroom. It's not magic or special. Not any more.

They try.

Of course they do; they try.

My best friends, determinedly upbeat, talking away to me and to each other, even when I'm clearly not listening.

I try too. I try to smile. Try to listen. Try to be their Emmy.

I'm fully dressed and waiting for Grey to finish putting on her make-up before a thought suddenly occurs to me. "Is Scottie going to be there?"

"No," Ella says. "He's giving it a miss."

"Because of me?"

Ella shrugs, which means yes.

I should feel bad, but I don't feel anything.

I wish I felt something. I pinch down on the skin at my wrist until it hurts, which helps.

Trix says, softly, "Are you OK?"

I make myself smile at her, say, "Yeah!"

She obviously doesn't believe me, but she doesn't push me for the truth, which I appreciate. I remember how, the very first time we met on our first day at Shona Lee, she leaned over to me and whispered, "I have never been so excited and so terrified in my entire life," and I knew we were going to be friends.

Grey turns on the spot, sliding the chain of her bag up over her shoulder. "Ready?" she says, in the voice that means it isn't really a question, but a command.

"Ready," Ella and Trix say together. I nod.

"Cool," Grey says, glancing in her mirror for the last time and tossing her hair. "Let's go."

"Do you think people are going to be weird with me?" I ask, not moving.

"No," Ella says, immediate and reassuring.

"Yes," Grey says. When Ella shoots her a very obvious glare, she rolls her eyes. "Well, they are. Lying about it won't stop it." She looks at me. "Sorry, Em. But we're here for you, so just let them be weird. Not your problem."

I must look uncertain because she reaches out and touches the side of my face, exactly the way I've seen her mother do to her. It's somehow both reassuring and intimidating.

"You're good," she says, very simply, in a way that gives me no choice but to believe her.

So I do.

There are usually multiple Shona Lee parties over the summer – probably at least two already happened while I was away – and it's a general rule that there's a running open invitation on all of them. If you go to Shona Lee, you can assume you're invited.

So even though we're not friends with Anderson Jay – beyond the intense, unspoken loyalty we all share as the chosen Shona Lee few – it's not weird when the four of us turn up on his doorstep, where we find Raef Selim smoking a cigarette by the open door.

"Hey," he says, smiling. Immediately, I calculate how many months it's been since his mother died – maybe nine or ten? – and wonder if that's how long I'll have to wait before I smile normally again. And then I wonder how long it will be before I stop relating literally everything I see to Beth's death, and if doing so makes me selfish, or at the very least self-absorbed.

And then I realize I'm just standing there, staring at Raef, who is looking back expectantly.

Shit, I think he asked me something.

Grey raises her eyebrows at me.

Fuck.

"Yeah," I say, attempting a half-laugh. I have a 50/50 chance of this being the correct response. "Sure."

I'm wrong. I can tell by their faces.

"Well," I say, then trail off, because what am I supposed to say? God, I was an idiot, agreeing to come here. What was I thinking? I'm not ready to be around people yet. I should be at home, curled up on the sofa, eating Jaffa Cakes by the packet and crying about my dead sister.

"We'll chat in a bit, Raef, yeah?" Ella says, taking my arm and guiding me inside.

"Sure, see you later," Raef says, amiable.

It's loud inside the house. Music is thumping from at least two different rooms, discordant and weirdly unnerving, like an irregular heartbeat. As we walk through the entry hall, Ella's arm still through mine, there's a crash from somewhere above us, followed by something tumbling down the stairs. When I look over, a plant pot is cracked in two pieces, soil coating the stairs and the floor.

"Fuck's sake!" Anderson, clomping down the stairs, shouts this over his shoulder. "You fucking broke it!"

"Oh my God," Grey mutters, in her most judgemental, disdainful voice. "It's barely eight and we're already at this point? Remind me why we came here?"

"It was your idea," I say. Usually, Grey's lack of patience with people our own age acting like people our own age makes me laugh, but right now it just annoys me.

"I thought it might cheer you up," she says.

"So it's my fault?"

She blinks at me. "God, calm down, Em. I'm not getting at you. I was just saying."

"Also, I don't need to be *cheered up*," I snap. "What the fuck is wrong with you?"

"Woah, OK," Trix says, trying to laugh, her voice a nervous shake. "Let's go get a drink or something, OK?" When neither of us says anything, she says to Grey, "OK?"

I can tell she's making eyes at her, because Grey bites down hard on her lip before she smiles at me, very tensely, and nods. Grey never, ever, lets a jibe go unchallenged, let alone something as aggressive as "What the fuck is wrong with you?" so clearly my trump card of grief is still valid. Maybe I should be grateful for this, but I'm not. I still feel all hot and annoyed, like my skin is itching. I hate everyone, even my friends. Even *Grey*. Especially Grey.

"Can we go?" I say.

"We just got here," Ella says, uncertainly.

"I want to go," I say. Trix opens her mouth, but I talk over her. "Actually, forget it. You guys stay. I'll just get a cab home."

"I thought you were staying at my house tonight?" Grey says.

"No. I want to go home." I do a quick mental check of what I have with me, if I've left anything I actually need at Grey's house. No, thank God. I'm free.

"Emmy," Grey says, using her firm voice again. "Look at me." When I do, she touches my arm. "You're spiralling. Take a second."

I wonder what it would feel like to slap her right now. Would how much I'd regret it balance out how good it would feel for that one split second?

"Oh, shit! *Emmy.*" The voice is beside me, loaded and loud, and I turn to see Olivia Valero, one of the true Shona Lee elite among elites, widening her eyes at me. "You're really here."

I mean, what the actual fuck am I meant to say to that?

I say, "Yeah."

"Sorry about your sister, or whatever," she says.

Or whatever.

Olivia isn't a bitch, not really. She's just not my friend, and she's the kind of person who gets an easy ride because she's beautiful and cool, so she's never needed to cultivate things like real empathy. So, this might sound like a peak bitch comment, but the truth is actually more mundane, and maybe even a little bit worse. For her, it really is just an *or whatever.* Someone else's problem in someone else's life.

"Thanks," I say. "Or whatever."

Her eyebrows lift slightly, but she doesn't say anything else.

"That was really sensitive, Liv," Grey says. "Have you been practising?"

Olivia doesn't reply, just curls her lip slightly in disdain, then walks away without a word.

Grey rolls her eyes at me, but there's a tentative smile on her face that is so un-Grey-like it catches me off-guard. "See how nothing changes?"

"I think that was her trying," Trix says. "Like, actually trying to be nice."

"How depressing," Grey says. "Em, if you want to leave, then that's obviously fine. But can we dance first? One song?"

I hesitate.

"One song," Trix repeats, nodding.

"With us," Ella adds. "Before you go."

She takes my hand and starts leading me towards the living room, where the music is pulsing out of the doorway. I'm just trying to decide how strongly to object when the song changes, and it's like a shot of electricity directly to my heart. Like I've been plugged into something. For the first time in a long time.

Beside me, Grey lets out a shriek. "*Yes!*" She spins around, eyes alight, to grin at me, and I can't help it, I really can't. I grin back. She shrieks again, actually clapping her hands, and bounds into the room, Trix right behind her. Ella follows, tugging me after her, and I go, willingly.

"Are You Gonna Be My Girl", by Jet, is like the unofficial Shona Lee anthem. No one remembers why, or how it started, but if you get a group of Shona Lee kids together and play it, magic happens. Does that sound cheesy as hell? It is. But in the best way.

It's a shortcut to happiness, this song. It's the kind of song where, while it's playing, it feels like it's the only thing that matters. Like you could just live inside it and be OK.

Everyone is singing/shouting along. It's hot and loud and perfect. The music fills the room. I move and dance and bounce on and off the beat. I even laugh.

And for those three minutes.

Three little minutes.

Everything is

almost

OK.

OK doesn't last. The song ends.

(The song always ends.)

"Happy" comes on, and I'm so aware that I shouldn't be happy, that I'm not happy, and I hate that I can't just hear the song and *be* happy. Suddenly, so suddenly, I'm angry again, like I could set fire to the whole world just to get it to stop.

I tell my friends that I need some air and leave, hoping they won't follow me, but of course they do. Friends turned babysitters. Grief-sitters.

I don't want to, but I can see the disappointment in Grey's eyes, like she wanted the break from my vibe-ruining grief to last a little bit longer than three minutes. I wanted that too. But I'm allowed to think that; she isn't.

"Just go back in," I snap at her, and her eyes widen in bewildered surprise. "I don't need you hanging onto me."

There's a flash of hurt on her face, but only for the briefest moment, before she covers it. "Let's get a drink," she says.

"Or we can get some air," Ella suggests.

"Or you can just give me a minute," I say, too harshly. "Please? I want some space."

Grey opens her mouth to say something, but stops when Trix touches her arm. She shrugs. "OK, go, then."

"Fine," I say.

"Good," she says. "But, Em?"

Trix bites her lip, anxious.

"What?" I ask.

"You know it's not our fault, right?" Grey says. "Beth being dead. It's not our fault."

52 DAYS GONE

The boy in the kitchen

The only sensible decision I make that night is to walk away from them instead of responding to Grey. I walk without thinking, which is why I head away from the front door and deeper into the house, through the hall, towards the garden. There are so many people around; way too many. When they see me, they all say things like, "Oh! Emmy!" and "Shit! Emmy!" Always that exclamation.

I go back inside without talking to any of them and find my way into the kitchen, which is empty except for Anderson Jay himself, on his own, thumping out ice trays into a bucket. His back is slightly to me so he doesn't hear me come in, but I can hear him humming "The Rhythm of Life", from the musical *Sweet Charity*, which is weirdly endearing. *Endearing* is not a word I'd have chosen for Anderson before.

They're not exactly flattering, the words I would have chosen for him. Shona Lee is a small school, and everyone knows everyone pretty well, especially by reputation. And the thing with Anderson is that he's slept with about half the girls in our year. (So people say, anyway.)

Grey thinks he's trash. "Hot trash," she says, "is still trash."

(But Grey thinks all Shona Lee boys are beneath her.)

Anderson Jay and Keela O'Connell both got suspended for getting caught mid-fellatio in the PE cupboard during one lunch break in Year 10. (Or so the rumour goes.)

Keela transferred out not long after that. Anderson shrugged the whole thing off, the way boys can.

He still got the lead in *Hairspray* that year.

He's been the cream of the Shona Lee crop since his first day in Year 7.

He and I have basically never had a real conversation about anything outside of Shona Lee and schoolwork. We've always just moved in different circles. Two years ago, we had to do a composition assignment together in Music. It surprised me at the time that he didn't act like a dick, didn't mention my famous sister or The Jinks, which he definitely could have done; most people did.

I've never given much thought to liking him, but I've never disliked him, either.

Right now, he feels like the only person who doesn't think he knows me. So when I walk into the kitchen, and he's standing there with his ice trays, I don't grab a beer and leave. I take two beers and go over to him.

I say, "Need some help?"

He looks up at me, curious, but smiling. "Hey, Em," he says.

(There is no reason for me to already be "Em" to him,
    except that he can see into the future,
        just like I can,
            for him and me and this night.)

I smile back. He takes the second beer. He says, "Sorry about—"
But stops when I put my hand up. There's a brief silence and then he says, "You all right?" Like I'm normal, and this is normal.

And I say, "Yeah. Not too bad. You?"

    And that's it.

        That's all it takes.

                What I find out
            that night with Anderson
        is that it's very easy to become
    someone you never thought you could be.
        In fact, it turns out it's as easy as
            "Need some help?"
                And a smile.

In the kitchen we
    talk
    smile
    drink beer
    knock out ice into buckets

And then

In the garden we
    talk
    laugh
    drink beer
    stand close

And then

In the living room we
    dance
    shout
    laugh

And then

In the hallway we
    stumble with
    his arm around my shoulder and
    a smile on my face and
    my back is against the wall and
    he steps close and
    kissing and tongues and hot and forgetting

And then
    up the stairs

hand in hand
fuzzy drunk and high on kissing (and a mistake in the making)

And then
his bedroom door
opening
and then closing.
A bed
a boy
and me.

I've never kissed anyone like this before,
never been kissed like this.
I feel like I'm watching myself because it doesn't seem real.

I didn't think I was this person,
the person following someone towards a bed,
lying down.

The "someone" isn't Scottie.
This "person" isn't even really me, either.

Anderson says, "You want to? You want to?"
And I say, "Yes. Yes."

It goes,
him, heavy, on top of me.
Legs entangled, tongues, fingers.
The scrape of foil, the smell of rubber.
Push, hard, inside.

It hurts (it really fucking hurts) but I don't make a sound, so he
probably doesn't notice. *Push push thrust.* I'd planned to move like girls

do in videos, moan a bit maybe, say something sexy, but actually I just lie there while he thrusts and he doesn't seem to notice.

I think, in an actual sentence, *So, this is sex.*

And then it's over.

He rolls off me, says something that I think might actually be, "Thanks."

I want to be cool, but my body is feeling things my mind can't control, and so I cry, and he's annoyed, I can tell, but he's trying to hide it, which I guess is nice.

He says, his voice almost irritated like boys get when they're anxious, "You did it before, didn't you? You and Wilde, you did?"

I know he can tell by my face that I didn't, because he says, "Why didn't you tell me? I would've..."

But would've what, I don't know. Would've cared more, maybe? Would've made it nice?

But why did he need a reason for that?

Scottie would have made it nice, but that's OK. I didn't want it to be nice.

So why am I crying? Crying harder now, trying to hide my face so he can't see, and also so I don't have to see whatever's on *his* face.

I put my clothes back on, shake my head when he tries to talk to me, leave.

I summon an Uber and go home without talking to anyone. There are messages from my friends, asking where I am, but I ignore them too.

It's later than I'd realized, and my house is dark and quiet. I let myself in, kick off my shoes and go upstairs. When I reach the top, the door to my parents' room opens.

"Emmy?"

It's Mum, using her mum-voice. Soft, searching, not quite worried, but anticipating the possible need to worry. I hadn't realized just how much I'd missed this voice until this very moment, just normal mum-voice, and I feel tears rise in my eyes. I whisper, "Yeah?"

"You're home," she says. "I thought you were going to stay with Grey?"

"I changed my mind."

"Did something happen?"

Anderson's tongue. His fingers. His penis.

"No."

It is the most unconvincing *no* in the world, and I wait for her to ask me again. Just one more time will be enough. I want to cry on her, like all those times I let *her* cry on *me* these last few months. She will ask me what's wrong and she'll stroke my hair and I'll say, *Beth. It's all Beth. Beth is gone and it's always going to be Beth.* Everything that will ever happen to me will happen in a world where I can't tell Beth. This, the first time I've had sex, and all the sex I'll ever have with all the people I'll ever meet. All the parties I'll leave in tears. Every heartache, forever exacerbated by the fact that I won't be able to tell her about it. Forever dwarfed by what I've already lost.

"Good night, then," Mum says.

In the dark, I just nod. My tears are flowing freely now, tracing lines down to my lips. I think about kissing Anderson, how his mouth felt against mine.

"I love you," Mum says, then shuts the door before I can reply.

* * *

My room feels too empty, too quiet, so I go on a hunt for Sebastien. I find him in the last place I look, which of course should have been the first place, because he's in Beth's room, lying on her bed. I take my place beside him, very carefully, very slowly, and am rewarded by the fact that he doesn't move, not even when I let my head rest very gently against his fluffy back. I close my eyes, try to summon my sister into this moment when I need her so badly.

She would say, *You OK, there?* with a smile in her voice. I would tell her everything, and she'd lift her arm so I could crawl in for a hug. It would be warm and soft, like she was. Safe.

I keep my eyes closed. Sebastien has started purring.

Beth would say, *So, how was it? Any good?*

I don't know... Like, maybe? Kind of? What does good feel like?

This would make her laugh. She'd say, *When it is, you'll know.*

Helpful! Can you at least give me some tips?

I wait. I open one eye, then both of them. The room is still and quiet, and the friendly-ghost version of Beth I've conjured in my head is gone. Of course I can't imagine what her tips would have been, because I never got to hear them.

We never talked about sex, not really, because I was always too young. I knew we would one day, when I'd graduate from being her kid sister to being just her sister sister, her friend. That would be the kind of relationship we'd have as we got older together. Beth used to say, *Em, just wait until you're old enough for us to go drinking together. I bet you'll be hilarious when you're drunk. Oh my God, we'll have so much fun.*

I guess she just … forgot about that. That we had plans together. That there were so many things we were supposed to do. Together.

Sebastien lets out a chirp beside me, making me start in surprise. It's what Mum calls his "wake-up chirp", because he makes it anytime someone touches him while he's sleeping.

Was it me? Did I nudge him by mistake?

Or…

"Beth?" I whisper. "Are you there?"

My heart is fluttering like a trapped bird.

"Beth?"

I wait. I hope.

But there's just silence.

It all looks a lot clearer in the morning.

Which is to say, I regret having sex with Anderson.

I wish I didn't. I hadn't planned to regret it. But I do.

Mostly because I can't tell anyone.

I can't tell my friends, because they are also friends with Scottie, and I don't want him to know. Plus, they don't like Anderson — especially Grey — and I'm really, really not in the mood to face any judgement right now.

I can't tell Mum, because she's my mum, and also because we just don't seem to talk any more, not like we used to.

I can't tell Beth, because she's dead, and apparently doesn't seem in any great hurry to haunt me, even when I need her.

So I have to sit with the knowledge that I've had sex. Alone.

(Which is a really shit way to sit with this kind of knowledge.)

There's only one person I can talk to about it, and so, I message Anderson.

I go to his house.

We have sex again. It's better.

I tell him, after, that I don't really understand what's happening.

Which I guess isn't a very flattering thing to say. He looks kind of hurt.

I remind him that he didn't exactly want to have sex with me. It just happened.

And he says, "Shit, Emmy. You're literally still in my bed."

Which I am.

And then he laughs and kisses me.

Later, when I'm at home in bed, he messages me.

Wanted to say this earlier.
I know things must be so shit
for you right now. I hope this
thing with me is good.

It's a nice thing for a sixteen-year-old boy to say.
I reply:

It is good.

Present tense?

Present tense.

I know it's probably a mistake. I don't care.

Grey
Hey Em, you OK?

Emmy
Yeah

You sure?

Yeah

Do you want to talk about last
night?

No.

Do you want to talk about
anything?

No.

OK...

OK.

59 DAYS GONE

Change

I decide to get a haircut.

   Because my life is so completely out of my control, clearly,

      if people I love can just up and leave it without warning

         if people can bully and bitch and ruin lives with no
         consequence

            if someone like Beth can die like Beth did and the world
            just carries right on.

But I am in control of my hair, so:

I want a haircut. A major, drastic life-change kind of haircut that will make people who know me go "Oh my God!" when they see me.

I tell Mum that I need to have my hair done without adding that I want to change it completely, and she hands over her debit card without asking any questions.

I tell the hairdresser that my sister died and so I want a new haircut.

She looks alarmed, then awkward. "Um," she says.

Long pause.

"OK. So ... what do you want me to do with your hair?"

(Thousands upon thousands of people die every single day, and still people don't know how to react if you mention just one of them.)

She talks to me for a few minutes about what I want my hair to look like, then disappears.

Later, an older woman comes over to me; it turns out she's the manager of the salon.

"Hello," she says to me. She has a very kind smile. "Would you mind if I take over from Alys?"

I shrug.

"I'm Diane," she says. "I'm very sorry about your sister. Would you like to tell me about her while I take care of your hair?"

Which is nice of her.

When I leave, I want to tell Diane that I will remember her for the rest of my life. That I will never, not ever, forget the way she listened and nodded and smiled as I told her about my sister, even without knowing that my sister was famous, someone she would have heard of, probably had talked about, at length, while she cut other people's hair, part of a band whose songs would have played in the salon. That there was more care in the way she patted my shoulder when she was finished than I've felt since the day Beth died.

What I say is, "Thanks."

I walk into the kitchen to find Mum sitting with Auntie Char and a pile of papers. When she sees me, her whole face jolts with shock.

"What did you do?" she says, the words like a gasp.

Which is a stupid question, because it couldn't be more obvious what I did.

"Cut my hair," I say. "You know that. Remember how you gave me your card?"

"Don't snark at me, Emmeline," she says. "You know you should have discussed this with me first."

"Why? It's my hair."

"That's very much not the point."

"Are you seriously going to have a go at me about this? Remember when Beth dyed hers *blue*? And all those tattoos she got without asking you first?"

"Don't bring Beth into this."

I laugh, because this is such a stupid thing to say it doesn't deserve a proper response.

"Emmeline! Go to your room."

I roll my eyes, hard and dramatic. "As opposed to...?"

"What's gotten into you?" she asks, sounding like my mother from three months ago and not the one who can barely hold a conversation with me. "You've never had an attitude."

That's a Beth word if ever I heard one. It's what the teachers used to say about her before she got so famous she dropped out of school. Not just attitude; attitude *problem*. She wrote a song about it, actually.

They say I've got an attitude/But I just—

"Emmy," Mum says, voice tense, and I jump.

"What do you want me to do?" I snap, probably more harshly than I would have done if she hadn't interrupted the sound of Beth's voice in my head, which is becoming increasingly, frighteningly rare. "Go back in time? Glue it back on?"

"OK," Auntie Char says, reminding us both that she's sitting right there. "Let's all take a second, OK? Emmy, your mother's just had a surprise, that's all. Obviously, this is a change you felt you wanted to make— Where are you going?"

I'm on my way out of the kitchen, because if I stay there and listen to Auntie Char trying to be understanding while Mum glares, I will definitely cry and ruin the whole *attitude* thing. "Going to my room," I throw over my shoulder, proud that my voice doesn't shake.

I stomp up the stairs, and neither one of them follows me.

When I get to my room, I go to the mirror and stare at myself, taking in my new reflection. Diane gave me exactly what I'd asked for: a side shaved buzz cut, a few inches lobbed off the length, the colour now a deep, rich chestnut brown with caramel highlights. It looks amazing. So amazing it doesn't feel like it really belongs to me; more like I've stolen it off someone else's head.

But it's mine. When I touch my fingers to the strands of my side fringe, my reflection follows suit.

I'd planned to take at least fifty selfies to send to Trix and Ella and Grey, maybe a video too. I wanted us to talk about something real again, something that wasn't soaked in pain. To smile and laugh and just be sixteen with my friends. I wanted to be that Emmy again, just for a while, for their benefit as well as mine.

But when I try to take the first selfie, I can't summon a smile, even a fake one. Not even for three seconds.

I don't know what I wanted Mum to say.

Actually, that's not true. I do know what I wanted her to say.

I wanted her to say, "Emmy! Wow!"

And I'd say, nervously, "Do you think it looks OK?"

And she'd say, "It looks brilliant."

And, "Beth would love it."

Dad gets home late again. I don't expect him to come and say hello to me, but he knocks on my door and ducks his head into my room with a smile.

"Let's see this haircut, then."

I'm sitting at my desk, scrolling through the results of a Google images search for "Lizzie Beck hair". I turn to face him and point at my head.

His smile widens. "Bold."

"In a good way?"

He nods. "It looks great."

"Aren't you mad?" I ask. "Mum was mad."

"No, I'm impressed," he says. He gives me a smile that is part conspiratorial, part understanding, and reaches out to give my shoulder a chummy nudge with his knuckle. "I didn't know you had it in you."

It should make me feel good, hearing that. I should enjoy being on the receiving end of one of those smiles, the kind I used to see him direct at Beth all the time. Like they were friends as well as father and daughter. Like he liked her as a person, as well as loved her as a daughter.

But it doesn't make me feel good, and I don't enjoy it. It just makes me sad.

60 DAYS GONE
Secret

Anderson likes my hair.

It's a giant betrayal to go and see him first, instead of my best friends, but I do it anyway.

"Wow!" he says, when he opens the door to me. His eyes have gone wide.

"Do you like it?" I ask. It doesn't look as good as it did in the hairdressers, now it's up to just me, mousse and a hairbrush, and to be honest I'm a bit nervous about it.

"It looks so cool," he says. He still looks a little stunned, which makes me laugh. "Holy shit, Emmy. You're like a whole different person."

"Good," I say. "That was the general idea."

He gestures for me to come inside, and I do, letting my smile grow wider when his back is to me on the way up the stairs to his room. His TV is on, so I ask him what he's been watching, and he says it's a video game, not a TV show. I make the mistake of asking him about the game and he spends — I am not kidding — twenty minutes telling me about *Assassin's Creed*. It's sort of sweet, how excited he gets when he talks about it. (But, also, really boring.)

"Is that what you want to do?" I ask, when I finally spot a gap in his monologue. "While I'm here, I mean?"

For a second, I think he's actually going to say yes, all enthusiastic, but then his face flickers with understanding and he smiles wide, setting the controller down and coming towards me.

"What's the other option?" he asks.

So. Anderson and me. I guess we're ... a thing?

Some kind of something. But not a thing thing. A multi-night stand. That also includes daytimes.

Something that doesn't need a label, that's what I mean. That's what I want, obviously. I'm not in a rush to share what's going on between us, even as days turn into weeks and I'm seeing him more and more.

And when Anderson says, "This is, like ... a secret, right?" I say, "Totally. I haven't told anyone." And I really mean it, honest. I don't even want to think about what my friends would say. And I really, really, *really* don't want to think about Scottie.

For the most part, not thinking about Scottie is pretty easy. This thing-not-a-thing that Anderson and I have is nothing at all like what Scottie and I had. Scottie and I did stuff, went places, hung out with friends as well as on our own. We went on *dates*. I met his parents, messaged his sister on her birthday.

Anderson and I spend our time, almost exclusively, in his bedroom.

My mind does drift to my ex-boyfriend, though. Of course it does. I think about how completely different Anderson and Scottie are, in basically every way. Anderson is objectively better looking in a model-esque way that I'd never previously found attractive, but now, however inexplicably, do. He's tall and thin, almost lithe, with dark brown hair, cut short and classic. His skin and teeth are perfect. His smile is so confident. One day, he'll be a picture in magazines, sharing the frame with someone else beautiful and famous. His name was made for headlines.

Beth would have said, *Sounds like a twat, Emmy.*

And I'd say, *You don't get it.*

And she'd say, *Oh, I do. Sadly, I do. Are you sure you get it, though?*

(How typical of Beth, the champion of poor decision-making in life, to become the voice of my inner conscience in death.)

I'm *not* sure, though. That's the truth. Sometimes, I get a flash of feeling like, *Emmy, who are you? What are you doing?* But I push it down, and it goes away.

I haven't seen my friends since the party, and I'm barely replying to their messages. I'm being a terrible friend, and probably not a great person, either.

But it's just so much easier with Anderson, the two of us in his bed, and I don't even know why.

Although, I guess it's not that hard to guess why. He never knew Beth, and though he knew me while she was alive, it wasn't in any real way, and not how all the people who know me and love me do. So that means I get to tell him all my stories of her for the first time, which means that I get to hear them again, fresh.

I get to introduce her to someone again. Show him what it is we have all lost. *Beth.* (Not Lizzie.) (I don't even talk about The Jinks if I can help it. When he asks what they're doing now, I tell him, *they're done,* which is what I want to be true but probably isn't, what with Dad always being at the office nowadays. Something must be happening, though no one tells me what it is.)

Anderson is more empathetic than I realized, because he seems to get this. In messages, he calls her Beth. He asks me for more stories. Asks me questions about her, about the band, her life. (Not her death.)

He's a good listener. Which is also a surprise.

All that's true, and it matters a lot, but honestly? I mean, if I'm *really* honest with myself? It's not the real truth, or at least, it's not *why* I keep going over to his place, letting him be my distraction.

When I'm with him, even though I know, deep down, that it's not a good thing to be doing, I *feel* again. Isn't that an embarrassing cliché? But it's true. When he kisses me, I feel it. When he touches me, I feel it.

It's not even that it feels all that *good,* not really. But feeling anything at all, anything that isn't numbness or low-key rage, is worth the confusion, worth how I might feel when it all, inevitably, goes away.

That's what I tell myself, anyway.

74 DAYS GONE

Fight

It has been far, far too long since I saw my friends. Even in our group chat, I've been lukewarm, and I know it's not fair. I'm being a bad friend, grief or no grief, Anderson or no Anderson, and there's only so long I can expect them to put up with it. So I message them, apologize for being a bit distant — That's obviously OK, Em, Ella says. Grey says, Apology accepted — and ask if they want to meet up.

What I find, as I walk across the grass of the rec, where we've arranged to meet, is that I'm actually excited to see them. Not fireworks and cartwheels excited, but still. The surprise of happiness at seeing them in the distance is nice.

They're all staring at me, agog, as I approach, like I'm a complete stranger, which makes me laugh because it hasn't been *that* long.

"Holy shit!" Trix calls out to me. She beams, bringing her hands together under her chin, endearingly excited. "Emmy! I love it!"

Which is when I remember my hair. The big, massive identity change that I haven't, at any point, bothered mentioning to them, my best friends. Shit.

I try to cover myself by striking a pose, as if I've planned this whole thing. "Surprise!"

"You look so cool!" Ella says, reaching up a hand as if to touch my hair, then changing her mind. She grins at me. "Wow!"

I glance at Grey, hoping for a similar reaction from her, even though this is Grey, and Grey never gets openly excited about anything if she can help it. When I see her face, my heart sinks.

"Doesn't it look amazing?" Trix prompts.

Grey doesn't smile. Her mouth is a set line, like she's gritting her teeth. "Emmy, what have you done?"

Annoyance, instant and burning, rises in me. For God's sake. Can't she pretend? Just this once? For me?

"You don't like it?" I ask, stating the obvious to force her to do the same.

"It's not you," Grey replies. "It doesn't matter if I like it or not. I want to know why you've made yourself look less like yourself."

"I didn't," I say, deliberately obtuse. "The hairdresser did."

She rolls her eyes. "You know what I mean."

I want to ask her what *she* thinks she means by it being *not me*. Does she really think I'm the same person I was before Beth died? That even one single cell of me is the same? Of course I've changed. *Of course* I have.

"Why are you being like this?" I ask. "Just say you like it, Grey. It's just hair."

"But it's not just hair, is it?" Grey says. "It's the fact that you're not acting like yourself."

In my peripheral vision, I see Trix shifting anxiously on the spot, looking over at Ella, who is biting the corner of her bottom lip, eyes on Grey.

"What?" I don't even know if I'm saying, *What do you mean? Of course I'm acting like myself*, or *What does "acting like myself" even mean any more?*

"You," Grey says. "How you've been. I know you're grieving, but breaking up with Scottie and then acting like you guys aren't even friends? Changing your hair like this and not saying anything? And getting with *Anderson Jay*?"

Shit. "You ... you know about Anderson?"

"You mean, did you kiss him in the middle of a party in front of basically everyone we know? Yeah, you did, and so yeah, we know."

Just the kiss, then. They don't know we've been sleeping together. My heart rate, which had spiked at "getting with Anderson Jay", eases with relief.

"What's wrong with that?" I ask. "It was a party."

Grey's eyes go wide, and for a second she just stares at me, like she's waiting for me to laugh and say, *Gotcha!* "Emmy, this isn't you. That's what's wrong. You know it isn't you. So, no, I'm not going to 'just say I like it' when you turn up looking like a totally different person. I care about you too much to lie to you, and I'm starting to feel like maybe you need to hear this? Like, from someone? The way you're dealing with this ... it's not OK."

"*This?*" I repeat. "You mean, my sister dying?"

"Yeah. Look, if you need to hear it, then I'm going to say it. Shall I say it?"

"Grey," Trix says.

Ella adds, her voice unusually hard, "Seriously."

"Yeah, seriously," Grey says, deliberately misunderstanding her. "Emmy. We all know why you're doing all of this."

I know what she's going to say. "Why?"

"You're trying to be like Beth."

There's a silence while I fumble for what to say. I feel like I'm watching myself figure it out. Like I'm not in my own head when I say, cold and sarcastic, "Because I got a *haircut?* Really, Grey?"

She blinks at me, a frown creasing her whole forehead. "Em, you know what I mean. I know you do. I know you."

You used to know me. You don't know me now.

"I love your haircut," Trix says, but her voice is too tentative and it's not going to cut across whatever is going on between Grey and me right now. Still, she continues, "But, Em… You're…"

I turn to her. "I'm *what,* Trix? Grieving wrong? Seriously? What would you know? What would *any* of you know?"

"We know *you,*" Grey says again, and for a moment I think it's unusually generous of her to use "we" for the three of them, when she's always been proud, even a little possessive, of our tighter twosome within our quartet; the two of us always the "we". But then I realize what it actually means. That *they* have become the "we". So what does that make me? "Look," Grey says, because she's still going. "I will tell you this if you need to hear it. You'll hate me, but you need to hear it."

"Go on then," I say. "Tell me what I 'need' to hear."

"OK, can we stop?" Ella says. "Can we calm—"

"You're grieving, yeah," Grey says, talking right over her. "But you're also in denial." She shakes her head, like, *are you really going to make me say this?* "Emmy. You're kind of acting like you lost an imaginary version of Beth, not the real her," she says. "Do you know that you're doing that? Beth didn't just, like … become perfect. Just because she's dead. You know?"

"*Grey*," Trix says, part command, part plea. I know she's saying it to protect me from whatever she thinks Grey is about to say, but I can hear in her voice that they've talked about this together, all three of them, the new "we"; they've talked about me and Beth and her being dead and me apparently handling it all wrong, and right now if I could choose to die instead of have this conversation, I really think I would.

"You don't want to be more like her," Grey says. "Not by this crazy hair change or any other way. Beth was a trainwreck. Remember?" A sharp stab, directly into my heart. I think, *Stop. Don't.* "Remember when she turned up high to your sixteenth birthday? And she wanted to drive us all to a club and we had to be like, no, Beth, and you had to call your mum because you were so freaked out? Or all the times she *didn't* turn up because she was drunk or high or whatever. Like the Year 9 showcase, you remember that? You told everyone she was coming and she just never showed. Yes, she's dead, and that's fucking awful and sad, but you can't just erase all the shit *because* it's sad. Beth was so fucked up. That's why she's dead. Don't be like her, for fuck's sake. Be *not* like her."

My stabbed heart, leaking proverbial blood into my emotional chest, starts beating very hard. Too hard.

"That's not…" I try, and fail. "That doesn't mean…"

What I want to say is something   profound
      and   heartfelt
  about my sister's love and
        how her bad qualities and decisions
           don't take away from the good in her,
  but my head can't form a
      single coherent sentence.

And I *hate* that I'm

        faltering   right now

instead of standing strong and defending Beth, who would have
     fought whole armies

        for me, who was so far from perfect, who is

           fucking *dead*.

"I don't think it's healthy to pretend she was this tragic angel," Grey
continues. It's not that she's enjoying this, not at all. But I know her
well enough to recognize the way

    she's holding her shoulders,

      the sharpness in her eye;

        she's so certain she's right.

Somewhere inside of her, she's proud of herself for speaking what
she really thinks is the truth.

For being tough love Grey on soft grieving Emmy.

She says, "Sure, she is now, but she wasn't before. She was *awful*."

"Grey!" Trix actually shouts it this time. Her whole face is rigid
with anxiety, her eyes darting between us both.

This would probably be enough to stop most people. But not Grey
Alvarez. "She was! Em, *you* used to say that! You used to say you were
embarrassed by her! You used to say, why can't I have a normal sister
instead of that tr—"

And then she has to stop speaking, because I've slapped her. OK,
not really slapped her. My hand is more a claw than a palm, pawing
at her face. She lets out a scream, words that I think may be, "Oh my
god, you psycho bitch," and then we are, somehow, fighting. There's
hair pulling, actual slapping, the sharp sting of nails into skin.

In my whole life, I've never physically fought with anyone, not
even Beth.

It does not feel good.

"Oh my God, *stop!*" It's Ella, frantic but completely ineffectual,
trying to pull us apart, that eventually gets through to us both.

Something about the sheer helpless panic in her voice stops us.

All four of us, I realize, are in tears. Even Grey.

When I let myself look at her, I see the savage red of scratch marks down her cheek. Three vivid lines, caused by … me. Mortification heats me up from the inside, fresh tears rise in my eyes. I've physically hurt my best friend. I've clawed at her face like some harpy from a TV show.

"Oh my God," I say, because it's all I can manage. I should say sorry, I know I should, but I can't.

Because I'm not sorry.

I'm not.

"Holy shit," Grey says, but quietly, shock winning out over anger. Her hand at her face. She looks at me, eyes still wide. Beside her, Trix and Ella are staring at me. All of them, waiting.

When I turn and walk away, they don't follow.

I push it all down.   Down, down.

I message Anderson, ask him if he wants to hang out.
    But he's spending the day with his friends,
        so I'm alone.

I go into town and walk around by myself.
    In and out of shops, staring at shelves.
    Trix messages me, and I ignore her.

I feel like I've stumbled into the wrong life.
    Like I took a wrong turn somewhere, and if I could find my way
back, I could be Emmy again, like I was before, like I'm meant to be.
    I'd be with my friends, hand in Scottie's, smile on my face. Beth
would be a message, a phone call, away.
    I would be so much lighter.

I get a message from Anderson after the sun's gone down.
    Still want to hang out? he asks.
    I know what he means.
    I know that if I say no, he'll barely care.
    But I say yes, I go over to his house, I lie in his bed.
    I've become someone I don't recognize; someone who wears my face.

It's not that I miss Scottie, because I don't.
    It's that I wish I was still the person who would miss Scottie in this
moment.

I used to think it was stupid when people talked about losing
themselves.
    Because, how can you lose yourself? You *are* yourself.
    But now I get it.
    I really, really get it.

50-78 DAYS GONE
Conversations with my therapist
(the quiet during the storm)

THE POINT

I don't want to be here.

OK.

I'm only here because I have to be.

That's OK.

Is it?

Sure. I get paid either way.

Ha. Ha.

How are you feeling today? Shall we start there?

You don't need to bullshit me. I know you know why I'm here.

What makes you say that?

You know I'm here because my sister is dead. You know she was famous. You know who she was. So you already know it all.

I do know you've recently experienced a bereavement, yes. But I'm more interested in what you have to say than what I may or may not already know.

Why?

Why … am I interested in what you have to say?

Yeah.

Well, that's my job, Emmy. To listen to you.

So you only want to listen to me because it's your job.

And you're only here because you have to be, right? So I suppose we're both here under some kind of duress.

Hmmm.

I saw that smile. You don't have to hide it. I won't tell anyone. Everything here is confidential. Even when you laugh at my bad jokes. How are you feeling today, Emmy?

Fine.

That's good, that you feel fine today. How did you feel yesterday?

...

...

...

What's the point of this?

Of talking to me?

Yes. What's the point? Seriously.

Well, talking helps, to put it simply. There's general agreement around that idea.

Yeah, if it's, like, financial problems, or someone's having an affair, or you're depressed, or whatever. Not when someone's died.

Why do you think that?

Um, because you're not going to bring the dead person back to life, are you?

...

Are you?

No, Emmy. I'm sorry. But why does that mean it isn't helpful to talk?

It won't bring Beth back.

No.

It won't help her.

No.

She's gone.

She is, Emmy. But you're still here.

THE ANGER

Do you feel any anger towards Beth?

Anger?

Yes.

No. Why?

It would be very normal if you did. Anger is one of the recognized stages of grief. Especially with … when there are circumstances like these.

You mean suicide.

Yes.

How can I be angry? It's a sad thing.

It is a sad thing. But it's not just a sad thing. If you felt angry … it wouldn't mean you were any less devastated by Beth's death. It wouldn't mean you loved her any less.

…

Do you see what I'm saying?

Yeah.

If you do want to talk about that – or anything like it – I'm here to listen to you.

I mean … obviously I'm angry. I'm so angry, all the time. But not at Beth, not at all.

Do you want to talk about those feelings? Where do you feel you're directing that anger?

At everyone.

I see.

The whole fucking world.

…

…

How about me? Any anger towards me?

Yeah. But not, like, as intense.

Well, thank you, Emmy. Can you tell me some more about what's making you angry?

The journalists, for all the articles they wrote before, and the ones they're writing now since she died. How hypocritical it all is. They act like it was nothing to do with them, you know? Like someone else wrote all that awful stuff. And people on social media, they're just the same. They keep talking about how upset they are, how sad it is, like they have any … any right to it, you know? But they don't. It's mine. Ours. My family's. We lost Beth. They lost nothing.

Those are very understandable feelings. When the loss is so huge, and so personal, it will be difficult to watch other people also feel a sense of loss. But … your sister was a public figure; a celebrity. People tend to form a particular kind of attachment to famous people, or even just the idea of them. It's known as a parasocial bond. Losing that can be very painful, in its own way. It's not the same as your loss, but nevertheless it is a loss. Have you ever grieved for the death of someone you didn't know?

Sure, but not actually. And I never trolled someone to death and then cried about how sad it was they died.

I can see why it would feel like everyone was part of that, but—

I know they're not. You don't have to say it. I'm just saying how it feels, OK? Like you said, right?

Absolutely.

And my parents.

Your parents?

The anger.

Right, I see. Do you want to talk about that?

Mmmm.

Take your time.

I just don't see what the point of this is. It won't change anything.

I disagree.

You're a therapist – you're not meant to disagree, you're meant to affirm my feelings. And my feelings are: Beth is dead, complaining about my parents won't bring her back.

It won't, no. Of course that's true. But there are other changes that can happen that aren't about what has already happened. Changes in you; in your state of mind; your process of coping with your grief. Talking will help you.

OK. I think I'm done for today, though. Can we stop?

THE ALTERNATIVE

I've kind of been thinking about what you said before. Last time. About being angry. At Beth.

Oh?

Yeah.

…

…

What have you been thinking?

That maybe I am. Kind of angry.

Do you want to talk to me about that? Take your time, if you need.

I feel like … she never gave me a chance.

To help her?

Not even that. A chance to know. What was really going on for her, you know? Like, in her head.

Why do you think that was?

I don't know, because I'm five years younger? I think she just saw me as her baby sister. Like, I was always so much younger than her. Even though I'm sixteen now, and that's how old she was when she won "Great British Sounds" and got really famous. So she should have known that I could handle it. Handle her. I feel like … she got all of me. There was nothing about me she didn't know. I told her everything. But her … I only got one version of her, and I thought it was real.

What makes you think it wasn't real?

The fact that she's dead?

Why does that make it less real?

Because it wasn't the whole truth. She could have told me. She could have said what it was really like, instead of thinking she had to be … whatever she thought she had to be with me. And I feel like … I feel like maybe that's my fault. Like I should have made sure she knew that she could be real with me, that I was old enough for it.

Can I suggest an alternative?

What do you mean?

Well, you feel strongly that she was projecting a certain … version of herself, when she was around you, for your benefit. Is that right?

Yeah.

Well, have you thought that maybe it wasn't solely for your benefit? Maybe it helped her too?

…

Maybe it was important for her to have that relationship that was separate from the pain in the rest of her life. Maybe she loved being who she was with you. Maybe it wasn't a burden; maybe it was a gift.

…

It's OK to cry, Emmy.

I never … I never told her that I…

What? What didn't you tell her?

That I loved her anyway. I used to pretend all that stuff didn't happen, and she let me, everyone let me. They let me just pretend. But I knew, and I should have said.

Beth knew you loved her, Emmy. That's all that mattered.

But I can't ever tell her.

…

I wish she'd let me have the chance to tell her.

That's understandable. That's very normal.

She died before I could get old enough to be on the same level as her. I wish she'd waited. Isn't that selfish? But I do. I wish she'd waited long enough for us to be adults together.

…

Aren't you meant to tell me it isn't selfish?

I think you already know it isn't selfish, Emmy.

I really loved her.

I know you did. And so did she.

THE HAIR

I changed my hair.

Yes, I can see that, Emmy.

Do you like it?

Does it matter to you if I like it or not?

Oh my God, you can just say yes, not everything has to be all therapist.

Yes, I like it. It suits you.

Thanks. Mum hates it.

Does she?

Uh huh.

The haircut? Or the change?

...

Do you want to talk about why you felt you wanted such a drastic change?

Uh, because it's just hair?

So a safe way to experiment with drastic change?

Oh my God.

If you tell me, I won't have to guess.

I know what you think.

What do I think?

That I'm trying to be more like Beth. Or that I've done it *for* her.

Is that a haircut Beth would have chosen?

Well, no.

Is it a haircut Beth would have expected from you?

      ... **Well.** ... **No.**

So why do you think I'd think it was about her?

      Because isn't everything?

No, not really. Sometimes hair is just hair.

      ...

...

      Beth would have thought it was cool.

...

      She'd have been so excited. She wanted me to be braver.

      ...

      ...

Do you think she'd like it?

      Yeah.

I think so too.

THE PROBLEMS

I was wondering if you'd like to talk to me today about Beth's problems.

> **Beth's … problems?**

Yes.

> **What problems?**

I'd like it if you told me.

> **But you clearly know there were problems, because you said it like that. So you tell me.**

This isn't an attack, Emmy. Not on you, or your sister. But I think it might be helpful for you to talk about it. In this space, where you're completely safe from judgement, where everything you say is confidential.

> **"Problems" seems like a pretty judgemental word, but OK.**

What word would you use?

> **…**

Does it make you uncomfortable, talking about the issues Beth faced? Or even just thinking about it?

> **…**

It's OK if it does. It's a difficult thing for anyone to come to terms with, especially when the person you love has chosen to die. There are very complex emotions involved. It can be difficult to remember the past without reframing it entirely. Maybe you feel that it's somehow disloyal to Beth, now she's died, to remember the difficult times?

> **I thought you weren't meant to put words in my mouth.**

I'm not trying to do that, Emmy. We don't have to talk about this today if you'd rather not. But do think about it, in your own time.

Can I just ask…?

Yes?

Do you know about Beth's problems because you heard about them from my parents, or because you read it in the papers?

…

…

I'm not going to lie to you and pretend I've never, in the course of my everyday life, come across discussion about … Lizzie Beck. But I know that the persona of a famous person is likely very different from their real self, and at the very least is just one part of their real self. Equally, I do have notes on the circumstances that brought you here to talk with me, and yes, they have come from your mother. But they are very brief; just some basic background. I'd much rather hear it from you.

What do the notes say?

I don't think there would be much benefit in telling you that, Emmy.

…

…

Maybe you should talk to your mother about it. Do you talk, the two of you?

Yeah, of course. She's my mother.

I mean … really talk. About your grief, and losing Beth.

…

It might be a good place to start. You can tell her we talked about the notes, and that you have some questions. You may find that she wants to talk; even that you do too.

OK.

OK, you'll talk to her? Or OK, stop talking about it?

Both.

THE PLAN

I know what I want to talk about today.

That's great, Emmy. Tell me.

There's this thing I'm scared of, that I can't talk to anyone about, because they won't understand. You probably won't understand, either, but you're still probably the best person.

I'm glad to hear that. Go on. I'm listening.

...

Take your time.

I ... I was always going to follow Beth. That was the plan. Like, always. She got famous, and she opened all the doors for me that she possibly could – like, you know my school, Shona Lee? She got me the audition there. They're not open auditions; you need to have a referral, and she got me that. Beth got famous through reality TV, which is basically luck, but me, I was going to get there because I'd learned from her. She used to say it would be legit, me and my music. We used to talk about it all the time. She really liked talking about it. Or, like, I thought she did. Anyway, the longer she was famous, and the worse things got for her, people started saying things to me like, Oh, you don't want to turn out like Beth. In a way, like... that'd I'd agree? Like it was obvious? But I ... I never stopped wanting to be like her. Even when things were bad. I still thought she was just ... the greatest person. I loved her so much. People didn't ... they didn't see her the way I did. And, like, obviously I wasn't going to get into drugs or anything. I don't think she would have let me, anyway. She was protective like that, of me. But

she was always so bright. She was like my light, always. And … and…

…

   …

Take as long as you need.

This is so fucking stupid.

It's not stupid at all, Emmy. It's OK to cry. Your sister, who you loved dearly, is gone. Of course you're crying. Make sure you drink some water. Take your time.

   …

…

   …

…

And now she's dead, and people are saying it even more. Like, I don't think they even realize they're doing it, but they're acting like they think I'm scared of turning out like her. They're saying to me, don't worry, Em, you won't end up like Beth. But I'm not scared of turning out like Beth; not at all. What I'm scared of is – and I feel like I can't talk to anyone about this because I think they'll think it's mad or stupid – I'm scared that I won't turn out like her. That I'll just be … I don't know what the word is. Like, smaller. Ordinary. Beth was always, like, the dial turned up to a 100, you know? She felt things so much; everything. Maybe that was part of the problem. She was never just a bit sad or a bit happy. She had so much fire and passion. I know that made things hard for her a lot of the time, but I always wanted that for myself. Just a bit of it; to feel that way. And to make other people feel, the way she could. And now she's gone and I … I…

It's OK, Emmy.

I miss her.

I know.

I can't carry on without her.

You can. You will. … You are.

78 DAYS GONE

"*Tomorrow*"

The Jinks @thejinks

@thejinks Tune in to @TheMorningShow tomorrow at 10.30
for a major announcement from The Jinks!

That's it. That's the tweet.

I stare at it, my phone heavy in my hand, looking for clues. I know it was written by someone on the management team, not any of the band members or even their publicist, because it's so bland. Just one exclamation mark, no kisses.

A major announcement. What can that mean?

I know what it means. Of course I do, because it can only mean one thing. They wouldn't go on "The Morning Show" to announce that the band was over, would they? Even though they *should*.

I feel nauseous. It's going to happen; the band is going to carry on without my sister, without Lizzie Beck. Jodie is going to get what she wanted, and no one will ever know that she was forcing it into motion before Beth even died. It's the perfect outcome for her, isn't it? It's not fair. It's not right.

I screenshot the tweet and message my dad. What is this?

He replies far more quickly than I'd expected: Let's talk tonight. Pick a takeaway, I'll be home by 7 x

My heart sinks even lower. If I hadn't already guessed by the tweet, I know it by Dad's message. The Jinks are relaunching. The thing I'd always known, at the back of my mind, would happen eventually. But not so soon, not this soon. It's *too* soon.

Dad arrives home at exactly 7 p.m., a takeaway bag in his arms. He closes the front door with his elbow, smiling when he sees me coming down the stairs.

"Hello, love," he says. "Can you help me lay the table?"

I go into the kitchen ahead of him, hearing him call to Mum up the stairs. Last I saw her, she was sitting on her bed, staring into space, so I doubt we'll be seeing her anytime soon, but I don't bother saying so.

"So just tell me," I say, opening the cupboard to pull out three plates. "They're relaunching, aren't they?"

"Maybe we should wait for your mother," he says, glancing towards the kitchen doorway as if she's about to walk through it.

"Tell me now," I say. "I've waited all day."

Dad hesitates, then sets the takeaway bag on the table and starts pulling containers out of it. "OK, yes. The band is officially relaunching, and they'll be announcing it tomorrow morning. It's good news. We can all be happy about it."

I stare at him, pausing in motion, the plate I'm holding hovering over a place mat. "Happy?"

"Yes, happy." There's determination in the way he says this. "We have precious little to celebrate at the moment. But this is good."

"How is it good? Why is it good? How can this even be happening?"

He frowns at me. "What do you mean? You're not surprised, are you? You've always known they were still going to be a band; you've seen me going to work every day. Surely you knew this was going to happen?"

"Eventually, maybe," I say. "But not for ages. And I thought I'd... Why didn't you tell me in advance?"

"I am telling you in advance," Dad says, looking genuinely confused. "This is in advance."

"The night before?"

"Emmy, calm down," he says. "Why would I tell you earlier? So much of this has been up in the air for the last couple of months.

We weren't even sure when we'd make the official announcement. It's enough that I have to carry all this stress around. The last thing you or your mother need is to carry it as well."

"I always knew things earlier before," I say.

"Not from me," Dad says. Or starts to say, because he stops himself, a flash of pain passing over his face. He doesn't finish the thought, and neither do I. *From Beth*. Beth always told me things way in advance. She'd send me photos from shoots they were doing, text me from meetings, record voice notes of the band's demos. I guess she wasn't really supposed to, technically. But Beth was never really one for "supposed to".

"What are they going to say?" I ask.

"You should watch it," Dad says.

"Obviously, I'm going to watch it," I say. "But what are they going to say? Will they mention Beth?"

Something happens to Dad when I say this. He flinches, like I've reached out and slapped him. He puts down the container he's holding and looks straight at me. "Jesus Christ, Emmy," he says. "*Of course* they'll talk about Beth. This isn't..." He stops, closing his eyes momentarily. "No one is forgetting about Beth, I promise you that."

"But this is what they wanted," I say.

"No," he says, sharply. "This is not what *anyone* wanted, and don't you dare say it is. Have some respect."

"But Jodie—"

"That's enough, Emmy." He doesn't say it angrily, more tiredly. "Just watch the interview, and we can talk about it afterwards, OK? But it's been a long day in a long week in a long month in the worst fucking year of all our lives. Can you just give it a rest?" He looks towards the doorway, shaking his head. "For God's sake, where is your mother?"

I shrug. Mostly because I'm trying not to cry.

"Can you go and get her, please?" he asks, tensely, like maybe he's containing some emotions too.

When I go upstairs to their bedroom, I find Mum exactly where I saw her last, sitting on the bed.

"Dad says come down for dinner," I say, like we've switched roles and I'm the parent.

Mum breathes in a sigh. "OK, love."

Dad looks almost relieved when she and I walk into the kitchen together. He's sitting at the table, an untouched plate of food in front of him. He doesn't say anything as we sit down and start sharing out the food between us.

After what feels like a long few minutes, Mum looks up at him. "Good day?" she asks.

He nods. "We've made the decision," he says. "We're going ahead with the relaunch." My face must do something at these words, because he amends, "*They*. The band. Are going ahead with their launch as a three-piece."

Mum raises her eyebrows in acknowledgement, but other than that she barely reacts, just starts spooning rice onto her plate. All she says, her voice placid, is, "When?"

And Dad says, "Tomorrow."

79 DAYS GONE

The Jinks

> *(Camera pans across the studio floor to rest on*
> *the smiling faces of Mellie Wright and Colin Arvin)*

Colin: Good morning!

Mellie: Good morning! It's Thursday, it's 10 a.m., and, people, it's nearly the weekend.

Colin: Almost!

Mellie: It's been a long week, hasn't it? Is that just me? I woke up thinking it was Friday.

Colin: *(chuckling)* A whole day to go until Friday, I'm afraid! But we'll be here with you for the next couple of hours to see you through to the afternoon. In just a few minutes we've got Hassan Montel giving us the lowdown from LA, followed by Marisa Marlow here in the studio, putting new school uniforms to the test.

Mellie: Coming up at 10.30, we've got an exclusive interview with The Jinks, their first since the tragic death of Lizzie Beck in June.

> *(Sombre moment staring directly*
> *into the camera, sadness in her eyes)*
> *(beat)*

Mellie: *(brightly)* And at 11 we've got Claudio Costa answering all your food questions. Can you freeze fresh parsley? We'll find out.

10.30 a.m.

Colin: *(soberly)* Welcome back. We're joined now by Jodie Soto-Hahn, Aiya Mehta and Tam Lord, the three remaining members of The Jinks.

(Camera pans slowly over to the three girls, sitting close
on the opposite sofa from Mellie and Colin. They are
unsmiling, all dressed in dark colours — Jodie in black)

Mellie: *(gently)* Girls, thank you for joining us today. This
must have been an incredibly difficult time for you,
following the death of Lizzie Beck.

(The Jinks all nod, no one replies)
(a few seconds go by)

Mellie: *(smoothly)* So my first question for you is, how are
you? How have you been coping these past few months?

Aiya: We're doing... *(voice cracks, she smiles weakly)* Well,
we're doing... *(small, sad laugh)*

Tam: We're doing the best we can. Just trying to look
after each other.

Aiya: It's been really hard. For all of us.

Jodie: For everyone.

Aiya: Yes, for everyone. And so, as a band, all we can do
is try to support each other as best we can.

Mellie: Absolutely, absolutely. And you've come here today
to make an announcement, is that right?

Tam: That's right. *(She looks at the girls)* We've had people
asking us, for a long time, when we'd have new
music out, when we'd start touring again. And we've
been planning for a while, you know, how to do
that. But now, of course, things have changed so
much, so we haven't been sure exactly what that
would look like, or if we even wanted to carry on
as a band, without ... without Lizzie.

Aiya: We've talked about it a lot between us, and with
our management. To decide what the right thing

to do is, for us as a band but also to honour Lizzie's memory. We could never have imagined being a three-piece instead of a four-piece band.

Tam: Never. And we wanted to be sure it was what the fans would want, as well.

Aiya: Right, yes. That was so important to us. But what they've made clear — and the fans have been so amazing these past few months, we owe them so much, they've been so supportive — what they've made clear is that they do want The Jinks to carry on.

Mellie: And that's what you're going to do? Carry on?

(Aiya takes a deep breath, glances at Tam and Jodie as if for courage)

Aiya: Yes.

Mellie: *(smiling)* That's wonderful. Tell us about it. You're planning a tour, is that right? Starting with a memorial concert?

Aiya: That's right, yeah. We're hosting a one-off special at the Royal Albert Hall on September 30th, to honour Lizzie's memory and to raise money for charities dedicated to mental health. We'll have some special guest stars, some friends of the band, that we'll be announcing a little way down the line. And then, in October, we're going to go on tour together. It will be an intimate tour; smaller venues, rather than arenas. We want it to be something special, for our fans, and us. Some way to… *(she falters)* Well, it didn't seem right to just … you know…

Tam: This is new territory for us. And, of course, we're still grieving. So it didn't feel right to go on an arena tour.

Mellie: Will you be playing all your hits?

Aiya: Oh yes! It will still be a Jinks tour! But there may be some surprises in there too, some new arrangements.

Jodie: Because we have to make new arrangements, with three voices instead of four.

(awkward silence)

Mellie: Of course. That sounds just wonderful. And the memorial concert at the Royal Albert Hall… I imagine it's not a coincidence, that venue?

Aiya: It seems right to have it there. What with … with it being five years since Great British Sounds and the Proms. We always said that … Lizzie, she…

Tam: Lizzie always said we'd be back there one day.

Aiya: *(nodding, tearful)* It's the right place for it. And they've been incredibly generous to us, agreeing to host us for the night. We're grateful.

Mellie: And we'll be sure to be there cheering you on, won't we, Colin?

Colin: *(brightly)* Oh yes, front row.

Mellie: You have so many people supporting you. Grieving with you.

Aiya: *(choked)* Thank you.

Tam: It means so much to us. We really can't say enough how much.

Jodie: *(softly)* I just …

(A silence falls; all eyes on her. Aiya looks worried)

Jodie: … can't believe she's gone, really. Still.

Mellie: *(not missing beat, extravagantly sympathetic)* You miss her.

Jodie: *(looking down at her lap)* Yeah.

(Aiya takes her hand)
(Camera zooms in on Jodie squeezing it tight)

Aiya: We all miss Lizzie, and we always will. But the last thing she would have wanted is for The Jinks to end. And at some point … you have to move on, you know?

(sage nods)
(Aiya blinks back tears)

Mellie: Thank you so much for speaking to us today, and for sharing your news with us. We really do wish you the very best. The whole country is cheering you on.

Aiya: Thank you. Thank you so, so much.

Mellie: *(to camera)* We'll be right back.

(an advert for cat food starts)

Mum and I watch the interview together. Her on the sofa, me kneeling on the living room floor in front of the TV. Neither of us says a word until it's over.

"Can you believe that?" I say. My head can't seem to choose an emotion — angry? Sad? Shocked? Heartbroken? — and so I'm half laughing instead. It feels wrong, but I can't stop. "Can you actually believe that?"

Mum is calm. "Which bit, Emmy?"

"All of it!" I'm standing now — not sure when that happened — and my hands are gesticulating in front of me, almost of their own accord. I notice, with some surprise, that they're shaking a little. "They ... a *tour*. An actual tour! And Aiya saying they'd *never imagined being a three-piece*. They just ... lied. They *lied*."

"They would have been told what to say," Mum says. "You can't blame them for that."

I thought she'd be on my side. Angry, like me. "I can blame them for lying."

"Emmy," Mum says, very softly. "The girls ... this isn't their fault."

It is. It *is* their fault. They get to sit on a posh sofa in designer clothes on national TV and tear up about my dead sister for ticket sales, like none of it happened, like things can just carry on.

Why isn't Mum angry? Why isn't she crying and raging, like I want to be? I can't do it on my own. I'm so sick of doing all of this on my own.

She actually looks concerned, like she's worried about me. She's leaning forward on the sofa, forehead furrowing. "Emmy," she says. "Sit with me. Talk to me."

Now she wants to talk? Now The Jinks are back together, now I apparently can't blame them, now everyone is moving on? *Now?*

"They wanted to have that interview in *June*," I say, pointing to the TV, which is now showing Mellie Wright talking cheerfully to a chef. "The three of them and their tour. The only thing that's changed is that Beth is *dead* instead of…" I falter, trying to think about what Beth would actually have been doing if she was alive but also not in the band. I come up completely blank. I shake my head. "Beth *is* dead."

"Yes," Mum says, her voice gentle, but firm. "She is dead, Emmy. And the girls … they're…"

"Not?"

"Well, yes. Darling, I'm sorry that you're so upset. I thought you were more prepared for this."

How? Why? Why would I be prepared? Who does she think I've been talking to all this time that would have prepared me, if not her? Or Dad?

"Can you think of this as a good thing?" Mum asks.

Something about these words, in this order, unlocks something inside my head. In the moment after she speaks, a memory flashes into my head, so vivid it's like I've stepped right inside it. Mum kneeling on the floor of this very living room, holding onto Beth, who was crying in that out of control way that is more like wailing, loud and unselfconscious. The noise had summoned me from my room, and I'd stopped in the doorway, confused, maybe even scared. Mum was saying, "Shh. Lovely Bethie. It's OK." Over and over, like a mantra, stroking her hair. Through the incoherence of the sobbing, I could make out, "I've lost everything. I'm no one. I'm nothing." Mum said, "No. No, my darling. You're wonderful. My Bethie. Think of this as a good thing, darling. A *good* thing."

What did I do, in that moment? Did I go into the room, kneel beside my broken sister, take her hand and tell her that she was not nothing, that she hadn't lost everything, that I loved her and needed her and was proud of her? No, I didn't.

I backed out of the doorway and crept back upstairs before either of them saw me.

I ran away.

I go upstairs, into my room, sit at my desk. Flip the lid of my laptop open.

Twitter. *Come on, come on.* People are never nice on Twitter. Surely, they'll see through this. They will.

@backtoparris Got to say, good on The Jinks for that interview. Must have been hard. #themorningshow

---

@kerrysouthlee Cried buckets at The Jinks interview #themorningshow

---

@waitingfordaylights So weird seeing Jodie, Aiya and Tam without Lizzie. When Aiya held Jodie's hand, I cried. #themorningshow

---

@forthehijinks Now is the time to support our girls. Let's show them we love them! #themorningshow #thejinks

---

@thisjinksygirl THE JINKS FOR EVER ❤

"No." I actually say it out loud. Alone, at my desk. "No."

Twitter never had a good word to say about Lizzie Beck, not until she was dead. She could really, really have used a good word or two. Maybe it would have made a difference. And *now* they're being nice? *Now* they think it's "time to support" them?

It's not fair. It's not right.

Something occurs to me suddenly, the breath catching in my throat, and I go to The Jinks' profile page to check that … no. They've done it. Their Twitter header is just the three of them. Aiya, Jodie, Tam. No Lizzie.

The Jinks @thejinks

For more hijinks, we are: @aiyamehta @jodieso @tamlord

thejinks.com

8.4M FOLLOWERS

Beth wrote the hijinks bit, way back when the band was brand new, and so was the Twitter account. No one ever seemed to think to change it. Until now, to remove her handle from the profile, as if she were never there, never part of it. But she was. She was first on the damn list.

I click on the link for their website. The website I've seen so many hundreds of times, I know it by heart. Or did.

Not any more.

The website has been redone completely. The photos of the band are all new three-piece pictures. New styling for the three of them, new poses.

There's an In Memoriam page for my sister, called We Love You, Lizzie. It's black and white, full of photos of her smiling face, the tribute that had been read at her funeral written out in full.

But that's it.

The rest of the website is stripped bare of her.

I feel sick. My hands are shaking.

How can they do this?

How can Dad let them do this?

How can Mum be so calm about it?

I'm making a noise, I realize. A horrible whimpering noise, like an animal. I try to stop myself, clenching my hands into fists, then releasing them, trying to breathe.

But the world is cantering forward and there's nothing I can do to stop it or even slow it down. I am small and insignificant and minor and no one cares what I think or feel or need.

So I just cry.

HEADLINES

The Jinks make heartfelt tribute to Lizzie Beck as they announce new tour

Tears for Lizzie: The Jinks confirm relaunch in tearful television interview

Memorial concert announced to "honour" Lizzie Beck

(Pictured) Sobbing Jodie Soto-Hahn comforted by Aiya Mehta outside television studios following relaunch announcement

Lizzie Beck remembered in The Jinks' first interview following her death

Support for The Jinks floods in from across the entertainment world

Hope and Healing: Why we're so happy The Jinks are back

New Look for New Look Jinks: What The Jinks' new style tells us about the band's future

Dad comes home so late he may as well not even bother. It's past midnight, and Mum's already gone to bed.

"Hello," he says in surprise, when he comes through the door and sees me sitting on the stairs, waiting. "I thought you'd be asleep by now."

I study his face for some sign of ... what? I'm not even sure. Sadness? Guilt? He just looks tired, but in that energized way that comes with a busy day managing a major British pop band, like he's running on Pro Plus and coffee. This is Dad as I haven't seen him for months. Manager Dad. Shirt sleeves rolled up, phone in hand or at his ear, a confidence radiating from him that I used to find comforting, even safe. Now, it feels all wrong. Like I'm glimpsing Dad from another life, one I'd thought was gone for ever. How can this Dad exist without Beth? How can he be the manager of a band she isn't in? In a *world* she isn't in?

"How did it go?" I ask, instead of what I want to ask, which is, *How could you?*

"Good," Dad says, nodding. "Really good, actually. There's been a very positive response from the press and the public, which is what we were hoping for."

I should be happy that he's talking to me like I'm an adult, but I'm not. I want him to treat me like his grieving daughter.

"What did you think?" he asks. I don't say anything, so he adds, "It was a good interview, don't you think? The right tone."

What does that even mean? Who cares about the right tone?

"I just don't understand why they couldn't have ... waited."

"Waited for what?"

"Just... I don't know. A decent amount of time? Like, a respectful amount? It's barely been three months. That's nothing."

"What would you consider a respectful amount of time?" he asks me, but genuinely, like he really wants to know.

"At least six months after," I say.

"Six months after is the inquest," Dad says. "The headlines will

266

be full of that. Launching at that time would be seen to be them capitalizing on the extra press, which would be obscene."

I swallow. "A year, then."

"The anniversary?" Dad says. He's using his devil's advocate voice. "That's a bit cynical, don't you think?"

"I... You know what I mean."

"There is no right time," Dad says. "That's what I'm trying to explain to you. But there are *worse* times, and we've tried to avoid those. Shocking as this may be to you, Emmy, we *are* trying to do the right thing. By everyone. The girls in the here and now, and Beth's memory."

My throat closes up. I look away.

"What did you think of the memorial concert?" Dad asks. "I thought you'd like that."

"I hate it."

For a moment, he closes his eyes, like he's gathering his strength, or just doesn't want to look at me. "Why? A night for Beth; isn't that a nice thing?"

"No, it's disgusting," I say.

"Oh, Emmy."

"Oh, Emmy, yourself," I say, or try to say. It actually comes out more like a sob, and I stand up abruptly to turn away and jog up the stairs to my room.

He calls after me. "I was going to ask you if you'd want to sing!"

I pause at the top of the stairs. "Sing?"

"At the concert."

I backtrack, almost tripping over my feet. "Are you serious?"

"Yes."

"At the Royal Albert Hall?"

"Yes."

This is so huge, so unimaginably huge, that I don't know what to say. A thrill of traitorous excitement zings through my body just thinking about it. A stage like I've only ever dreamed of. But those dreams were from a different life, so I shouldn't be excited, should I?

"Does Mum think it's a good idea?"

A pause.

"Well, I haven't spoken to your mother about it yet."

"Right. Why not?"

"Emmy … it's been a long day. Can we talk about this in the morning?"

"OK," I say.

In the morning, when I get up and go downstairs to find him, he's already gone to work.

80 DAYS GONE

Distraction

Anderson
Want to come over?

Emmy
I'm not great company today tbh

How come?

Long story.

Is it the stuff about The Jinks?

Yeah

Need a distraction? ;)

idk maybe

Or you can talk to me if you want.

It's so complicated though

How come? Isn't it cool that they're still going?

No, it's all lies

Serious?

Yeh. The relaunch with the three of them was planned in June.

You mean right after Beth died?

No. Before.

Wait what??

They wanted Beth out of the band. They basically kicked her out.

wtf?????

Jodie planned the whole thing. She wanted Beth out so she could lead the band without all the shitty press Beth always got them.

This is crazy. Is that true? Are you sure?

100%. I was there when it was all happening.

And then Beth... Fuck.

Like I said. Complicated.

But that's fucking insane?? That they're just going ahead with the relaunch anyway??

I KNOW RIGHT

Fucking hell Em!! You should go to the press. HUGE story.

lol no, I can't

Why not?

Obvs not going to do that. My dad's still their manager.

You should tell him it's fucked up

I did! No one cares what I think

I do. Come over. We can talk more about it.

Even though I'm not great company?

Sounds like you need to talk about it. Come over. I'll listen.

Were you always this nice?

ha don't tell anyone x

On my way over x

Trix
Hey, I saw the stuff about
The Jinks yesterday. Hope
you're OK, it must be hard?
Here if you want to talk.
Love you xxxx

Call me anytime xx

Ella
I miss you, Em xxx

Grey
Just so you know, I'm here
whenever you're ready to
be a friend again. And if you
need someone to talk to. X

Anderson and I talk for what seems like hours. He listens, generously patient, and he doesn't even act freaked out when I get upset and cry. He just makes me tea, like Scottie would have, and asks more questions.

We don't even have sex, just talk.

I wish I could tell Grey that Anderson is not, at all, the trash we always thought he was. He's sweet. (But I'm still not talking to Grey.)

It's petty, but it feels good to think, when she messages, I *do have someone to talk to, actually.* I don't reply to her, and not to Trix or Ella, either.

I'm secretly hoping that Anderson will ask me if I want to hang out again tomorrow, Saturday, but he doesn't. Not when I leave, and not when we message later that evening.

Emmy
Sorry for talking so much about Beth. It kind of took over, sorry.

Anderson
No, you're all right. Good to talk about it, it's fine.

You sure?

Yeah. Such a headfuck, wow. I'd go crazy if it was me.

I kind of am going crazy lol

He says I can always talk to him about Beth, which is so nice, especially when he follows it up by asking me more questions. What it was like being her sister, how well I knew the rest of the band, whether I'd talked to any of them since she died. What my life was like before June, whether I'd hung out with them all, who my favourite was, who I hated the most, now. I love being able to talk about it with someone who doesn't know it already. At least, someone who isn't being paid, like my therapist. Turns out she was right about talking; I make a mental note to tell her at our next session.

Send me a pic of the two of you? he asks. A sister pic, not a fame pic.

I love that he asks for this. I send him a picture of Beth and me from my camera roll, taken last Christmas. Cheek to cheek, both of us smiling. After I've sent it, I let myself just stare at it for a while, remembering the feeling of her arm around me, the smell of her hair.

You look alike, he says.

We don't, not really, but I send a smiley face anyway.

Maybe one day I'll be as cool as her.

You're already pretty cool.

It's embarrassing, how wide this makes me smile.

I spend Saturday by myself, on the internet.

Chocolate digestives and a cup of tea, curled in the sun room with a sun-drunk Sebastien, watching old YouTube playlists of The Jinks. I go back in time so far that I end up watching the backstage series from "Great British Sounds" that I only watched once and then forgot about. I love seeing the joyful naivety play out in front of me, the girls sixteen (Aiya seventeen) and excited, utterly clueless about the ways their lives were about to change, having piggyback races across the stage during rehearsals, plaiting the keyboard player's hair while he smiled indulgently, giving each other fake interviews with posh accents while they cupped their chins thoughtfully for the camera. It should probably make me ache, make me hurt, but it doesn't. It makes me smile. I even laugh.

I need to get used to this, that's the thing. The Jinks are going to be back, and clearly I need to accept that. Maybe if I can convince myself I'm OK with it, I could even consider what Dad said about singing at the Royal Albert Hall, for the memorial concert. Every time I think about this possibility, a secret thrill shoots up my spine, and I remember that incredible night of the Proms, when The Jinks were on that stage, the most unlikely of stages for a band like them. How brilliant they were despite all the negative press, how they proved themselves worthy when all the snobs had been so sure they wouldn't. I had been there, sitting with Mum in the stalls, so overcome with pride I'd cried through the whole performance. The Royal Albert Hall is more than a venue, more than a stage. It is special; transformative. Maybe it can be that for me too, the thing that finally makes it all start to get better.

If I can ever actually sing again. I've tried not to let myself think about it too much, but I'm starting to worry more and more that I haven't sung a note since before Beth died. At first, I'd assumed it was a shock thing, and that it would come back. But it hasn't come back. Not just the physical ability, but the desire.

I try Googling it, but I just get lots of results about laryngitis and drinking plenty of water. I could probably be more specific, but to be honest I'm a little scared to be. I don't want the answer, because then I'll have to face it.

What will happen to me if I don't sing? Not just with the concert – which, let's face it, is a big question mark anyway, what with the possibly insurmountable issue of me hating the remaining band members – but also with school? My life? I can hardly go back to Shona Lee if I don't have music in me any more. But then what will I do?

The thought makes me feel panicky, somewhere deep inside.

So I push it away.

Dad doesn't come home from work that evening.

This wasn't unusual, once. In the before time, Dad used to work crazy hours and travel all over the place; sometimes whole days would go by before Mum or I saw him. When there was a Beth-related crisis, which to be honest was a lot of the time, he'd stay at the office all night to deal with it.

But Beth's gone now, so why would there be a crisis?

"Is something wrong?" I ask Mum, when she tells me he'll be working so late it won't be worth coming home.

"I didn't ask," she says.

82 DAYS GONE

Exclusive (part two)

World Exclusive: Backstabbed Beck

- Lizzie Beck BULLIED by jealous bandmates

- Kicked out of The Jinks just DAYS before suicide

- Relaunch of three-piece was planned in JUNE

- Jodie Soto-Hahn orchestrated COUP and COVER-UP

Tragic singer Lizzie Beck was bullied out of hit British band The Jinks just days before she took her own life – an exclusive source has now revealed – in a secret coup led by Beck's former bandmate and best friend, Jodie Soto-Hahn.

These shocking details are surfacing just days after The Jinks publicly announced they would continue on as a trio – only three short months after the tragic death of star Lizzie Beck – with the group's remaining three members.

[Image Description: Lizzie Beck and The Jinks in happier times, L-R Jodie Soto-Hahn, Lizzie Beck, Aiya Mehta, Tamryn Lord]

Today, a source close to Lizzie Beck and the band confirmed Lizzie Beck was no longer a member of The Jinks at the time of her death and had in fact been forced to leave the group after a fight with fan favourite Jodie Soto-Hahn, who had also been Beck's best friend since childhood.

This week's big relaunch of The Jinks as a three-piece was sold to fans as a sad move made necessary by Beck's death, when ditching Beck and continuing on without her had in fact been the group's plan for months.

Today's devastating revelations are sure to raise questions over the return of The Jinks, who to this point have enjoyed a huge amount of support from the public and their fans in the aftermath of Beck's suicide.

It is uncertain if the planned memorial concert for Lizzie Beck will go ahead at the end of this month. Jodie Soto-Hahn was not available for comment.

My entire life, I've been Beth's little sister. For five years, I've been Lizzie Beck's little sister. Occasionally, I am a Shona Lee student. Sometimes, a singer. (Or "aspiring singer".)

Now, I am a new word:

Source.

I am a *source close to Lizzie Beck.*

I am the worst thing to be in the world of the famous. I am the enemy. A traitor. A betrayer.

Beth would have been so ashamed of me.

I am so ashamed of me.

After I read the article, I throw up.

#1 Jodie

TRENDING WITH **Jodie So, Jodie Soto-Hahn**

#2 #JodieSoIsOverParty

#3 #JodieIsSoOverParty

#4 The Jinks

#5 Lizzie

TRENDING WITH **Lizzie Beck, RIP**

@thisismybirdhouse FUCK ME. You think you can't be surprised any more, you know? Who knew Jodie So was a stone cold bitch?!

@augustjune11 Holy shit! *grabs popcorn* #JodieIsSoOverParty

@chordless91 Big shock, members of a girl band are two-faced bitches. Definitely front page news there.

> **@ninestopshome** Sure, but Lizzie Beck is actually dead, so this goes beyond that, right?

@devongirl211 I don't know how the law works but really feels like there should be some kind of charges against Jodie Soto-Hahn and the other two for this.

> **@florence10mcgill** It might not be true.

> > **@swiftieuk028** Of course it's true. Jodie would just deny it otherwise. Who would stay quiet right now if it wasn't true?

@backtoparris PSA for the people tweeting that Jodie Soto-Hahn drove Lizzie Beck to suicide: libel is a thing and you should really look it up, OK? You're welcome.

@waitingfordaylights Idk, maybe this is childish but I'm actually really fucking sad about this stuff about Jodie So. I loved her and Lizzie when I was a kid. They were like friend goals when I was being bullied at school. Listened to The Jinks non-stop. Can't believe it was all a lie.

> **@kerrysouthlee** I know what you mean, but it doesn't mean it was ALL a lie. They probably really were friends like that at the beginning, and it just went bad.

> > **@waitingfordaylights** That's even worse?!

@kaleidoscopedreams Why are people saying this isn't a story? It's a HUGE fucking story to anyone who loved The Jinks. This ruins everything.

@thepinktoadette Fucks sake, have you people learned NOTHING? Stop hounding **@jodieso** you heartless monsters.

@rosaliejjones Well, I guess @jodieso is getting the attention she always wanted now.

@lcfc83294 **@jodieso** hope you fucking kill yourself

@sophyphilo12 **@jodieso** lizzie beck died because of you

@green032291 **@jodieso** FUCK YOU

@jebens0n **@jodieso** Was it worth it?

@j1nksfan00 **@jodieso** Lizzie trusted you. We ALL DID. Burning my Jinks stuff.

@kerbjoska **@jodieso** kill yourself

@998eksalo2 **@jodieso** kill urself

@lcfc83294 **@jodieso** hope you die fucking whore bitch

I don't know what to do with myself. Dad is still at the office. Mum is in bed. I try to hug Sebastien close to me, but he's a cat and he doesn't understand, just yowls in outrage when I squeeze him too tight. When I relent and let him go, he bolts out of the room.

Who can I call? Not my friends, because I pushed them away, because they don't even know about Anderson, because how could I begin to explain this? Not Scottie, because we don't talk any more.

I call Anderson. He doesn't pick up. I message him CALL ME NOW. He doesn't.

When Beth died, I thought that how I felt would be the worst I would ever feel. I thought it was the lowest anyone could go.

I was wrong.

I go to Anderson's. I don't even really know why. It's not like he's going to say anything that will make this better. Most likely, he'll say something that will make it worse.

But I go anyway, because I can't not. I message him when I'm outside, tell him that I'll stand right there on his doorstep all day if I have to, however long it takes for him to get some fucking balls. (I'm proud of this; it's the kind of thing Beth would have said.)

He opens the door abruptly, not even a minute after I've sent this message, and stands there in the doorway, very clearly not inviting me in.

"Go on then," he says as a greeting. "Yell at me."

"That's an interesting way to say sorry," I say.

"Look," he says, and I can tell by his voice that he's practised whatever it is he's about to say. "I told you it was a huge story. You were just sitting on it. People should know, and now they do."

"How selfless of you."

"No, not selfless, but yeah, smarter than you." I'm trying to figure out why the way he's acting seems familiar, and it comes to me in how he says "you". It's exactly how he was after we first had sex, when I cried and he realized that it had been my first time. His own guilt is making him stressed and anxious, and he's turning it back on me. Like I'm the one at fault here. "Fuck, Emmy. You were just OK to let everyone think Jodie's all sweet and perfect when what she actually did was fuck over your sister? Don't you think Beth deserves for people to know the truth?"

I let out an embarrassing, loud, sob-laugh. "Like you did any of this for Beth."

He sets his jaw, crossing his arms, and shrugs. "True, though."

I say, "Is that why you slept with me? To try and get a story to sell?"

He looks at me for a long moment, like he's trying to figure something out.

And then he laughs.

A real laugh. It doesn't hurt because it's mean; it hurts because it *isn't* mean.

He's laughing because he thinks it's actually funny.

"No, Emmy," he says. "I slept with you because I wanted to."

He says, "This wasn't some grand plan. It just happened."

I think it would be easier to deal with if he was lying.

If I could feel like I'd been manipulated. Tricked into sex by a shitty guy ruthlessly waiting for the chance to sell my pain to the tabloid press.

But it was just sex for him, like I'd thought I understood. And then I handed him an opportunity on a plate.

"How much money did you make?" I ask, and these are the words that make him uncomfortable, make him shuffle his feet and look at the floor. My words are grubby. Shona Lee students don't talk about things like money.

But Shona Lee students don't leak stories to the press, either.

He shrugs. Doesn't look me in the eye. Mumbles, "You want some of it?"

For a second, I think I might launch myself at him and claw out his eyes. Honestly, it's like an impulse I actually have to stop myself indulging. He must see it on my face because he looks momentarily terrified, taking an actual step back from me.

"Fuck you," I say. I mean it to be bold, but my voice shakes. "Fuck you."

He digs his hands into his pockets, his shoulders lifting again. "Fair," he says, voice flat. "Are you done?"

"Yeah, and so are we," I say. In my head, it sounded sharp and cool and savage, but out loud I hear how cheesy it is, how embarrassing. He looks embarrassed *for* me. I know I'm going to cry so I turn on the spot and walk away, forcing myself to take it slow and not run. He doesn't call after me, and before I've even made it to the road, I hear him close the door.

Dad knows it was me.

I can tell by his face.

He comes home late, even later than usual.

His hair is ragged, like he's spent the day running his hand through it.

He looks wrecked.

I'm waiting on the stairs, because I want to be brave and face what's coming.

The anger, the disappointment.

But he just stops in the hallway, looks at me, keys still dangling from his fingers.

He doesn't seem angry, or even disappointed.

Just really, really sad.

"You should be in bed," he says. "It's late."

"Aren't you going to yell at me?"

He shakes his head.

For a moment I think he's going to walk away from me, into the kitchen, but then he says, quietly, "I want you to just think about what this has done to Jodie. What is happening to her right now. And how you felt when it was Beth being treated like this by the press and the public. Just think about that."

He looks at me, and I have to look away. He says,

"You don't need me to yell at you."

I start to cry. Uncontrollably, like a child. Sputtering tears.

"I didn't mean to."

"I know," he says, even though he can't know, even though he's probably spent the whole day thinking I did it on purpose. "Go to bed. Get some sleep."

83 DAYS GONE
Jodie (part 2)

I don't feel any better in the morning. When I check online, "Jodie" is still trending on Twitter, higher even than the band, or "Lizzie Beck". The commentary is vicious, so bad that even the more thoughtful comments are just stoking the fire of the vitriol. Checking her mentions makes me feel physically ill.

One of the morning chat shows has a discussion about it, even though they don't know anything more than what the story was yesterday. They're talking about the harm fame can do to young women, and how they should have more support to deal with it.

Which, obviously.

There's no comment anywhere from Jodie, and not from Aiya or Tam, either. No official statement, no tweets, just nothing.

I guess they're laying low, which makes sense.

For the first time in a long time, I'm actually alone in the house. Dad is in London, of course, dealing with the crisis, and Mum has gone back to work for the first time since she went on compassionate leave in June. Just for a half day, she says, to see how it feels. She had it planned since before all this *source* stuff — something she seems to be leaving Dad to deal with — and I'd told her it was fine for her to go.

I've decided I'm going to try and force myself to sing something, now there's no chance of anyone overhearing, now I've reached a point where things can't get worse. I walk up and down the stairs a few times, trying to energize myself. I try a few vocal warm-up exercises, surprising myself with my familiar voice. It really is still there. I close my eyes, breathe in through my nose.

I open my mouth, and the doorbell rings.

I falter, startled, my eyes opening. It's probably a journalist chancing it, trying to get a comment from us about the story. I could ignore it, but if I do, they might spend the rest of the day trying, which would be really annoying. The doorbell rings again and I head down the stairs, deciding that I'll just say, "No comment," firm and polite, like I've been taught, and close the door. I'm practising it in my head as I reach the door, already opening my mouth to say it—

But it's not a journalist.

It's Jodie.

My entire body goes cold with shock. And guilt.

Jodie.

Jodie, who ignored the message when I called her a lying bitch, who has never come to the house, who hasn't tried to speak to me this whole time.

Jodie, who I just threw to the wolves, whose career I might have destroyed.

"Emmy," she says. I'm confused because she doesn't say it angrily. In fact, she kind of says it ... worriedly. "Emmy, don't shut the door."

I hadn't been going to shut the door. I just stand there, confused.

"Can I talk to you?" she asks. Pleads, really. Rich, famous, golden girl Jodie Soto-Hahn. "Please, Emmy."

I don't understand what's happening. Is this a trick to get me to let her in? And then once she's safely inside she'll start screaming at me for ruining her life?

"I know you won't want to hear anything I've got to say," she says, confusing me even more. "But please, can I just have a chance?"

I step aside, and her relief comes out in an audible hitched sigh. She follows me inside, closing the door behind her.

"Do you ... want a drink or something?" I ask. Maybe I should call Dad.

Jodie doesn't answer me. She's staring at the display of framed family photos on the wall. I can see that her eyes have fallen on the picture of Beth, eight years old, grinning out with all her confidence and charm. I'm in the picture too; three years old, in her lap, looking up at her instead of at the camera.

Fitting.

"Do you know what my mum keeps saying to me?" Jodie says, out of nowhere, as if I could say yes. *Your life isn't destroyed, because you still have it.* Her face is impossible to read. "I'm still here. I still have a chance to fix things."

I wonder what she means by *fix things*.

"Some things," she amends, like she can hear my thoughts. "I can fix some things." She turns to me. "That's why I'm here."

"OK," I say.

We go to sit in the kitchen together. I ask her again if she wants a drink, and she asks for wine, which isn't what I meant, but I get a bottle out of the fridge anyway and pour her a glass. The smell makes me think of Beth, which is ridiculous, because it's not like she's the only person in my life who ever drank wine. But still.

I hand the glass over and Jodie sips at it.

I realize, suddenly and brutally, that this is the first time Jodie and I have ever been alone together. Ever. No Beth between or beside or behind us. No Beth, not ever again. I don't understand why grief can still feel like a surprise, but it hits my entire body like a wave against rocks. I even make a noise, a little cry-gasp, and Jodie looks up, alert.

Jodie, who is not my sister, but is now the closest I will ever get.

I'm crying like I just found out Beth had died. Crying like a child, even though it's been months and I should be getting over this by now, like everyone else seems to be.

I feel arms around me, and it's Jodie, stood up from where she'd been sitting at the table, hugging me sideways. She cups my head with her hand and strokes my hair.

I break away after a couple of minutes and she stands there, arms still partly held up, empty. "Why are you here?" I ask, in a voice that comes out half choked. "I don't understand."

She opens her mouth, then closes it again. Glances behind her at the wine on the table. "We should sit down," she says.

When we do, her hands go immediately to the glass, cupping around it, the way people hold mugs of tea.

"Those stories in the press," she says. "I ... I couldn't stand thinking of you reading them and believing them. It kills me to think that you'd think it was true, any of it. That I'd ... that I'd do that to Beth. So, I know that I've…" She keeps stopping, biting her lip, sipping from her glass again. "I know that I'm meant to not be talking to you, but I had to come for this. I'm sorry, maybe it's selfish, but I need you to believe me."

I have so many questions. So many. The first is, *What the fuck?* And then, in no particular order:

What do you mean, they aren't true?

Don't you know it was me who leaked the story?

Not meant to be talking to me? What? Why? Since when? Says who?

Why do you need me to believe you? Since when do you care?

I say, "Believe what?"

"That none of it is true," she says. "Those stories; what 'the source' said, whoever that was. It's not true."

I stare at her, trying to read her face. Maybe she *does* know it was me. Maybe this is part of some elaborate scheme to maximize my guilt.

But her face is all open pain and worry. Earnest.

"It is true, though," I say. My voice comes out flat. "Like, I really don't know what you're trying to say here. Did you just come here to lie to me?"

Her entire face crumples. Right in on itself, like I punched her. "Emmy, no. No, I'm not lying. I swear I'm not. God, I … please, just let me talk, OK? Will you just listen to me?"

"Why?" I ask. "Why do you care what I think?"

"Because you're … because Beth…" Her breath is starting to come out all jumbled up and loud, like she might hyperventilate. Shit, she *is* hyperventilating. "F—fuck. Fucking *fuck*."

I don't know what to do. She's almost wheezing now. I pour her a glass of water and hold it out helplessly, watching as she closes her eyes, pats her chest with one hand, tries to breathe through her nose. She presses the glass to her forehead, but doesn't drink from it. Jodie Soto-Hahn is breaking down at my kitchen table, and I just stand there and watch.

It takes a long time for her to calm down. When she's breathing normally again, she sips wine, not water.

"Sorry," I say, even though I'm not certain whether I actually am sorry about anything or not. "I didn't mean to make you—"

"It's OK," she interrupts. "It's not your fault. That's been happening a lot lately." She shakes her head, closing her eyes, and sighs. "This has just been the worst fucking..." She opens her eyes and looks at me. "Well, you know. Grief is fucking heinous, isn't it?" She looks down at her glass, tapping her nails against the rim. "You think I hated her," she says. It's a statement, not a question. "That's why you believe the papers? And why you sent me that message on Instagram?" Tap, tap, tap on the glass. "You think I don't have any right to miss her. You think I'm ... you think I'm the bad guy. All three of us: Aiya, Tam and me."

"Aren't you?" I say.

Quietly, she says, "I feel like I am, yeah." I'm about to consider myself vindicated when she adds, "But not for the reasons you think." There's a silence that I wait for her to fill with the truth. "I don't know how to do this." She shakes her head. "Can you tell me what it is you think I've done? So I can at least set you straight? And if it's what's in the papers, why did you send that message back in June?"

This, at least, is easy.

"You wanted Beth out of the band," I say. "You were trying to push her out, all three of you." Her mouth falls into a rigid line, her fingers tighten around the stem of the glass. Now I've started, the words fall out. "You were tired of all the bad press she got the band, and that you couldn't just *be* a band, because she kept fucking things up for all of you. So you wanted rid of her, you and Aiya and Tam. You tried to make her leave, and when that didn't work, you tried to get your management to kick her out instead. And then she died, and you got what you wanted, and now you're carrying on the band as a three-piece, just like you planned, even though she's dead. And you're using the fact that she's dead for more publicity. *And* you're trying to make out the three of you care that she's dead, that you cared when she was alive, when all you ever wanted was to be rid of her."

She's staring at me, waiting to be sure I've definitely finished. After a long silence, she says, almost sarcastically, "Wow. Why did you even let me in the door if you think that's who I am?"

I say nothing.

"Right," she says. She tips back the last of her wine and sets the empty glass on the table. "OK. That's all bullshit."

"You have to say that."

"Actually, I don't," she says. "Remember, I came here to talk to you. That's a choice I made. Why would I do that if any of what you just said is true?"

"Because you don't want me to think it's true."

"Shit, Emmy," she says. "If that stuff were true, and that is the kind of person I am, why would I *care* about what you think?"

This gives me pause. I frown, and she frowns back.

"Can I have some more wine?" she asks, very politely.

"Isn't it a bit early for … more wine?"

"What a judgemental sixteen-year-old you are," she says. "Yes, it is. Please?"

I pour her another glass.

"I'm trying to figure out," she says, watching me slide the wine glass back across the table towards her, "why you think all of that stuff. Where you got it from. And it must be Beth, before she died. Right?"

I nod. "She told me about how you wanted her out of the band."

"Right," she says.

"And obviously," I add, "my dad was part of it. And he used to talk about it too."

She looks up at me. "Malcolm talked about it as well? And he said that we were trying to force her out?"

"Yeah."

"Did he ever say *why* we'd want that?"

I hesitate, trying to remember. All I can think of is Beth's rants, in messages or over the phone or sometimes right here in this kitchen, rambling and mostly incoherent, about how they were bitches and snakes and liars. She was usually drunk or high, like she seemed to be so much of the time in the days and weeks before… I push the thoughts away. I don't want that Lizzie/Beth hybrid in my head. I want my dazzling sister, Beth. The one who made sense.

"He said…" A memory of an argument has invaded my head. Beth screaming at Dad, the sound of smashing china, his thunderous voice telling her he would section her if he had to, that this was his job on the line, that she was a waste of talent, a waste of fame, a waste of everyone's time and energy and money. I'd put my headphones on and buried myself under the covers. I'd been messaging Scottie. I remember writing, Beth's being a psycho again.

A cold, thick shame rises in my blood, making me feel dizzy. That's what I wrote. These things happened, and I know they did, even if I've let grief give me a selective memory.

Jodie is watching me carefully, like she can see inside my head. She says, again, "It's not true. It's so much more complicated than that."

"That's just the kind of thing people say. It doesn't mean anything."

Her eyes close momentarily, she shakes her head. "Well, can I explain it, and then you can decide if it means anything or not?"

"Did you try and force her out of the band?"

She hesitates, bites her lips together. "Yes." I open my mouth, but she speaks before I can. "Can I tell you why?"

"Why doesn't matter."

"It actually matters a lot. Emmy, Beth needed to leave the band for her own good. I was trying to help her. She needed to get some serious help, to be away from the press and the public eye. It was killing her. I didn't hate her, Em. God, I loved her. She was a bitch, but I loved her. I didn't want her out of the band for the sake of it.

I wasn't thinking of me and Aiya and Tam, I was thinking of *her*. Beth. My best fucking friend, Emmy. She was like my sister. I wanted her *better*. I wanted her *safe*." Tears are gathering in her eyes. There's pain in her voice. "We all did. I was trying to help her." Her voice breaks. "I was trying to save her."

I stare at her, letting her words settle into my head, trying to make sense of them, scanning for truth. Can it be true? It feels true, the way she's saying them. But no, it can't be true.

"If it was about helping Beth, why would anyone need to fight?" I ask. "It wasn't you versus Beth. It was you three versus management. They were on Beth's side. They were fighting for her."

Something happens to Jodie's face when I say this, and for a second I can't tell whether she's going to laugh or cry. She does neither, just takes another long sip of wine. "Holy fucking shit," she mutters, mostly to herself. In her normal voice, she says, "Right. OK. So let me get this totally straight. You think that me and Aiya and Tam were the bitches trying to get rid of Beth because … what … we were jealous of her?"

"Not jealous." Maybe jealous once, but not in the last couple of years. "You were tired of her being in trouble all the time, dragging the band down. You wanted her gone so you could get on with being famous."

"Right," she says. "Right. So we were the bad guys, heartlessly kicking Beth out of her own band for an easier life —" she looks at me, eyebrows raised, and I nod — "not caring at all about her and what effect that would have. Bearing in mind we were the ones seeing her every day, and knew how bad her mental health was, and knew the shitload of stuff you don't know about, because you're younger and everyone — especially Beth — wanted to protect you from it. But that's what you think? That we're the bitches?"

To be honest, I've sort of lost track by now of the point she'd been making, but I nod again when she gets to "bitches". Because that bit, I know, is true.

"Right," she says again. "And, so, we're the bitches, and management were the heroes — the men, let's not forget that bit, right? — trying to stop us being unreasonable, standing up for Beth, trying to save her career?"

She sounds incredulous. So incredulous that a flicker of doubt question marks in my head. I don't know what to say. I just look at her, waiting.

She shakes her head. "Emmy, management weren't trying to save Beth, they were trying to *keep Lizzie Beck*. All the stuff that was painful for Beth — for all of us — was what got the headlines for the band. It kept us in the public eye, all the time, even when we didn't have music out. When she was fucking up, our streams went up. Of course, we didn't give a shit about that. Me and Aiya and Tam. We didn't care about how many streams "Daylights" was getting. Not when Beth was destroying herself. She needed to get out of that whole toxic mess, because no one was helping her, Em. Helping her meant making hard choices, like getting her out of the headlines, away from social media. Long-term help. That's what we were trying to do. And fucking management —" she spits this out — "were like, *no, no, we can't lose Lizzie. The Jinks can't work without Lizzie.* Making her believe it. Saying they'd do all this stuff to help her, stuff we knew they wouldn't actually do. Do you know what it was like, sitting in those meetings? I felt like I was losing my mind. Literally, like I was losing my mind. And then Beth would talk like we were betraying her, trying to get rid of her. It was so fucked up. What were we meant to do? We pushed harder. We made an ultimatum. The three of us on our own or we'd walk."

I laugh. The kind of bitter bark I've never heard out of my own mouth before. "Right."

"You're right that we weren't fighting Beth, we were fighting management. But we were fighting management *for her.* To *help* her."

"But now she's dead."

"I know she's fucking dead!" She screams this at me. Actually screams,

the words jagged, like they'd wrenched at her throat. "I know that! I know that every second of every day. I have to live with that. Goddamn it, I thought I was doing the right thing." She chokes a sob. "But she — she thought that I'd betrayed her. She *died* thinking I'd..." She turns away from me, her hand reaching up to her face. "I'm sorry. God, I'm so sorry."

I don't know who she's talking to. Beth? Me? Herself?

"But you're saying my dad was in on this," I say. "That he was just ... selling Beth out for more streams on Spotify? Do you expect me to believe that?"

She closes her eyes and sighs, like she's tired. "I'm saying it's a lot more complicated than you seem to think. No, obviously he wasn't selling her out. Not, like, consciously, anyway. But was he acting in her best interests, or the best interests of management?"

"You keep saying 'management' like they're not real people."

"They don't fucking act like real people."

"You're talking about my dad."

"Your dad," she says, hard, for emphasis, "is great. Yes. I love your dad, he's been amazing to me, to all of us, especially over the last fucking awful few months. But, like the rest of them, he's made a lot of money off us, Emmy. I'd have to be pretty naive to not realize that. They all have. Yes, he loved Beth, more than anyone. He hated her being in pain; of course he did. No one wanted Beth to be happy and stable more than him. But he still fucking did it all, though! He still convinced her to stay in the band when she *should have left*, talked us into carrying on with her over and over. Em, what I'm trying to say is, this is so much more complicated than you're making it out to be. People are complicated. There aren't good guys and bad guys. We all loved Beth. That wasn't ... that wasn't the problem. And it wasn't enough."

"You're still a band, though."

"What?"

"The three of you. You're saying all this, and yeah, maybe it makes sense, but if that was true, why would you be carrying on now? How could you carry on working with them after what they did to Beth? Why *should* The Jinks carry on without her?"

In profile, I see Jodie bite down on her lip. Quietly, she says, "Like I said, people aren't perfect. We're not perfect. I'm not perfect. I hate them for what they did to Beth. What they did to all of us. But this band ... it's still my life, Em. It's everything I... I've worked so hard. I've put up with so much shit. *So much shit*, Emmy. Why should I give that all up?"

"Because it's the right thing to do?"

She snorts. "In the music industry? No such thing. No one benefits from a sacrifice like that. Is it selfish? Yeah, probably. But it's my band too. I don't want to give it up. And, hey, you know what? Beth – really Beth, the Beth we both loved – would want us to carry on."

I want to tell her that she's wrong about that, but she's right, and I know it. Strip away all the noise and bullshit, and Beth loved the band, loved the girls. She *would* want them to go on and be successful. Would probably even support them doing it on the back of her death and the press it had generated.

I can see her in my head, standing right next to me. I'd say, *But it's wrong, isn't it?* And she'd screw up her face like she did when I said something stupid and say, *Why? I'm dead, Em. I don't care.*

My heart twists.

"Anyway," Jodie says, her unBeth voice wrenching me back to reality. "We're looking for new management."

I wonder if Dad knows that. Should I tell him? I won't tell him.

"Will that fix things?" I ask.

Her mouth quirks into an entirely humourless, ironic smile. "Nothing can fix things. Beth is gone. But it might give us a better future, who knows."

"Maybe you should have done it before."

She shakes her head. "Beth would never have gone along with that while your dad was in the management team. That was part of the problem. Things were always so unbalanced. And when things went wrong, like they did all the fucking time, management were always on her side. *Always.* Even though she was the..." She stops herself, breathing in a sigh. "None of this matters any more."

"She was the what?" I ask. "The problem?"

She snorts. "I was going to say bitch, but that works too."

"You were literally just saying you did all this because you cared about her, but you're already back to calling her a bitch, so..."

"Beth *was* a bitch," she says, face screwing up as she looks at me dead on. "You know that, Em. She was your sister. I'm not going to pretend she was a saint just because she's dead and I miss the fuck out of her. She was a nightmare, a lot of the time – why are you looking at me like I'm talking shit?" She shakes her head, incredulous. "All of the shit still happened. Remembering that doesn't mean I miss her any less."

She stares at me, waiting, but I don't say anything. What am I meant to say?

"Do you know that she slept with my boyfriend?" she demands, suddenly, like she'd just decided to say it in that moment. "Do you?"

"What? No ... I—"

"No, you didn't know. Because we kept it out of the press and of fucking course she didn't tell you. She cared so much about what you thought of her. Didn't much care about what I thought though, did she? Fucked my boyfriend because she was mad at me – who *does* that? And now they all think I was the monster? That I *bullied* her?" She's crying again. "Fuck! Fuck, fuck, *fucking* Beth."

I try to make sense of it, as Jodie touches the pads of her thumbs to her eyes, shaking her head. Beth made mistakes, of course she did, but she had a good heart and she loved Jodie. Why would she hurt her like that?

"When did she sleep with your boyfriend?" I ask.

She sighs and shrugs, like it's irrelevant. "About a year ago."

A year ago. I try to summon that time in my head, the context of it.

"And she just ... told you?"

"He did." Jodie's boyfriend was Sutton Reilly at the time, a rugby player. I'd never met him, but Beth had told me he was "sweet but dim". "He felt bad about it." She shrugs again. "But I guess he would say that, wouldn't he?"

"I don't really understand what you're telling me," I say.

"It's what it sounds like. Beth and I were having one of our blow-ups, her at her worst. You know what that was like; don't pretend you don't. And it was so bad — *she* was so bad, properly off her head then — that she fucked my boyfriend. Because she could. You know that interview I did with the *Mail* about my anorexia? That was in exchange; to stop them printing the real story. Management sorted it all out, and I had to talk about being anorexic in a national newspaper, because it would be *too damaging for the band* for the real story to get out."

Fuck. This is really bad. What she's telling me, it's awful. She's making Beth sound monstrous. And the worst thing is, I don't think she's lying to me. I want her to be, but she isn't. This happened. This was my sister, as much as the Beth I knew.

"No wonder you hated her," I say. My voice comes out soft.

"I didn't hate her," Jodie says. "I mean, I did. Then. But not for ever. The thing with Beth is ... she was self-destructive. She didn't mean to do the things she did. Most of the time, anyway. That doesn't stop how much it hurt, but I do know why she did that stuff. I still loved her. Besides, I feel like I should say this, but my boyfriend could have said no. He knew Beth. He knew how vulnerable she was — fuck, she hated it when we used that word — but he did, he knew. So he should have said no for her, as much as for me. He took advantage. That's true, whether she was a bitch or not." She lets out a small, pained laugh. "Look, I'm still protective over her, still defending her. And she's already dead. Isn't that crazy?" She shakes her head. "God, Em, I miss her. I miss her so much. I wish I could just ... tell her I love her, and I forgive her, and things are OK."

Softly, I say, "Things aren't OK."

She opens her eyes again. "No, I guess they're not, are they?"

We're both quiet for a while, like we're taking a breather from the heaviness of the conversation. Jodie sips at her wine, eyes on the table.

After a while, when I've done as much processing as I can manage, I say, "Can I ask you something?"

"Sure, of course."

"Why didn't you reply to me when I sent you that message on Instagram? Actually, why didn't you contact me at all? Not even once?"

Jodie frowns into her wine glass, then at me. "I wanted to. We all did; Aiya and Tam as well. But your dad told us not to. Didn't you know that?"

I shake my head.

"He said I'd just upset you more if I spoke to you after Beth died. That you'd take it badly, whatever I said. Aiya wanted to talk to you and your mum before we relaunched the band – she thought it was the decent thing to do. But your dad said he'd already spoken to you." As she watches my face, a humourless smile appears on hers. "He didn't, then?"

"No. He didn't. Not until, like, the day before."

She lets out a loud sigh. "I love your dad, but he can't half be a dick sometimes. I really should stop believing him when he says things." She touches her forehead with her fingertips, closing her eyes. I can see the stress on her face. "I'm sorry, Em. I should have just messaged you anyway."

I think about it, trying to imagine how I would have reacted if she had messaged me. Badly, probably, if I'm honest. Dad was right about that, but I'm not sure that means it was the right thing to do. Why does everything have to be so complicated? When did there stop being easy answers?

I wonder if what Jodie said is true, if Beth really did sleep with her boyfriend solely because she was mad at her and for no other reason, or if there was more to the story. I'll never know now, because I only have Jodie's version. I'll never reach an age where Beth would have thought I was old enough to talk to me like a friend instead of a younger sister, where she could have been honest about things like that.

"You knew her better than me." I don't know I'm even thinking it until the words fall, unbidden, from my mouth.

Jodie looks at me in surprise. "What do you mean?"

"Just what I said."

She shakes her head. "You guys ... sisters. There's nothing like that. I was always so jealous, you remember? That the two of you had each other. I always wanted a sister."

"That's not the same as knowing her," I say.

"I don't think..." She trails off, considering. "I don't think it's about knowing her *better*. In a different way, sure. But not *better*. Maybe it's more like ... your story of Beth is different. You know? I have a story of me and Beth, and who she was to me, and in your head, there's another story. You don't know mine, and I don't know yours, because they're *ours*. But neither one is wrong, or less real." She waits for me to agree or disagree, but I don't know what to say, so I say nothing. "I really am sorry I didn't come and talk to you earlier," she says. "That was obviously the wrong thing to do. But ... OK, this is a shit excuse, I know, but this has been a really hard few months. Like, impossible."

"Same," I say.

"You *can* talk to me, though," she says, almost tentatively. "You can message me, or even call me, if you want to talk about Beth, or anything else. I should have said that from the start. But maybe I was ... I don't know. Maybe I was too ashamed. The story in the press is wrong, but I do feel ... God, guilty isn't even the word. I let her down. That's the truth. I know that." She seems almost to be talking to herself more than she's talking to me. "I should have been there. Done more."

"I think everyone feels that way," I say. "Everyone who knew her."

She gives me a small half-smile. "I don't know if that makes me feel better or worse. Thanks, Emmy. And thanks for letting me in and listening to me ramble."

"Does my dad know you're here?" I ask, the thought occurring to me for the first time.

She smirks. "Ha, no. He thinks I'm hiding out at my house. That's what I'm *meant* to be doing. There's this whole strategy." She waves her hand, as if it doesn't matter. "I don't want to think about that now."

I watch her from across the table as she lifts her glass of wine again, eyes closing briefly with each sip. The tension seems to have gone from her face and shoulders, like she thinks the difficult bit is over and she can relax.

But there's one question left, and it's been thrumming in my head for the past ten minutes. *Should I tell her that I was the source?*

If I tell her, will I make things bad again? Or is that irrelevant, when the truth is the truth?

If I don't tell her, she'll never find out it was me. There's no way she would; there's no one to tell her. Except my dad, that is, and he wouldn't.

So I can get off scot-free, if I want to.

"Jodie?" I ask.

"Yeah?"

"Do you know who the source is?" Maybe Dad's already made up an alternative scenario on my behalf. Lied for me, like he used to lie to protect Beth, all the time. Invented someone on the investigating team leaking information for money, like what happened with Beth's voice memo. That would make sense. A plausible lie, and one with no casualties.

Jodie looks at me for a long time without answering, her eyes moving over my face. Sometimes, you can *see* people thinking. Right now, I watch Jodie move the pieces into place, seeing our entire conversation through a new filter.

I just stare at her, waiting.

"Yeah," she says finally. "I think I do."

I say, "I'm sorry."

She says, "I'm sorry too."

We both loved Beth.

We were both loved by Beth.

We are both sorry.

Maybe that can be enough.

She was kinder to me than she needed to be.
>   I can see clearly enough to appreciate that.
>   In a way that maybe I wouldn't have yesterday.

She came all the way here to sit down with me, to talk, to explain.
>   And not just talk in the way everyone tells me I should be talking,
>   *you need to talk to someone,*
>   *but are you talking to someone?*
>   She talked to me *about Beth* in an actual real way.
>   No sugar-coating, no sweet grief-soaked reimaginings, no hiding
from the truth.
>   She didn't get awkward, didn't try to change the subject.

Is this what I've been missing, the thing I've wanted this whole time?
>   Not just to talk, but to talk *about* her?

I've got a lot to sit with now.
>   A lot to think over, to reshuffle in my mind.
>   And when I'm done, see what's left.
>   See who I am
>   in the end.

When I hear Mum's car in the driveway, I put the kettle on. She walks into the kitchen, already frowning.

"Who was here?" she asks, without a hello.

"OK, how do you know that?" I ask. "Are you psychic?"

"There's perfume in the air," she says. "You don't wear perfume."

"It's Jodie's," I say.

Mum's whole face transforms. "Jodie?" When I nod, she says, "She didn't wait for me to get back?"

"She was here to see me," I say. "We talked for a while."

"To see you?" she repeats. "Why?"

Which is kind of an insulting question, if you think about it.

"To talk about the whole source thing," I say. "She wanted to explain what had actually happened. Which is nice, because, you know, no one else has bothered to do that."

Mum sinks herself down onto one of the kitchen stools. "Emmy, I'm not sure I've got the strength for wherever this is going."

"Well, I'm making you tea," I say. "So that will help." I wait, but she doesn't say anything else, so I say, "Do you even know the source was me?"

She closes her eyes, rubs them with her fingers. "Of course I know that, Emmy."

"Don't you care?"

She breathes in and out in a long sigh, then opens her eyes. "Yes, I care. But I didn't think you'd need me talking to you about it on top of everything else. I thought your dad had spoken to you."

I sputter out a laugh. "Oh yeah, because that was so helpful?"

"And now you've spoken to Jodie," she continues, as if I haven't spoken. "Did that help?"

I swallow. "It would have helped more if someone had talked to me earlier, to be honest. So I didn't have to get it so wrong, and now maybe I've ruined... I've hurt Jodie and..."

"You haven't ruined anything," Mum says. Which I'm pretty sure isn't true. "I'm sorry, Emmy. I didn't realize you were ... misinformed about that situation. With the girls and the band. I thought you knew that it was a far more complex situation than Beth may have led you to believe. Of course, I understand now why you thought the way you did, and I'm sorry that I didn't realize. I really am. At the time, I was so worried about Beth, *so* worried, and then…" She lets out a long sigh, shaking her head. "I haven't been thinking clearly. This has all been so hard. So impossibly hard."

I put the cup of tea I've made on the table in front of her. "It is true, then? Definitely true?"

"Which bit?" I must look frustrated, because she says, "I'm sorry, Emmy, but this is a lot to keep up with."

"Basically that Jodie and the girls wanted Beth out to protect her, not to hurt her. That being in the band was bad for her."

Mum nods. "My understanding is that that is the truth, yes."

"And that management were the ones who wanted her to stay in the band? Because, like, all press is good press?"

She hesitates. "Yes."

"Including Dad?"

Mum is quiet for a moment. She's looking away from me when she says, "There aren't any right answers here, and there weren't any then. They all made mistakes. Jodie made mistakes; Beth made mistakes. But I want you to understand – it's really important that you understand this, Emmy – that there wasn't one thing that made Beth choose to take her own life the way she did. I don't want you taking from this that Beth died because she had to leave The Jinks. There is no single 'why', OK? You understand that?"

I nod, even though I'm not sure I do, not really. Maybe I never will.

"Thank you for my tea," Mum says.

I know this means the conversation is over, but she's let me have more of it than I've had for a long time, so I don't complain. "You're welcome," I say.

83 DAYS GONE

Love. Love. Love.

That evening, I get my first ever WhatsApp message from Jodie.

Jodie
Hey, Em. Hope it's OK to message you like this. Actually you know what

[audio message – 01:23]

I feel the smile of recognition on my face before I even realize I'm smiling. An audio message, just like Beth used to send. I give myself a few seconds to feel it, the pain and warmth in the familiarity, before I tap the message to listen.

OK, hey, sorry. This is so much easier than typing it all out. How are you? Hope you're good. I just wanted to send you this file — you'll see it after I send this. I've been thinking a lot about our conversation, and trying to see it all from your point of view. Beth, I mean. Me and Beth and the band. I know how she was, and I can't even guess what kind of stuff she must have said when she was… Well. You know. Not quite herself, I guess? She used to say Mad-Beth, but I don't know if you used to use that phrase too? Anyway, maybe you're still not sure if you should believe me. That I didn't hate Beth, and that she knew that. We had a complicated relationship — I know I said that a lot, but we loved each other too. Really. Em, if I could have saved her I… God. Sorry. You think it's going to get easier, you know? As time goes on? Anyway, I'm forwarding you one of the voice messages Beth left me a couple of weeks before she died. I think it sort of shows everything I've said. I hope it's OK to send you this — it might be upsetting to hear, I don't know. But it's the truth, and I think that's the most important thing. And you'll hear how she felt about you, which I know you knew, but it might be nice to hear it again. God, Em, she loved you so much. You were like pure golden light to her. OK, I'll just send—

actually, maybe I should say— you might listen to this and think that I should have done something. But I want you to know, she used to leave messages like this all the time. Drunken rambles, really. This is one of the nice ones; sometimes they were really … well, horrible. Bitchy. This might sound like the kind of one-off that should have raised alarm bells, but — you'll understand this — life with Beth was one long alarm bell. She ate red flags for breakfast. Anyway. Sorry, I'm going on and on. Have a listen, and I hope it helps.

Here it is. Let me know if you want
to talk xxx

[fwd: audio message – 01:28]

I stare at the forwarded audio message for a long time without playing it. I guess I always knew that Beth left voice notes for other people, that it wasn't something she only did for me. But it had never occurred to me that one day I'd be able to listen to one of them. Not just to hear her voice again, but to hear her saying something I hadn't heard before.

And the other thing is this: I know that Jodie has sent me something *true*. And that's scary. She has done the one thing no one else has done, which is to not coddle me, to not try and hide the frightening parts of Beth from me, even in retrospect. What I'm about to hear is a Beth I didn't know, a version of my beloved sister that was just as real as the Beth in my head. Once I've heard it, I can never unhear it.

I tap on the message.

I close my eyes and listen.

Hey, Jodie. Hey, Jo-Jo. Hey, Jo-Jo-So.

Hey, Jodie, you know you're the love of my life, right?
I think you really are. Not Leo love. Real love. You're my
best friend in the world. I'm sorry I messed everything up.

Remember when we were kids and all we wanted was to be
famous? And then we got it and it ruined us? Well, not us,
I guess. You're fine, you're great. Just me. I don't know why
I'm like this, Jodie. Jo, I'm so scared. I'm so scared, I—I
can't see a way out of this. I don't… I need you, I'm sorry.
Please. Can we just try again? I—I'm sorry I said all that
stuff earlier. I know I've said that before, but I really am.
Jodie, I'm so broken. Jodie.

Jo, if I have to leave the band, I'll leave the band, but
I can't lose you. Jodie. Remember that time we had that
water slide in my garden and you and me and Emmy played for
literally hours in the sunshine? I remember that as being,
like, the most perfect of perfect times, you know? How old
were we, like, twelve? I wish we could be twelve again.
Not famous, and Emmy's all cute and tiny, and I'm still…
When did things go wrong, Jo? Jodes, it's not true about me
sleeping with that producer, I swear. You don't believe it,
do you? He came on to me, yeah, but I said no. Honestly.
Jodie, maybe *you* can leave the band too! Maybe we should
just stop the band. What do you think? You can go solo and
I'll wait for Emmy to get a bit older and then maybe the
two of us can be like First Aid Kit or something, wouldn't
that be cool?

No, I know, I couldn't bring Em down like that. She's going
to be so amazing on her own. You'll look after her, right?

Better than me. Fuck, Jodie, I don't know what happened to me. I don't know how to get back. Jo. Jo-Jo-So, I love you so. You're the love of my life. You and Em. I wish I was good enough for both of you. I'm sorry. I love you. Love. Love. Love. OK. Bye. I love you.

The message is a barely coherent ramble. Beth slurs her words, stumbles over sentences, repeats herself. Listening to it is agony. I want to reach into the message, into the past, and pull her out of it. Hug her close and tell her it's OK, she's so loved. That Jodie loved her all along, and so did I, and so did Mum and Dad and Auntie Char and, God, even Leo. I'd say, *Don't leave, Beth. Don't leave me.*

But it's too late for any of that. So I just listen to the message again, and then again, and then again.

So, I was wrong about Jodie.
I was wrong about Beth leaving the band.
I was wrong about Anderson.

What else am I wrong about?

84 DAYS GONE

Leo (part two)

Leo seems nervous to see me.

His attempt at a smile keeps twitching off his face, and his hands are shaking. (I don't know if that's because of me specifically, or the remnants of some kind of withdrawal. Obviously, I don't ask.)

It's late on Tuesday morning, and I'm at the Ivy Lodge Rehab Centre in Banbury, sitting on a bench in the grounds of the facility. Somewhere near by, Mum is still in our parked car, reading a book while she waits for me. (The book – she showed me before I got out of the car – is *The Year of Magical Thinking*, which Auntie Char bought for her. "Take your time," Mum said. She even smiled.)

I've been waiting a few minutes, and now Leo has come out to see me, asking if it's OK to sit down beside me, and I've nodded, and he's sat down.

"You all right?" he asks.

It's a weird question for a guy whose girlfriend died on the other side of his wall to ask her surviving sister when she visits him in rehab. But then, what else is he going to say?

"Not too bad," I say. If your girlfriend dies, are you still her boyfriend? Is Leo Beth's former boyfriend? Her ex? Why, when there are hundreds of thousands of words in the English language, is the lexicon of death so inadequate? "You?"

Leo shrugs. He's thinner than I remember. His face is sallow; his eyes dim. "Still here."

It's what Beth used to say when I'd ask her how she was during the low times. *Still here.* The words hurt.

The grounds and garden of Ivy Lodge are beautiful, all flowers and pathways and benches and plants. The frame of the metal bench is cool against my legs. Leo asks if I mind if he smokes. The impulse is there to say no, just to make him more uncomfortable, but I don't. I say it's fine, and he lights up.

I stay silent as he takes the first drag, trying to figure out what I want to say. Finally, he says, "How come you're here?"

"I don't know," I say honestly. "I just felt like I should talk to you."

"Why?"

"Because maybe you understood Beth in a way no one else did," I say, realizing it as I say the words. But of course it's true. How can I understand the darkness in Beth if I don't at least face it?

"Because I'm a fuck up," he says, flatly.

"No, I mean..." I think about it. "Well, yeah. I guess. You both were. Together."

He inclines his head slightly in a resigned nod, like, *sure*.

"And I guess I just don't know why," I say.

"Why we were together?" He frowns. "We loved each other."

"No, I mean, like..." I trail off. What do I mean? I think back to what Jodie said about us having our own stories about Beth. That's what I want from Leo; his story of her. But that would be a pretty weird question to come out with straight off the bat. "Why do you think she did it?" I ask instead.

He shrugs again. "Well, her life was pretty shit, wasn't it?" he says. Blunt, even matter-of-fact. No one, not in the whole three months since Beth died, has said it like that.

"Was it?" I ask, and I hear how surprised I sound, as if this is actually news to me.

"Yeah. I don't get why we have to pretend it wasn't, be all, *she had so much to live for* and shit. Maybe that was true, but *she* didn't think so, and that's what matters, isn't it? How she felt? She thought everyone hated her, and that everyone who didn't hate her, like you and your parents, was burdened by her. And I could be like, *they don't hate you, babe,* but she had people on her fucking Twitter every single day giving her shit. Press calling her trashy and pathetic. Now, they're all sorry, saying it's tragic. Fucking hypocrites. I wish they'd at least be honest about it. It's like ... you know, gaslighting? Making out she was wrong to think she was worthless, when that's what they literally said, all the time. Of course she believed it."

I've been thinking a version of this since she died, deep in the secret conclaves of my mind, but no one has verbalized it like this, not once. Hearing it makes every part of me hurt, the way only truth can hurt.

"I'm not making out I'm perfect," Leo continues. "But at least I'll admit it. I was a shit boyfriend and I fucked her up a hundred ways, OK? I'm sorry about that. I'll be sorry until the day I die."

I don't say anything, because I don't know what I'm meant to say.

"You know, I don't even remember what we argued about?" he says. "That last night, we had a stupid fight – we were both high – and I don't even remember what it was about. That's fucked me up, trying to remember."

"Do you think it matters?"

"No, but that's not the point. I should be able to remember every single second of the last night I spent with my girlfriend before she died. But she made me sleep in another room and I don't even remember why."

"What could it have been about?"

"No idea. Anything. We fought about everything, all the time. Shit, we were so fucked up. Maybe I shouldn't tell you that." He looks at me sideways, an uncertain, guilty glance. "How old are you again? Fifteen?"

"Sixteen. And I know you were fucked up. You cheated on her. Twice."

He looks away. "I know."

"Maybe you were arguing about that."

"No, that was done."

I'm not sure what he means by this, but I can't quite bear to carry on this line of questioning, to think too much about the last few hours of Beth's life being lost for ever because Leo was too high to remember any of it. So I say, "Did you know what was going on with The Jinks? Before she died?"

He nods. "Jodie thought she needed to be out of the public eye for a while, so she could get proper help."

Hearing him say this makes me realize how much I wanted him

to say, *Jodie was forcing her out of the band, she's a bitch, she always hated Beth.* How much I wanted the easy story to be true, so I could have someone to blame.

"Do you think she was right?"

"Probably. Jodie is sound. Beth hated that, but she was usually right. And way more sensible than Beth and me. But they had all those meetings about leaving the band, and then she died anyway, so..." He shrugs. "Who knows if it was right or not."

"Have you spoken to Jodie?"

"No. We weren't exactly mates. She told me once that if I kept Beth hanging on she'd end up dead."

He says this with no emotion. Flat, almost lifeless. I look at him, trying to understand what I'm feeling. For the first time, I can understand why my dad cares so much about him. I get to feel sad about Beth dying; an unfathomable, agonizing sadness, but still just sadness. Leo has guilt, too. Not a guilt he's invented out of the confusion of grief, but actual, weighted guilt. How does a person even begin to deal with that?

Drugs, I guess. Hence, rehab.

We're both silent in the seconds and then minutes following his statement. He smokes his cigarette, one slow inhale and exhale at a time.

"Can I have some?" I ask.

For the first time, there's a flash of warmth on his face when he smiles. "Fuck no," he says. He coughs out a laugh. "I'm haunted enough as it is. Beth would never let me sleep if I let you smoke."

"Don't you think she'd be pleased?" I ask. "If I was braver?"

"No," he says, surprising me with his vehemence. "No fucking way. She wanted to protect you."

"From ... cigarettes?"

"From *everything*." He pinches the cigarette between his finger and thumb. "In a good way. She loved you more than anyone."

I almost smile. It's nice to hear.

"I just don't know what to do with myself now," I say. "Without her."

Leo is silent for a while, like he's thinking about it. I don't even know why I've bothered saying it to him, because it's not like Leo has any wisdom to share, and I wouldn't take it from him even if he offered it. But I find myself waiting for an answer, anyway.

"Just … have a good life," he says. It's not what I expected him to say. "The best life you can. That's what Beth would want for you."

"Yeah, well, I can't have a good life now, can I?" I say. "Not now she's fucked off out of it."

"Nah," he says. "You'll be fine."

He says this like it's actually true.

"How do you know that?"

He shrugs, tossing the cigarette butt to the floor and crushing it with his foot. "I just do," he says.

How do I feel after talking to Leo?

Not better, exactly. Maybe ... calmer? Kind of like I've let go of something. I'd planned to tell him about me being the source, but we talk for almost an hour and it doesn't come up. He doesn't tell me anything new, not really, so there's not really any reason why I should feel like talking to him has made a difference.

But it has made a difference.

"How was he?" Mum asks, when I open the passenger door and slide into the car.

I don't even know how to answer that. "OK, I guess?"

"Your dad says he's doing well." She reaches behind her to toss the book onto the back seat. "He's been visiting him every week."

"Are *you* going to visit him?" I ask.

She shakes her head, not looking at me. "I'm not quite ready for that," she says.

I could leave it there, like she obviously wants. I could let this go the way it's gone for the last few months; the two of us not talking properly about things we need to be talking about.

I ask, "Why not?"

Mum pauses, her hand stilling from where she was pulling her seatbelt into place. She looks over at me, a question on her face. I try and make myself look as grown up and mature as possible, the daughter she can talk to about difficult things instead of avoiding or sugar-coating them.

"I can't forgive him," she says finally. "I know that's not right. I understand why your dad has, and why he wants to help him. But when I look at him, I see Beth dying alone in his bedroom."

I swallow. I'd hoped she'd trust me with the truth, but now it's come, my instinct is to turn away from it. I force myself not to look away. "I felt like that too."

"But not any more?"

I consider. "Talking to Jodie made me see things a bit differently. I just didn't realize how much I'd got wrong."

"I don't think it's so much about getting anything wrong," Mum says, "as living through a period of intense emotion and grief. For me, it's hard to feel that most things matter after losing Beth. Honestly, even getting out of bed has felt like a pointless task a lot of the time. So I see all these things happening around me, and I... It's hard to care, that's the truth. Isn't that terrible? I shouldn't admit that to you. It's shameful."

"About me as well?" I ask. I'm scared to ask, but I have to ask.

"What do you mean— Oh, God, Emmy, no. Not you. Of course I care about you, always. You're *all* I care about. If it weren't for you, I'd..." She stops herself. "You're the shining light of my life, my darling." I can tell she's struggling not to cry. "Can I take you home now?"

85 DAYS GONE

Progress

Here's where my thoughts go now: how do people pull themselves out?

After talking to Jodie and Leo, and hearing their versions of Beth, I've felt her beginning to become clearer to me in a way I hadn't expected. Less my-sister-Beth, less popstar-Lizzie, and more of the whole person she was. Take all of the noise away, and she was depressed. That's it, isn't it? One word I barely associate with her, even though it underlined everything, because all the other words were always so loud.

People face depression all the time. People get suicidal, and they live. How do they pull themselves out?

Because they do. Every day, people do. There are tunnels of darkness everywhere, and some people get lost, and some make it out. What's the difference between them? Why do some survive, and others don't?

I know these are questions no one can answer. I know there *is* no answer. But I want to know anyway – I *need* to know – because how can I carry on in this world *not* knowing? How can I love people in the way you're meant to – easily, fully, with complete trust – if I will always be wondering whether I'll lose them this way? If I understood it, maybe I can stop it happening to someone else one day. I know it's too late for Beth. But what about everyone else?

There are so many things that could have happened that night that would have stopped what happened happening. Tiny things, even. If someone had phoned Beth, just by chance. If Leo had decided to try to smooth things over earlier. If I'd messaged her asking her something – anything – to pull her attention away. If she'd changed her mind. If the kitchen had caught fire and the alarm went and she and Leo had to evacuate. If a pipe had burst outside and the street flooded. If it had started snowing, right in the middle of June. If Yellowstone had erupted. If an asteroid had hit the ocean.

I don't know which scenario is harder to deal with: that Beth was always going to die that night, or that she wasn't. The thought that I could have done something, or that I couldn't.

Maybe what I really need is to accept that I'll never know, and find some way for that to be OK. And maybe the way to do that is to loosen my grip a little – just a little – on the Beth I'm holding onto, and put more of my emotional energy into the people who are still here. The ones who can not only hear my questions, but give me answers too. And smiles. And hugs.

I know what I need to do.

NOT THE SPAGHETTI, FERNANDO!

Emmy: Hey

Grey: Hey

Trix: Hey ☺

Ella: Emmy!

Emmy: You guys free today?

Trix: Of course!

Grey: Maybe

Emmy: What does that mean?

Grey: To clarify, is this to see you?

Emmy: Yes

Grey: Then yes, we are free.

Ella: We're meeting at the rec
with Bonsai later. Come
meet us! 2pm!

Emmy: Is that OK?

Trix: OF COURSE!

Grey: We're not going to beg

Ella: Grey ffs

Trix: Come join, we'll wait.

Emmy: I'm a bit scared now

Trix: Grey is all bark, no bite.

Emmy: Is she, though?

Grey: Ruff

Ella: I'm bringing doughnuts

Emmy: I'll be there

Trix: ☺

Grey: xx

When I get to the rec, my friends are already there, sitting in a triangle, mid-conversation. As I approach them, the gaping chasm I've been cultivating between us over the last three months suddenly becomes very, very clear to me. Maybe I'd always known it was what I was doing, but I just didn't have enough emotional energy spare to care about it, let alone think about what the consequences might be.

Consequences like, how the dynamics might change in my absence. My beloved Grey, who I have all but disregarded, growing inevitably closer to Ella and Trix. The three of them solidifying into a trio, bonding over their shared worry for me, through endless conversations about how they might reach me.

Our quadratic friendship has always been in perfect balance. Grey and me, Trix and Ella. Our own mini, mostly-unspoken twosomes within the comfort of our foursome. What if there's no room for me any more? What if I've made a wall between us that none of us can break?

I don't want to lose them. I don't want to scorch the earth of my entire life just because Beth is gone.

"Hey!" Grey's voice as she spots me first. She's shading her eyes from the sun, a smile on her face.

"Hi!" I try to say, but the word catches in my throat. Out of nowhere, I feel an overwhelming urge to run to her.

I manage to resist it, partly because Grey would be horrified if I did something that performatively emotional, but mostly because Bonsai, Ella's family Mastiff, is already bounding over from where he'd been sitting beside her to greet me. I fuss him, pressing a kiss into his fur, grateful for the second to gather myself.

When I look up, Grey opens her legs and arms, gesturing to the space between, then pats her chest with her right hand, and I swear I almost start crying. I sink down to my knees and scooch in, her arms sliding around my shoulders in a light hug. I slouch into the warmth of her, comforting and familiar. She smells like Grey; jasmine and mint.

She hugs me again from behind. Into my ear she says, "Missed you, Beckwith."

I do start crying then. I'm remembering how it felt when I met Grey, Ella and Trix when I'd first joined Shona Lee; like I'd found not just friends but, somehow, *myself*.

I hear rather than see Ella coming to sit by my side, touching my shoulder, saying my name in her gentle voice. Trix leans forward and takes both my hands while Grey hugs me, squeezing tight. We're all quiet for a minute while I cry and they hold me steady. The silence is broken by Grey, who half-laughs and says, "Holy shit, Emmy, we've wanted to do this since *June*."

The words aren't funny, but I find myself laughing, and then she's laughing properly, and so are Trix and Ella, and we're all laughing together for the first time in what feels like a really, really long time.

"Hey," Grey says, and I turn to look at her, moving out of the hug to sit back against the grass so I can see her properly. "I'm sorry about what I said about Beth."

"Well, I'm sorry I literally clawed at your face."

"OK, but you had a reason to react like that, and I was just…" She makes a face. "I shouldn't have said that stuff. It was horrible. I'm sorry."

Here's a thing. I'm not sure, not in almost five years of friendship, I've ever heard Grey apologize for anything, and I find myself unsure what to do with myself. I reach for Bonsai, rubbing his head.

"Reminding someone of the bad things they said about someone who's died is a shitty thing to do," Grey adds. "Really low."

I nod, wrapping my arms around my knees. "Well, yeah. It is."

"I felt like I was losing you," she says. "And it scared me. And Beth…" She trails off.

I take a breath. "Beth had issues, yeah. But I'm not Beth. And I can change my hair if I want to."

"I still think it looks great," Ella says.

I smile. "Thanks, Ell."

"I can get used to it," Grey says, which makes me laugh. "And, like I said, I'm sorry I said those things about Beth. Really."

"OK, two apologies in two minutes?" I say. "You're scaring *me* now."

She laughs. "That's your lot."

"Well, seeing as we're being all honest and open," I say. "I've got some stuff too." Grey's eyebrows go up, but she's smiling. Ella and Trix nod encouragingly. "Some things I should have talked about with you all earlier. Like, how I…" I take a deep breath. "Me and Anderson…"

"We already know about that," Trix says.

"It wasn't just, like, a kiss," I say. "We…"

They're all staring at me.

"Oh, Emmy," Grey says.

"Yeah."

"Shit," she says. "I mean, we did think, like, *maybe*? But yeah…" She glances at Trix. "You should probably know, though, that people kind of already know. Or, like, guessed."

I sit bolt upright. "What? Who? What do you mean, people?"

"Em," Trix says, almost smiling. "You literally did it at his house during his summer party. Basically everyone was there. If you wanted it to be a secret, you should've maybe not done it during a Shona Lee party?"

Grey nods. "Sorry, Emmy, but everyone knows."

"Everyone," Ella agrees, shrugging.

"Everyone?"

"Everyone," they say together.

I put my hands over my face, groaning, then look up. "Scottie?"

Grey makes a face. "Well, yeah. Sorry."

"Was he upset about it?" I ask. I can't understand why he hasn't messaged me.

She makes another face, like a wince.

"Oh, no," I say.

"I mean, yeah," Grey says, shrugging. "You guys were friends for years, then he was your boyfriend, then you dumped him and basically got right into bed with Anderson Jay. Obviously, he was upset about it. I'm pretty sure he's been dreaming about sex with you since he was old enough to wank."

"Grey," Trix says, rolling her eyes.

"Where's the lie, though?" Grey says.

"But why hasn't he said anything to me?" I ask, deciding to avoid that angle of conversation. "He hasn't messaged me once."

"What's there to say? Scottie's a decent guy, you know that. He knows you have the right to make whatever choices you want, now you're broken up. Plus, you've still got the whole grief trump card going on. You've got a licence to do some shitty things for a bit."

"That makes me sound horrible."

Grey shrugs. "It does a bit. And you have been. A bit. But, like we said, we get it. And we're here for you, mistakes or no mistakes. We can handle Scottie, don't worry."

"You had to *handle* him?"

"He may have said some guy stuff about punching Anderson."

"What?"

"It's fine. We talked him down."

"I can't believe all this went on and I just didn't know. Why hasn't anyone said anything?"

"Because it doesn't have to be a big deal, if you don't want it to be," Grey says. "Yeah, maybe people talked about it a bit, but just, like, *hey, did you know Anderson and Emmeline got together?* No offense, but people don't really care. Not for longer than five minutes, anyway. You were hardly the only two people who hooked up that night. Even Trix got fingered in the bathroom."

"Grey!" Trix explodes, her entire face flaming an instant, incandescent pink.

Grey grins wickedly at her. "Sorry not sorry."

Ella is laughing, her knuckles pressed against her mouth like she's trying to stop herself. "Grey, for God's sake."

"Oh my God, it's *Emmy*," Grey says. "Obviously I'm going to tell *Emmy*."

"*Word choice!*" Trix says in protest, her face still ablaze. "I object to your *word choice*."

"What the fuck other word would you use?" Grey demands.

I was right about one thing. They really have been bonding without me. How could I have missed all this?

"By who?" I ask Trix. "Renee?"

"Renee is old news," Ella says, answering for her. "This was Liv."

"Fucking *what*?!" I shriek. Trix puts her hand over her face. "Liv as in Olivia? As in Olivia fucking Valero?"

"It's not that much of a shock," Grey says, even though it clearly is. "You know Liv is bi."

"Yeah, but still." I shake my head at Trix, who still looks mortified, but also a little bit pleased with herself too. "I didn't know you liked Olivia."

She raises her eyebrows at me. "I didn't know you liked Anderson."

"OK, fair. God, if *that* happened, no wonder you don't care about me and Anderson."

"We do care," Grey says. "But we're not losing our minds over it, if that's what you thought. We can handle it, Em. If you want to let off a little steam with a fuckboy, we're not going to judge." She wrinkles her nose. "Unless you start thinking you want to trust him, or, like, actually go out with him. Then we will judge you very hard."

"And stop you," Ella adds.

"Yeah…" I say, slowly. "About that…"

Their faces drop.

"Oh, no," Grey says. "Don't tell us you're his girlfriend now."

"God, no," I say. "But … yeah. The whole trust thing…" I trail off. I don't even know how to tell this story, and I'm already questioning again whether I even should. But honesty is important, isn't it?

"What happened?" Ella asks.

I bite my lip. Swallow. Breathe in a sigh and let it out. "Did you see all the stuff in the papers and online this week? About Jodie Soto-Hahn being, like, a bully?"

"God, yeah, that was awful," Trix says. "I was going to call you, but I thought you wouldn't want to talk to me still."

But Grey's eyes have narrowed as she watches me, sensing what's coming. "Yeah...?"

Grey grew up on bad press. Headlines like the ones Jodie's been getting this week peppered her childhood. They're the reason her mother has been clinically depressed since before Grey was even born. She's from a household where the good times and the bad times were dictated by headlines. She's had cousins, aunts, old family friends sell stories on her parents, even on her. She is who she is because she was dealing with this kind of bullshit before she could read.

I might lose Grey over this. It might be something she can't forgive.

"That was my fault," I say.

"Your fault," she echoes evenly.

"Yeah."

"What do you mean?" Trix asks.

"Well," I say. "The source that they were quoting? You know, the 'source close to Lizzie Beck'?"

Quietly, understanding, Grey says, "The source was you."

I say, "Yeah."

I explain what happened as best I can, as honestly as I can, as quickly as I can. How I felt like I could talk to Anderson, how he seemed so nice, listening to me talk about Beth. How I'd been wrong about Jodie, and Beth having to leave The Jinks, but I didn't realize. When I'm finished, both Ella and Trix look a little confused, but there's a familiar slightly irritated crease in Grey's forehead. My heart sinks.

"So ... you *weren't* the source," Grey says.

"The source they talk about in the articles is me," I say.

"OK, but *you* weren't the source," she says. "*Anderson* is. God, Em, when you started talking, I thought you were going to say you'd called a journalist or something. Yeah, OK, obviously you shouldn't have trusted a twat like Anderson, and yeah, you should have talked to us, because we're your friends and you can trust us and we'd never sell you out like that, not ever, so you're a fucking idiot about that bit, yeah, but don't take the blame for this. It's all him."

"But—"

"Also, just to state the obvious, but how the fuck did it get to, like, September, and you still thought completely the wrong thing about Beth leaving the band?" Grey says. "I'm sorry, but that's on your parents. Why weren't they talking to you about it? That seems like a pretty big deal?"

Ella nods. "I was going to ask about that too."

"I don't think they even knew I thought that," I say.

"Yeah, well, they should have done," Grey says. "If you knew the truth to begin with, maybe you wouldn't have felt so angry about the relaunch stuff when it happened. Maybe you'd have been happy about it."

I hadn't even thought about that. There's something weirdly painful about thinking of an alternative timeline where I could have been on their side, rooting for them, happy the band is continuing. I could have messaged Jodie to say congratulations. I could have meant it.

"Something's got really fucked up somewhere," Grey says. "And, like, no shade on your parents, I'm sure it must be awful for them right now, but still. They should have talked to you. Sorry, Em, but they should."

"Maybe," I say. I don't say anything else for a while, taking it all in, and they let me. The four of us sit in comfortable silence, Bonsai rolling on his back in the grass beside us. Finally, I say, "Grey?"

"Yeah?"

"Did you really think Beth was awful?"

"Sometimes," Grey says, and the word brings on such an unexpected rush of love for her that I almost laugh. Only Grey would answer so honestly, after everything. Only Grey would trust that I was trusting her enough for the truth. "But we're all awful sometimes, right?" She smiles cautiously at me, and I let myself smile back. "The first time I ever stayed round your house, she was there, do you remember? She came home to surprise you because you'd told her that I was coming over, and she wanted to meet me. The famous Grey, she said. Em, I was born famous. But she just meant ... because of you. Because I was important to you, and that was important to her. She brought Crosstown doughnuts for us, remember? You were so excited when she came through the door. And she was, too, when she saw how excited *you* were. It made her so happy. I remember that."

I am crying, of course. Crying for the memory – which I hadn't remembered until Grey had brought it to life for me in this moment – crying for Beth, crying because this is all I've wanted to hear this whole time. My sister, remembered well.

And then Ella says, the slightest hint of a grump in her voice, "We were there too, Grey."

And Grey says, "Oh my God, this is a moment, Ell, let us have it."

And Trix says, "Are you sure it was doughnuts? I remember pastries. Like, patisserie ones. I remember because I said something about them being as good as the ones I'd had in Paris? And Beth went, *ooh la la!* And I couldn't tell if she was teasing me. Was that a different time? Am I remembering wrong? Why are you laughing, Emmy?"

I'm laughing because I've finally realized the one thing that hasn't changed. My life has – in so many irretrievable ways – and I have, and my family has. But my friends are the same. My friends are my friends, and they are still here, and I can hold onto this – to them – when everything else feels like it might be crumbling away.

Not everything goes. Some things stay.

86 DAYS GONE

Everything I ever wanted

I think I might actually be feeling a little bit better.

About The Jinks, about Jodie, about being the source, about Leo, about my friends. Maybe even … no, not about Beth being dead. That will never be better.

But still. Baby steps.

It's Thursday morning, and I'm thinking that I might ask Grey if she wants to meet up again, just the two of us, to do something normal. Spend the kind of day we would have spent in the before times, where it didn't matter so much what we were doing, just that we were together. The thought of it doesn't make me sink, like it has done all summer. It makes me lift.

"Morning, love."

The voice makes me jump when I walk into the kitchen – most of my attention on my phone – because it's Dad's voice. Dad, in the kitchen, at 10.23 a.m. on a weekday.

"What are you doing here?" I ask, looking between him and the clock. "Why aren't you at work?"

"You, actually," he says, smiling.

"Me?"

"What do you say to brunch?"

"Brunch?" I repeat, baffled. "You and me?"

"You and me and Jodie," he says.

Instantly, my positive mood disappears. Oh shit, this is it, isn't it? This is the overdue bollocking I've somehow managed to avoid since I leaked the secrets that may have brought down The Jinks and ruined Jodie's career.

I must look terrified because Dad laughs and says, "It's nothing bad, I promise."

It's nothing bad still means *it's something*. And something could be anything.

"OK," I say, cautiously.

"Great," he says. "The table's booked for eleven thirty. Go and get dressed."

* * *

Brunch is at a fancy hotel near the Skyscape Management offices. When we get there, Jodie is already sitting at the table, staring into space. Her make-up, clothes and posture are flawless in the kind of way that makes her seem distant; not quite real. But when she sees me walking over, she smiles, and it softens her.

"Hey, you," she says, standing to hug me. Not a Beth hug; a Jodie hug. Light and airy, not tight and warm. To my Dad, she says, "Hi, Mal."

I don't want to think about how obvious it is that it should be Beth here in this trio instead of me, Emmy, the little sister. I don't want to be aware of the wrongness. I want to just enjoy being allowed to be here, ordering brunch in a fancy restaurant with Jodie Soto-Hahn. But I'm thinking of Beth's distraught, drunken voice saying, "Hey, Jo-Jo. Hey, Jo-Jo-So," and it's making me want to cry.

"Hey," Jodie says. She reaches out and takes my hand. "You OK?"

I nod without speaking. She smiles at me, squeezes, then lets go.

Dad waits until we've ordered, received our food and finished most of it, before he claps his hands to his thighs and says, "So."

And even though I haven't really known for sure that anything is coming, I find myself relieved that the moment has come.

"So?" I repeat.

"Emmy," he says to me, smiling. "We have a proposition for you."

I think, *We?* I say, "A proposition?"

Dad looks at Jodie, that same smile on his face, like he's offering her the chance to speak first. She just looks back at him, so after a moment he turns to me. "Emmy," he says again. "How would you feel about joining The Jinks?"

All the air goes out of my lungs. Goes out of the *room*.

"Wh—*what?*"

"How would you feel," Dad repeats, dutifully, "about joining The Jinks?"

"Are you … are you *serious*?"

Dad chuckles. "I'm very serious, yes."

I look at Jodie again. She has a small half-smile on her face, but she's not looking directly at me, more at the space beside me.

"But that's crazy," I say.

"Is it?" Dad says. "Why is it crazy? You're certainly talented enough. You can sing, you can dance, you can perform. You're at home on stage. You know The Jinks inside out."

Dad has never said this many nice things about me in a row before, not ever. It's not so much that he didn't notice me, or even that he didn't think I was any good, it's more that I was the moon and Beth was the sun. That's just how it was. *Was.*

"Isn't this what you've been planning for?" Dad asks me. "To be a Beck? I thought you'd be excited."

"I … I am." *Overwhelmed* is a better word. There's excitement there, sure, but it's the kind of excited you feel when there's a bungee cord around your legs and someone's about to push you off an extremely high ledge. "It's a lot, though."

He laughs, lifting his coffee cup and taking a sip. "I'm sure it is."

"Wouldn't it matter that I'm much younger than you?" I ask Jodie.

She opens her mouth, but Dad is already answering. "No reason why it should," he says. "There's no rule that says band members should be the same age, and in this case, it makes so much sense, so there's extra leeway."

"You're the same age we were when we got famous," Jodie says, as if this will be news to me, as if I haven't thought about that at least once every single day since I turned sixteen. "And you'll have us to help you deal with it all. Aiya, Tam and me. We'll be like your—" She stops herself, and I know she was about to say "older sisters". There's a long pause, before she says, "We'll look after you."

I try to ask her with my eyes, *Are you still going to get new management?* Surely not, if I'm joining the band. Surely me and Dad are a package deal, just like it was when Beth was in the band. I look at Dad, wondering if he knows what they've been planning, if this is part of why he's offering me this chance. To save his job. The thought makes me feel hollow. I don't want to be that cynical; I don't want *him* to be that cynical.

"But … what about all that stuff you said?" I ask. "About the industry being … you know… Cruel?"

Dad's forehead has wrinkled with confusion. He puts his hand to his chin, scratches at his skin with his thumb. "When did I say that?"

"After Ricardo Patmore said that it was no loss that Beth died," I say. He can't actually have forgotten this, surely. It must be imprinted on his mind, like it is on mine. I glance at Jodie, whose expression is unreadable. I look back at Dad. "You said that it was an awful industry. So … like…" I pause long enough for him to pick up the conversation, because surely he won't make me say it. But he just waits, so I finish. "Why would you want me to be in it too? What if I … end up like…"

"You won't," Jodie says, before Dad can speak. Her voice is very, very firm. "Not a chance, Emmy. We wouldn't let that happen. And you are nothing like Beth."

The words stab. *Nothing like Beth.* My effervescent sister, who lit up the room. Lit up entire stadiums.

"Thank you, Jodie," Dad says. "That's exactly right, on both counts. It won't be like it was before. I've learned so many lessons … we all have. This is my chance to—" He cuts himself off. "We'll do it right this time. By you. With you."

This is his chance to what? Do it right? Am I just the do-over in this scenario? A beta test in the form of the second daughter? A way for him to make amends for everything that went wrong, and everything we lost?

I want to ask him, I really do, but Jodie is sitting right there, and this is a professional meeting, isn't it? Not a family one. Dad is not my dad right now. He's Malcolm Beckwith, manager of The Jinks, one of the UK's most successful girl bands, offering me the professional opportunity of a lifetime.

I consciously sit up straighter, trying to make my posture as perfect as Jodie's. She hasn't slouched, not even once. And these chairs are *really* uncomfortable.

"So how would it work?" I ask.

"Well," Dad says, smiling like he's been ready for this part of the conversation the whole time we've been sitting here. "First, we'd announce you as the special guest of the memorial. Like we discussed earlier; you remember." What I remember is that we didn't actually discuss it, but whatever, I let him carry on. "You'd sing Beth's parts of the songs; it will be seamless — a lovely tribute. And fitting too. People will understand it. And then, when the response is positive — which it will be — we'll announce that you're joining The Jinks on their tour, again as a special guest. And all of that will build to eventually confirming you as a full member, after you turn seventeen."

He really does have a plan. Hearing him talk like this makes it start to seem almost real, or at least like something that could be real. And I can see it, in my head. Me, standing on stage with The Jinks, as *part* of The Jinks. And why couldn't I? I've dreamed about it enough times.

But he doesn't know, does he? He doesn't know I haven't sung a note in months, that I haven't even played my guitar. Why would he? He's never home.

I open my mouth to tell him, but the words falter on their way out. He doesn't notice, just carries on talking. He's talking about rehearsals, and when I realize, my heart jolts with a surprising, visceral anxiety. We're onto rehearsals already? I haven't even said yes.

But of course I'm going to say yes.

I look at Jodie, who's turned slightly away from us both, concentrating on her fingernails. I try to imagine actually standing beside her on stage, being her equal. Standing where Beth stood.

"Emmy," Dad says, his hand landing gently on my shoulder, and I jump like he's grabbed hold of me. "I'm sorry," he says, surprising me further. "I'm rushing ahead; you're overwhelmed."

There are tears in my eyes, and he's noticed before I have. He really is paying attention for once. *And* he apologized to me.

It's like a whole new Dad. Or not a whole new one, exactly, but one I'd seen but not experienced myself. This is Beth's version of Dad, and now he's mine.

Maybe.

If I say yes.

"OK," I say, slowly, trying to imagine it. Even in my head, it's just a blur. "Would I still go to Shona Lee?"

Surprise flickers over his face, like this hadn't even occurred to him. "Why would you need to? This would be your future."

The idea of this probably shouldn't unsettle me as much as it does; students leave Shona Lee post-sixteen all the time when opportunities like this come up. But I'd always seen myself leaving Shona Lee at eighteen, fully educated, fully prepared, ready for the world. Cutting that short seems … well, a bit weird. But he's right, isn't he? Why would I need Shona Lee when I could have The Jinks? Be *part of* The Jinks?

Dad has started talking again. "We'll do an interview with one of the friendly morning shows – probably with Mellie Wright again," he's saying. For the first time, I realize he's using his work voice, one he's never directed at me before. "The band and you together, to announce you joining the memorial concert and to talk about the allegations against the girls. All of the questions and answers will be planned in advance, and you'll be fully prepped, so you won't need to worry."

"So, we'd be saying they're not true?"

"Of course," Dad says. "Because that *is* the truth. It will be very powerful for people to hear you talk about Beth. Though, you'll have to call her Lizzie, of course." He smiles at me. "You might need to practise that a little bit, to make sure it feels natural."

I nod, slowly, mostly to cover the instinctive uneasiness I feel at the thought of calling Beth *Lizzie*. It's not just that I'm used to always calling her Beth, it's that *Beth* only ever wanted me to call her Beth. It was such a clear line to her.

But then, she's dead now, so I guess it doesn't matter?

(It feels like it does matter, though. Quite a lot.)

"You don't have to say yes right now," Jodie says, and I see the way Dad's eyes slide towards her, like he *had* expected me to say yes right now. "And, obviously, you don't *have* to say yes, if you don't want to join this shitshow."

"Jodie," Dad says, in the way he used to say, *Beth.*

Jodie breathes in a sigh, smiling another sardonic smile. "A shitshow with perks," she amends. She inclines her head just a little to look me in the eye. "Think about it," she says.

* * *

So here it is. Offered to me on a plate.

Everything I ever wanted.

I used to dream — God, how I used to dream — about being in The Jinks. About living Beth's incredible, sparkling, exciting life. I'd have long, elaborate, entirely secret daydreams of Beth having to take a break from the band (for a non-life-threatening, unpainful, no-consequences reason that I never wasted precious daydreaming time thinking about in any detail) where I would take her place, just for a while, and blow everyone away. I'd step in at the last minute to go on tour, and everyone would say, "Wow, Emmy! You're incredible!"

And they'd all be so proud of me. Especially Beth.

If you'd asked me, that's what I would have said. *What do you want most in the world, Emmeline?* To be Beth. To have Beth's life.

And now I've got it, but to get it I've lost the one thing that made me want it in the first place. What kind of a head- and heart-fuck is that? It's a fucking Greek tragedy.

I want to scream into the void, *OK, I get it, I get the message! You can undo it, now!* I'll wake up and none of this will have happened, Beth will be alive — alive and still in The Jinks — and I'll be patient and grateful and happy to be me in the life I always took for granted.

Why are the most important lessons learned too late? It's not like I hadn't heard them my whole life. *Be careful what you wish for! Be grateful for what you have!* I thought I understood them. It's only now I really do that I realize I didn't.

❊   ❊   ❊

Dad's in a good mood on the drive home. He's talking about the set list they're putting together for the memorial show, the potential special guests they're talking to, whether I'd like to take a solo or stick with the band. I could play it cool, but I'm excited just listening to him. Maybe I shouldn't be, but I am, even though there's that shadow falling over it, the Beth-shaped shadow, like there is over everything. But I can keep the shadow out of view, if I tilt my subconscious a certain way. Pretend it's not there, at least for a little while. Can't I enjoy this? Dad asking me my opinion, smiling when I make a joke, listening when I reply to something he's said? It feels so nice.

I haven't actually said yes yet. I probably could, but every time the thought rises in my head, it doesn't quite make it out of my mouth. Something stops me, each time, though I'm not sure exactly what it is.

"There's no rush," Dad says to me when we pull into our driveway. "You take your time, Em. And you can ask me any questions, any time, OK?"

We head inside together, to find Mum already walking down the stairs towards us, most likely summoned by the sound of the garage door opening and closing. She pauses, looks at us both with an expression I can't read. Her eyes move from Dad's face to mine.

"Where have you two been?" she asks.

I don't know what's weirder; that she didn't know where we were, or that I didn't think to wonder if she knew we'd even left the house.

"Out to brunch," Dad says, too brightly.

"With Jodie," I add, mostly because I think it's a strange detail to leave out.

Mum looks at Dad. Dad looks at Mum.

I stand there between the two of them, still a few seconds from understanding.

They both speak at once.

Mum: "You better not have—"

Dad: "Ellen, listen—"

That's when I get it. The very obvious thing, the reason Dad wanted to take me for brunch with Jodie instead of having the potentially life-changing conversation with me in our own house, with my mother.

Mum doesn't know.

"Tell me you didn't," Mum says. For once, Dad doesn't say anything. "Malcolm. Tell me you aren't thinking of putting Emmy in The Jinks."

"Ellen."

Mum is about to explode, I can tell. Her whole face is red, and they haven't even got into it yet. I'm about to sneak into the kitchen when she turns her gaze on me. "Emmy," she says. Just that.

Both of my parents are staring at me like they're waiting for me to pick a side. But since when are there meant to be sides? They're my parents.

I glance at Dad, then back at Mum. "Yeah, that's what we were talking about with Jodie."

Dad closes his eyes briefly, breathes in a sigh. "OK, Em," he says. "You should probably leave us to it. I don't think you're going to want to hear this."

"Don't you *dare* try and be the good guy here." Mum descends the last few stairs in three angry, deliberate steps, and I use the opportunity to take Dad's advice and disappear. I scramble past her, up the stairs, and then park myself around the corner, out of view, so I can listen.

"How can you do this? How can you even suggest we go through all this again?"

"That's not what I'm saying; that's not what will happen."

"Beth is *dead!*" She screams this at him, these words that still hit like a shock, months on. "I won't make the same mistakes again. And I won't let you."

"We won't make the same mistakes," Dad says. He's pleading, really. I can hear it in his voice. "Ellen, it won't be the same. Of course it won't be. We've learned—"

"*What* have you learned? *Nothing.* I had two babies, Malcolm." There's so much pain in her voice it hurts just to listen. "Two babies. Only two. I have one left. You can't take Emmy. You can't have her."

"Jesus Christ, Ellen, will you listen to yourself? I'm not taking Emmy anywhere. But this is her life, and she deserves the chance to take an opportunity—"

"An *opportunity?* Like entering a talent show, Mal? Like sending in a video audition? That was just an opportunity, wasn't it?"

There's a long silence. When Dad finally replies, his voice is almost too low for me to hear. "I'm goddamn fucking sick of you trying to put this on me. What happened to Beth is not my fault. I lost my daughter too."

"But you've still got your band."

"They aren't my... Fucking *hell.* Listen to yourself. You sound unhinged."

"Emmy isn't Beth 2.0."

"I fucking know that—"

"You don't get a second chance with her. You don't get to risk her. It's not happening."

"It's not up to you... Look." I hear the strain in Dad's voice, like he's trying really hard. "Can you please just let Emmy think about it? This should be her decision, not yours. If she wanted this, would you really tell her no?"

"You're manipulating her. And me."

"I'm not. I'm offering her a chance at a life she's always wanted."

"How can you stand there and stay that? How? A life she's always wanted — *Mal.* Beth..."

"Emmy isn't Beth," he says. "She's never been like Beth. It won't be the same as it was. Can't you trust me?"

"No," she says.

There's a long silence. I strain to hear, wondering whether they've stopped talking, or just lowered the volume. After what feels like a long time, I hear the sound of the bedroom door opening and closing, then footsteps down the hall.

Then nothing.

Mum comes into my room to say good night, which is something she hasn't done for a long time, since way before Beth died.

She sits on my bed and doesn't say anything for a while, like she's trying to find the right words.

"I'm not going to tell you what to do," she says eventually. "And if you decide you want to be in The Jinks, then I will support you in that. Of course I will. I don't want you to think, if you were listening to me and your dad argue, that I wouldn't be on your side, whatever you choose. I just want you to really think about this, OK? Not for me, not for your dad, but for you."

I nod. There's so much I want to say, but nothing comes out. I want to ask her to really talk to me, actually talk to me, tell me how she feels about Beth, whether she thinks it was the band that killed her in the end, if she doesn't want me to join the band because the associations are painful, or because she thinks it's actually dangerous. If she regrets the choices she made when Beth was my age.

But she looks so sad, and I don't want to hurt her.

So I say, "Good night."

And she kisses my forehead, then leaves.

87 DAYS GONE

Choice

[Unknown number] [Add to contacts]

Unknown: Hey, Emmy! It's Aiya. Just wanted to say that I know you're still thinking about it, but the invitation is from all of us, not just Jodie. We'd be so excited to have you come join the band. No pressure though! Obvs it's a huge decision, but wanted to be sure you knew, we're all in this together. Maybe the four of us (!) should meet up to chat? Let me know! Lots of love xxx

[Unknown number] [Add to contacts]

Unknown: Hey, hope you don't mind me messaging you! Jodie gave me your number. It's Tam btw. I'm so sorry about Beth, and I'm sorry I haven't spoken to you directly before. She was a crazy hurricane, and I miss her every day. We had our differences, of course, but I loved her. We all did. I think it would be an amazing thing if you joined the band, and she'd be so proud. The Jinks needs a Beck. Hope you're good xx

Jodie
You want to talk?

> **Emmy**
> I don't know
>
> Maybe?

Did Aiya and Tam message you?

> Yeah

They're excited!

> Are they really?

Yeah!

Babe, it kind of sounds like you're not?

> I am!

You sure? Want to call me?

> I'm just a bit confused

Call me! I know I'm not Beth, but I'm pretty good with advice?

> OK ☺

Somehow, I end up talking on the phone with Jodie for an hour and a half. I never even used to talk for that long with Beth, who didn't like telephone calls and would often get distracted after twenty minutes if a conversation stayed on the same topic for too long.

We talk about the choice, the band, the press. I tell her about Anderson and the truth about being the source, and she actually laughs, tells me that I'll have to get used to that, "people being utter shits for money". She tells me not to feel bad, that it wasn't my fault, and it doesn't fix things in my head or my heart, but some of the guilt goes. She tells me about the meeting the band and management had had before our brunch, how Aiya and Tam had been excited right off the bat – I decide to go ahead and believe this – how the three of them had been talking about what it would be like non-stop. She suggests that, if I say yes, the four of us could go away for a week or so to just hang out, maybe sing a bit, see how it all feels.

She's warm and kind and excited. The whole conversation is like a fever dream of wishful thinking brought to life.

So why don't things feel clearer?

Throughout the whole conversation, the pendulum in my head swings from a yes to a no, lurching so abruptly that I'm left feeling vaguely nauseous. Sometimes the answer seems so obvious – *how could I say no to this?* – but then the confusion takes over, pulling me back down to reality. The reality being: Beth dead; this being her band; the fact that I'd accidentally caused the problem that my joining the band is designed to solve.

It's a headfuck.

Mum, who must have heard me on the phone, asks if I want to talk about it. I say no.

I make a batch of brownies. I think about how I still haven't told anyone that I haven't sung a note since June. I look at the calendar, count how many days are left before my first day back at Shona Lee. (Six.)

Dad comes home early from work. He's carrying a big, bright bouquet of flowers.

"Are those for me or Mum?" I ask.

"Both," he says. He seems happier than he's been for a long time. I'd almost call him relaxed. "Both of you."

He raises his voice a little when he says this, clearly wanting Mum to hear, but she doesn't come downstairs. He sighs.

"So," he says, turning to me with a smile. "Have you made a decision?"

"I..." Does he have to look so hopeful? So excited? "Not yet."

His smile flickers, but stays in place. "That's OK. That's OK, Emmy. It's a big decision. Did you hear from the girls today?"

"Yeah, all three of them."

"Good. Was it useful?"

I shrug. I know it's not helpful, the way I'm acting, but it's like I've forgotten how to talk.

"Why don't you tell me what your misgivings are?" he suggests. "Whatever it is that's stopping you saying yes. We can talk it through."

He looks at me expectantly, but I don't even know what to say, how to start. How can I articulate what my "misgivings" actually are when I can't even get them straight in my own head? There's just this vague feeling of wrongness, the kind you can try to look away from but can't quite ignore.

"Is it because of Beth?" he prompts, sitting down on one of the stools. I follow his lead, sitting opposite him.

"Everything is," I say. "But not just that."

He raises his eyebrows encouragingly, waiting.

"It's just ... is it only because of the bad press? You think putting me in will stop people saying that the bullying stuff is true, because I'm Beth's sister?" He begins to reply, but now I've started, I find I can't stop. "And will it actually solve the problems the band had? Or will it make more? And what if the fans don't like it? If they think

I'm just, like, I don't know … Lizzie-lite, or something. And what would Beth…" My voice gives out. "What would Beth think? Maybe she'd hate it. Me in her place. Me taking her place."

I stop to take a breath, trying to steady myself. Dad gets up, takes a glass from one of the cupboards, then pours me some water. He hands me the glass and I sip slowly, watching as he sits down again, taking his time before replying.

"It's what Beth would want," Dad says. "I really do believe that. For the band, and for you. I … listen, Emmy, I understand why you think this is a cynical idea. I really do. And maybe it is, in a way. But Beth…" He swallows. "Beth is gone. And she loved you, and she was so proud of you, and – truly – I believe she'd be thrilled to know you were joining The Jinks in her place. It would make her happy."

Maybe it would. It probably would. I think about the hours Beth spent with me when she was home, longer than she needed to, longer than even a good older sister owed the younger, singing with me, teaching me how to move, how to smile, how to charm a room. That was all preparation, wasn't it? For this. For following her, whether she'd be there to see it or not.

"And doesn't it make sense?" Dad continues. "You'll be so brilliant." Brilliant. It's what he used to call Beth. "Everything Beth taught you; wasn't it preparing you for this? I know it's not what any of us planned for, but it makes so much sense. Doesn't it?" He smiles at me. "You can be the next Beck. Little Beck."

Something happens in the room when he says these two words. A coldness, stirring more through me than around me. *Little Beck.*

The terrible blankness on Beth's face that day in London when the men with their cameras asked me if I was a whore like her.

The shock of the concrete against my knees when I stumbled over that bollard before she pulled me to my feet.

The shouting, the jostling, the laughter. *Hey, Little Beck!*

How Beth had cried when we were finally safe and away from them, alone in a taxi. How she'd apologized over and over, though

I told her she didn't need to. That was the reality, wasn't it? That was the truth of it, there in that taxi. All of the Lizzie gone and just Beth left, tearful and desolate, clutching my hand.

How can I believe that *Little Beck* is what she'd want for me? She didn't want me to *be* her, she wanted me to learn *from* her. She'd even said, *Promise?* And I'd said, *Promise*.

Maybe I can be a Beck one day. I hope so, perhaps more than anything. But I will be my own Beck, not a smaller version of who Beth became. And I'll never be Little Beck. Not ever.

Dad is wrong, he's so wrong. What Beth wanted was to help light the way for me on my own path, not trip over the tangled roots of hers.

She's going to be so amazing on her own, she had said in a voice note to Jodie, lost and distraught in her own life, but certain of that, certain of me. She believed in me — *me*, Emmy. Not as her miniature, not as Little Beck. Just me.

I close my eyes, even though Dad is looking at me, and I see Beth, right there, sitting beside me. She's wearing yoga pants and a black t-shirt, her hair loose, a bit tangled. She's not wearing any make-up. She's sitting with one knee bent up, her elbow resting on it, head slightly tilted as she watches me, a smirk on her face that is knowing and also, somehow, kind. I look at her, hard, in this moment I have invented, but in which she is also real. I see her shake her head, just gently. I see her mouth the word, *No*.

I would tear down the world to bring her back.

I open my eyes and look at my dad, who loved Beth, and also exploited her, and lifted her, and let her down.

I say, "No."

Does he take it well? No.

He tries to reason with me. Tells me I'm confused; mistaken. *You just need to think about it a little longer.*

He guilt-trips me. *What about Jodie and the band? What will happen to them, after what you did?*

He shouts at me. Tells me I'm selfish; immature. Ungrateful. *I thought you were better than this.*

He says, *Don't you want to be special?*

Which is when Mum comes storming into the room — and I mean storming; it's like a hurricane bursts right through the door — and tells him three things:

1) That I *am* special. Special and brave and wise. (Which is really nice.)

2) That he needs to listen to me, and to her, when we tell him what we want and/or need. ("For once.")

3) That she is leaving him, and taking me with her. ("If that is what Emmy wants too.") (It is.)

Dad just sits there staring at both of us, like he's been parachuted into a life he doesn't recognize or understand. Maybe I should feel emboldened and triumphant, but I don't. I feel sad for him. Really. Like if I look at him any longer, I'll start crying.

Mum says they can talk it over properly later. And then the two of us go to Wagamama.

87 DAYS GONE

Mum

"I'm so proud of you," she says.

It's the first thing she says after a car ride spent in silence. Now, we're sitting in the Wagamama car park, and neither of us has moved to get out. "So proud, Emmy. And so *relieved*, my gosh. I'm so relieved."

I look at her. "You think it's the right decision, then?"

"Yes. Absolutely the right decision. And so mature of you."

"But Dad—"

"Don't worry about your dad. He will be fine. We'll all be fine." She reaches out and takes my hand, squeezing it. "*You* are more important than anything. Any band, or any contract, or any press. Your dad feels that way too, even if he was a bit upset today."

I snort. "A *bit* upset?"

"Forgive him," she says. "He's channelled his grief into that band. Rightly or wrongly, that's how he's dealt with this. Now it's looking like that isn't the solution, and that will be hard for him to deal with."

I hadn't thought about it that way. "Is that what he's done? I thought he just, like ... really cared about the band."

"People deal with grief in all kinds of different ways."

"How have you dealt with yours?"

She bites her lip, looking away. "Oh, I don't know. Not well."

There's a silence. I wait, hoping, but she doesn't say anything else. I can feel the frustration building in me, slow and steady, until it bursts out of me in one sudden, "Can't you ask me?"

She looks at me in surprise. "Ask you what?"

"How *I'm* dealing with it? You haven't asked! Not once. Can't you just *ask me*?"

She stares at me, mute, her mouth slightly open, eyes glistening.

"*Please,*" I say, my voice thick. There are tears coming, I can feel them. "Please just talk to me."

"Emmy."

"Please. Why won't you talk to me?"

"Because I want to protect you," she says. "And I've already failed in that. I want to protect you from pain. I don't want you to have to know, not this early in your life, this kind of grief that I'm feeling. I—"

"But I'm feeling it too! It's not like yours is different from mine just because you're Mum and I'm the sister. We both lost Beth. And we're basically two of the only people who really know what that means. You can't just shut me out of that because it makes it harder for you. That's not fair."

She's crying, I'm crying. It's a whole, awful cryfest. "I know that, Emmy. None of this is fair. I'm sorry." She shudders in a breath. "I've been trying for so long to understand what happened. What I could have done. How she could have... Why I wasn't enough of a mother to just ... keep her here."

"But it wasn't your fault." Which is so obvious, the words sound awkward and clichéd coming out of my mouth. "You know that, right?"

"Knowing that it isn't my fault isn't the same as not feeling responsible," she says. "I brought her into this world. I was supposed to protect her from it. And I feel like... Oh, Emmy, I wish I hadn't let her enter that show. None of this would have happened if it weren't for that show. I should have said no. I should have stopped her."

"But you don't know."

She looks at me, wiping her eyes. "Know what?"

"How that would have turned out."

She's quiet for a moment, a small frown denting her forehead. "No. You're right. I can't know. Maybe something else would have made her unhappy. Maybe there would always have been drugs and bad boyfriends. Maybe I'd be sitting here saying to you, I wish I'd let her enter that show; maybe that would have been the making of her." She shrugs tearfully. "You can't ever know if the choices you're making are the right ones, not even in hindsight, not really."

"So what do you do then?"

"Make the best choice you can in the moment. Try not to be too hard on yourself if the outcome is a bad one." She tries to smile. "Sounds easy, doesn't it?" She wipes at her eyes again, calmer. "You're right; I should have talked to you earlier. I forgot how wise you are."

I smile. "Yeah?"

"Yes, my little wise one." She squeezes my hand. "I love you."

"I love you too. If I'm the wise one, what was Beth?"

She laughs, a genuine laugh. "You know the answer to that."

"The wild one?"

"Yes. My wild one." She closes her eyes for a moment, resting her head back against the seat. "My darling girl."

"I miss her."

"I know you do, darling. I miss her too."

"What do you miss?" I ask.

She half-laughs a tearful laugh. "Do you want a list?"

"Yes."

"OK. Well, I miss her face. That's the first thing. Her beautiful, lively face. She was so expressive, wasn't she? Especially when she was angry. I'd like to see her face again. If I could have one thing, that would be it. Her alive face." Her voice breaks, but she doesn't stop. "And I miss her voice. Her singing, of course, but also just her voice, talking normally. And her hands. I'd like to hold her hand again. Her hair. Oh, Emmy, when she was tiny it was so soft, her hair, just like yours was. I used to smell it when she hugged me. Her hugs, I miss those. She was a good hugger, wasn't she? She hugged like she meant it. Not everyone does that. Her eyes. Her wonderful, bright eyes."

I'm crying, but I manage to say, "Don't they count under face?"

"No," she says. "Related, but two different things to miss. Is this helping? Talking?"

I nod. "A lot."

"Do you have anything you want to ask me?"

I think about it, not wanting to waste this opportunity, because what if it doesn't come again? "What do you think the inquest is going to say?"

"The inquest? In what way?"

"You know. Why she died."

Mum is silent for a while, like she's trying to decide how much to tell me. *All of it,* I think at her. *Be honest.*

"I expect they'll conclude what we already know, really," she says, finally. "That Beth was very unhappy, and had been unhappy for a long time. That she never really got the help she needed, but that isn't the fault of any one person. That her job exacerbated her unhappiness in so many ways; the press attention, the abuse on social media. That the likelihood that she was going to have to leave the band made her..." She swallows. "Made her feel like she'd reached the end." I watch Mum's face carefully, see how her eyes fall closed, how she shakes her head slightly, slowly. "Emmy, suicide ... it's so complex, and to be honest I don't really know how to talk about it with you. I don't want you to think that Beth dying the way she did was inevitable, because I don't believe it was. But I also don't want you thinking that there was something you or I could have done to 'save' her, because I don't think we could have, really. Any more than if she'd had cancer, or been in a car accident. Sometimes people survive those things, and sometimes they don't."

"But you do think that having to leave the band was the last thing," I say. "Right?"

Mum grimaces again, like she's in pain. "I think *she* thought it was," she says, so carefully. "I think she reached a point where she couldn't see a way out. Emmy, this is so painful." Her voice breaks. "As her mother, to know she was ... that she felt... But I know I have to be honest about it. With myself, and you. The pain she was in; I don't want to turn away from that. I don't think her leaving the band was the end of her life, no. I think it would have been difficult for a while, but that she would have got through it, and found a new direction for her life, the way people do, every day. I believe she would have found happiness again if she'd ... if she'd waited longer. And I don't blame Jodie, Aiya and Tam for the choices they made, either then or since. It wasn't their fault. I expect the inquest will say something similar." She sighs, wiping briskly at her eyes again. "And, on a more practical level, you should know that they'll also say that she had drugs and alcohol in her system at the time of her death, and that that would have affected her decision-making."

"I knew that."

"Did you?" She looks surprised for some reason.

"Yeah, of course. I have, like, been around, you know? And, even if I hadn't been, Leo told me they were both high the night she died." Mum winces, like the words are painful, and I soften my voice. "Sorry."

"No," she says. "It's the truth. You don't have to be sorry. I do wish there was some way to protect you from it, though."

"You remember I'm sixteen, right? Not ten?"

She smiles. "Yes, Emmy. You're still my baby, though. Now, do you want to go in?" She points to Wagamama. "Or have we got too emotional to be seen in public?"

"Let's go in anyway," I say. "Be bold. Proud of our emotions, or whatever."

"Channel our inner Beths?"

"Yeah! Exactly."

She squeezes my hand. "Fantastic idea."

I squeeze back. "Mum?"

She pauses, from where she'd already been reaching to unbuckle her seatbelt. "Yes, my love?"

"Where do you think it all went? Everything that made Beth Beth? The stuff you just said?" She opens her mouth to answer, but I find I can't stop. "Like how bright her eyes were, and how she hugged. The physical stuff is gone, obviously I know that, but I just can't... She was so *alive*, she was like pure energy, and I don't..." I shake my head. My eyes are stinging again. "Where did that *go*?"

"Emmy," Mum says, very softly. The kind of softly that comes before something you won't want to hear. I wipe at my eyes, my heart cantering, because I know she's going to tell me that it doesn't go anywhere, it all just stops, because Mum is practical, she's always been practical, and she's never been one for false hope. "It went into you."

I startle, my breath like a cough. "What?"

"You," she says again. "So much of Beth's love and light is in you. And I don't just mean now she's gone; I mean for such a long time, she's been giving it to you. She wanted that so much, she used to say it to me, that she wanted you to have the good bits."

"She did?"

"Yes. You have so much of the best parts of Beth in you. How much she loved you; that's for you to carry, now. To keep like a gift. Emmy, for me … the only thing that could have made losing Beth bearable is knowing how much of her is in you. I see her in your smile and your eyes." She looks, suddenly, worried. "In a good way, darling. It's not a burden. I love you for you, *as* you."

This makes me smile, even as tears are flowing freely down my face. "I know. I get it."

She puts a hand to my wet face, her eyes on mine. "I was very lucky to have my girls. And I'm still so lucky – *so* lucky – to have you."

In Wagamama, I order edamame beans and cheesecake. Mum orders steamed dumplings and ice cream. We order everything to arrive at the same time, even the desserts, insisting that it is what we want when the waitress looks baffled.

We've been talking about what might happen to The Jinks without me when Mum trails off mid-sentence, hands cupped around her green tea, and says, "I didn't ask you."

"Ask me what?"

"How you're coping," she says. "You said in the car that I hadn't asked you how you're dealing with your grief. And you're right. I haven't asked you. I'm sorry. Tell me."

I try to smile. "Not very well?"

"I'm sorry. Is seeing the therapist helping?"

"Oh, yeah. A lot. But kind of in a … separate way? That probably doesn't make sense, but it helps my head, but not the rest of my life. Like, in her office, I feel better, and then I leave, and it's like, oh yeah, Beth is still dead, and I still can't sing."

She's been nodding along as I've been talking, but she stops when I say this. "Can't sing? What do you mean?"

"Just that. I can't sing any more."

For a moment, she looks like she's about to laugh. "What are you talking about, Emmy? Of course you can sing. You have a beautiful voice."

"I haven't sung a note since Beth died," I say.

"Because you haven't wanted to?"

"Not just that. It feels like I can't. Like there's ... like, a block. In my head."

"Because of Beth."

"Well, yeah, I guess. Obviously."

Mum goes quiet, but I can tell by the way her forehead has furrowed that she's thinking, so I don't say anything, either. We sit in silence for a while, but it's the comfortable kind, until the waitress arrives with the ice cream and the edamame beans, and we both thank her.

"You know that..." Mum begins, then stops, reconsidering. "The music wasn't the problem. With Beth." She looks at me like she's waiting for me to respond. When I don't, she continues, "The singing was always the good part. That was what kept Beth going. It wasn't the fame, it was the music. She isn't ... She isn't gone because she could sing. It's OK for you to sing."

"I know," I say.

The waitress reappears, depositing cheesecake and dumplings between us. "Can I get anything else for you both?"

"No, thank you," Mum says. "This is great."

"Awesome, enjoy," she says, then leaves.

"Are you sure?" Mum says, and it takes me a second to catch up. "I know it's confusing, emotionally. The line between Beth and Lizzie."

"Not really." But I've bristled at hearing her say "Lizzie", and I know she's noticed. I push my fork into the cheesecake, watch it crumble.

"Maybe you're concentrating your anger on Lizzie," Mum says.

"I'm not."

"But Beth *was* Lizzie."

"I know that."

"Lizzie isn't the reason she died."

I open my mouth to say, again, I *know that*, but I can't. I bite my lip, concentrate on my fork.

"Being Lizzie brought a lot of joy to your sister," Mum says. Her voice has got so soft, it's almost hard to hear her against the noise of the restaurant. "There's not a clear good side and bad side. It was all Beth."

"I *know*." But I'm crying.

I feel her hand close around mine. "I'm sorry," she says. "We can stop talking about this now. But can I just ask one question?"

I nod.

"Have you been up to the loft recently?"

"The loft?" I wipe at my eyes, reaching for my water. "No. Why?" (I know why.)

"Maybe you should," she says. "It might help."

The loft.

It's part of our house that I've been pretending to myself, since Beth died, doesn't exist.

Almost every single day, I've gone into Beth's room, sometimes just to walk around, sometimes to sit on her bed, sometimes to actually sleep in there. The room is pure Beth. You'd barely know — except for a few knick-knacks here and there, maybe — that she was also Lizzie Beck.

The loft is different. The loft is Lizzie's room.

In our old house, we had a loft hatch, but it opened up to a tiny space you could barely stand in, and Beth and I were never allowed up there in case we hurt ourselves or got buried under a collapsed pile of teetering boxes. It was where we kept the Christmas decorations, that kind of thing.

The house we moved to, our current house, is bigger. Lots more space, more rooms, and a proper loft, the converted kind. Bigger, even, than the bedrooms in the house we'd left. There are even proper stairs leading up to it, instead of a pull-down ladder.

Right from the beginning, it was Lizzie's room. I don't know if it was even something that was decided, or if it just happened, but that's how it was. It's where all the Lizzie-stuff ended up, because, let me tell you, there was a *lot* of Lizzie-stuff. You know something that comes along with being in a famous girl band? Paraphernalia.

I'm talking costumes from photoshoots, gifts from fans (and brands), posters, artwork, merchandise, clothes, awards, magazines, newspapers, just about everything you could think of. Over the last few years, when her Instagram follower count hit the millions, she started getting flooded with freebies and gifts from companies wanting her to wear their make-up and model their clothes, just for a few seconds, on her account. Piles and piles of stuff, every day. Mum and I used to sort through it on weekends, sometimes while on speakerphone to Beth, and decide what to keep and what to donate to the women's shelter in town.

All of that stuff, aside from the few precious hand-picked things that Beth saved for her bedroom, went into the loft. Mum kept it really nice as well; ordered, clean, tidy. The walls hang with framed sales awards, magazine covers blown up to five times their normal size and countless photos from award shows and appearances. A collage of success. I used to like going up there to just soak it all in, the visible perks of Beth's amazing life. Lizzie. Lizzie's life.

That used to be normal, going up there. Grey, Trix, Ella and I used to spend so much of our time there together, because as well as all the stuff, there's a sofa, a TV, a stereo. We used to talk about our future lives; what it would be like when we, too, were famous.

I think a part of me wanted to believe that the room just didn't exist any more. That it disappeared along with Lizzie, because it was never real, like Lizzie was never real. Beth was real, Beth lived, Beth had her bedroom that I could still walk around in. But that loft ... that life ... how can it still exist?

87 DAYS GONE

B & E 8 & 3

"One day," I said. "I want to be famous enough to have my own fame room."

"One day," Beth said. "You'll have your own house."

"A fame house?"

"No, your house. It won't be separate when it's you. Just make sure there's a room for me, OK?"

"Obviously."

The stairs still creak on the way up.

I turn the light on, closing my eyes as I do, then opening them with a slow inhalation of ... I don't know what. Dread? Hope? Both?

It looks just like it always did. Nothing's changed. Not the colour of the rug, not the order of the sales awards, not even the smell in the air.

I stand there for a few minutes, looking around, taking in the old familiarity. I know that if I go to the filing cabinet, I'll find press clippings going all the way back to "Great British Sounds", diligently sorted by Mum into order. I tell myself to walk over there and do that, look through them, let myself remember, but I can't. Maybe future me will be able to handle that, but I can't now. Will there come a point where I can be proud again, without the pain? Without that thought in the back of my head, wondering if it had all been a trade? That if she hadn't been famous, she'd have been OK. She'd still be here, and maybe we wouldn't be in this big house, maybe I wouldn't have gone to Shona Lee, maybe there'd never have been money and success and excitement, but she'd still be here.

I hear the creak from the stairs and turn to see Mum coming into the room, her arms crossing into a tight, self-comforting hug as she does. She smiles at me, warm and sad. "How do you feel?"

If I talk, I'll cry. I shrug.

"Come here, baby," she says, something she never calls me. She steps forward, opening her arms, and hugs me close, rubbing my back. "I loved her too," she says, softly. "We all loved her."

It feels nice to cry with her instead of on my own.

When she releases me, she wipes under my eyes with her sleeves, then smiles at me. "I had a thought. About what you were saying earlier."

"Which bit?"

"How you feel like you can't sing," she says. "Or won't sing. That there's a block on it for you."

I nod.

"I thought this might help." She crosses to the other side of the room, to the filing cabinet I was just thinking about. She opens the family drawer, reaches inside — she doesn't even need to search — and pulls out what looks like a DVD in a clear plastic sleeve. She gestures to me and I follow her to the TV.

"Home videos?" I ask. The DVD has B & E, 8 & 3 written on it in thick black pen.

"Just one," she says. "I'll let you watch it on your own." She slides the DVD into the slot and fiddles with the remote, not even flinching as the screen bursts into life with a child-Beth, beaming, mid-sentence. Mum begins flicking through, obviously looking for something specific, so easily it makes me realize that she's watched this video enough that it no longer hurts. Is that what she's been doing all summer? Watching old videos? "Here," she says, pausing the video and then turning to me, holding out the remote. "Watch this as many times as you want. See how you feel."

I hesitate, glancing at the image paused on screen. Beth, aged eight, looking not into the camera but slightly away from it, laughing. "OK."

Before she leaves, she kisses me on the cheek and reminds me that she loves me. "Both of you," she adds. "Always."

It takes me a while to press play. I don't even know exactly why, but I stand there, motionless, remote in hand, staring at child-Beth's frozen laughter. Whatever I'm about to see, Mum thinks it's going to be useful, so what could it be?

Play.

"Emmy!" Beth calls through her laughter. She reaches out a hand, eyes widening with encouragement. "Come and be on camera with me! Emmy!"

Off-camera, the sound of a young child crying.

"What's wrong?" she asks. Her eyes flick to the camera. "What's wrong with her?"

"Maybe she doesn't want to be on camera, Bethie." Dad's voice, off-screen.

"Why not? Yes, she does! Emmy!"

Beth ducks out of view. When she reappears, almost a full minute later, she's carrying me, three years old, face wet with tears. Beth beams into the camera, lifting me higher, jiggling me.

"See?" she says. Toddler-me hiccups. "Tell everyone why you're crying, Emmy."

Dad's voice, amused, "Who is 'everyone'?"

"The audience!" Beth says. She grins into the camera. "Hello, you!"

The sound of my dad's laughter, drifting.

"Can't sing," toddler-me says. Whimpers it, really. Sniffling, burying my face into Beth's neck.

"You can't sing?" Beth repeats, nuzzling my head. "That's why you're crying?"

A desolate nod.

"Why can't you sing, Emmbop?"

"Can't sing like you."

"Like me?"

More tears. Another nod.

"Can you sing *with* me?" Beth has started swaying slightly from side to side, moving me with her to some imaginary beat. "Then you'll stop crying?"

"'K."

"OK? Good. I'll start and you can sing with me, OK? You ready?" I watch as she gives my tiny self a squeeze, dropping a kiss onto my wet face. She's not looking at the camera when she starts to sing, but at me, eyes holding mine, a gentle smile on her face. *"Somewhere . . . over the rainbow. . ."*

Toddler-me and sixteen-year-old me are united in this moment of watching Beth sing. Both of us with wet faces and – I don't need a mirror to know this – identical expressions of adoration. Even at eight, Beth really could sing. Raw but sweet, light and bright.

She breaks off mid-lyric. "Come on," she says, bouncing me. "You know the words. Sing with me. *And the dreams. . ."*

My little voice comes out for the first time, shaky but determined, *"That you dare to dream—"*

"Yes! See! What do they do?"

"Really do come true."

"Yeah, they do! Good job. See? You *can* sing, just like me."

Toddler-me reaches out a hand and touches her face, and she laughs, glancing back at the camera for a split second. In this moment, in the loft in a house we couldn't have imagined, my hand reacts before my head does and I press pause at exactly the right instant. I stare at the screen, blurred as it is through my tears, at my sister and me, so long ago, in a moment captured, in a moment that isn't over, that will last for ever, that I can play over and over and over again.

I look into the past, into Beth's smiling, trusting eyes, and take the gift she's giving me. On behalf of toddler-me and who I've become, I whisper, "Thank you."

I rewind carefully, then press play. On screen, Beth says, "I'll start and you can sing with me, OK? You ready?"

I close my eyes, concentrate every cell in me on the sound of her voice and nothing else, take a deep breath.

Ready.

5 YEARS GONE
Emmy

Yasmine: Hello everyone, and welcome to this week's edition of Mind and Soul! Today we're talking grief, specifically grief after suicide, so trigger warnings for that, and we're joined by singer-songwriter Emmy Beck. Welcome, Emmy.

Emmy: Hi!

Yasmine: Your debut album is doing really well on Spotify — congratulations. You must be so thrilled.

Emmy: Thank you! Yes, I am. People have been incredibly supportive; I'm very grateful.

Yasmine: I really appreciate you coming on to talk to me today. Would you like to introduce yourself and your experience with grief?

Emmy: Sure, absolutely. So, I'm Emmy Beck, and my sister was Lizzie Beck. She died by suicide about five years ago now, when I was sixteen. She was one quarter of The Jinks, and my idol. I loved her so much.

Yasmine: That must have been devastating.

Emmy: It was, yeah. Do you know what, I've practised that speech so many times. Just so I can get through it without getting choked up. And it's been *five years*. Isn't that crazy?

Yasmine: That's one of the things I wanted to talk to you about, actually. We may as well jump right in. How has your grief changed over time? Has it helped, or is it still just as painful?

Emmy: That's an interesting question, because yes, time has helped, but also, it is just as painful, but not all the time. Does that make sense? It's sort of like a chronic illness that is always there, but sometimes there'll be flare ups that are worse, but they pass. That's the best way I can describe it, I think. Really, on a fundamental level… I just *miss* her. That's it. I still want to tell her things that have happened, big and small. I still feel so sad that her life ended the way it did, and she's missed out on so much of what her life could have been. I wish I could have a day with her right now, with us both the same age. Just one day, you know. *[chokes]* Sorry.

Yasmine: Oh, God, it's OK. Please don't feel you have to apologize.

Emmy: The world she left was a pretty different place, you know? It's changed so much since she was around.

Yasmine: Like you starting your own career in music?

Emmy: I was thinking more the pandemic, but yes, that too! *[laughs]*

Yasmine: Can you tell us a little about your journey into the music industry? How much of that was influenced by Lizzie?

Emmy: Oh, a lot. All of it, probably. Both in terms of what I've done and what I haven't done, if that makes sense. Because, obviously, there were a lot of lessons to learn from what happened to Lizzie, and I almost feel like it would be disrespectful to her memory to not learn them. So I've tried to make good choices, the kind of choices that I imagine she'd have made for me. She was protective, even though she obviously made a lot of mistakes herself, I'm not going to pretend she didn't, but when it came to me, yeah, she was protective. So I think keeping that in my head has helped keep me on track.

Yasmine: What do you think is the main choice you've made, then, with that in mind?

Emmy: To take my time, probably. I've been offered opportunities over the last few years that I decided not to take because I didn't think I was ready. I wanted to finish school, make sure I was really prepared, before I started trying to make it. And just… to say no. To say when things aren't OK. Lizzie was so exploited by the industry, and everyone — including her — sort of just acted like that was normal, like just part of being a singer. But why should it be, you know? People used to talk about how Lizzie was so outspoken and confident, like she took no shit from anyone. But in reality, she wasn't ever able to really stand up for herself. Maybe that's part of why she was so out of control sometimes, because she didn't *have* any control, over anything. No agency, or anything like that. The older I get, the more I see what a toxic world it was for her. I can't make that right, but I can do my best to make sure it doesn't happen to me, which I know is what she'd want for me.

Yasmine: So what does that actually look like, in practice, for you, at this stage in your career?

Emmy: Well… *[long pause]* Sorry, I want to make sure I say this right. Listen… I end up talking about Lizzie in every interview I do. Every single one. And I know why the questions come up; I get why people are interested. But I struggled for a while with that, thinking, shouldn't this be about me and my music, not her? Have they just invited me for this interview because I'm Lizzie Beck's little sister?

And am I just another one of those people using her fame to help my own career? I thought, maybe I should refuse to answer any questions about her. But that felt wrong too. So I just try my best to make sure that I'm shutting down anything that feels wrong or exploitive, of her or me or her death.

Yasmine: Do you need to do that a lot?

Emmy: More than you'd think. Some of the questions I get asked… honestly, some of it… it's like, can you hear yourself? One asked me if I blamed Lizzie for my parents' divorce. And when I was like, no, of course not, why would I, they said, it ruined your life, didn't it? Her killing herself? Just like that, those words.

Yasmine: Wow.

Emmy: Right? And they're just doing it for a reaction; I know they are. So I make sure I don't give them one, I just stay calm and say that it's inappropriate, and then they cut the whole thing out of the final interview anyway. It's funny; I said earlier how much the world has changed since she was around, but some things really haven't.

Yasmine: Can I apologize on behalf of interviewers everywhere?

Emmy: [laughs] Thank you, but you don't need to. It's good to be able to talk about it like this, though. I think being transparent about it all is a good thing, too. I'm grateful for the opportunity to do that. But… could we maybe get back to grief?

Yasmine: Oh yes, of course. Could you talk a little about how you feel being twenty-one? The same age Lizzie was when she died? Has that changed anything for you?

Emmy: Yeah, it has. It was such a turning point for me. I'd been so scared of it for so long, but now I'm here, it's a strange kind of relief? I don't know if I can describe it, really. I don't think relief is the right word. But I think I breathe a little easier than I used to.

Yasmine: That's really interesting. Do you wish you could tell your earlier self that? That it would get better?

Emmy: No, because she wouldn't have listened, and that's OK. That period of relentless grief was so awful, but necessary. You can't hide from it or skip past it, you just have to live through it.

Yasmine: So, on that note, what would be your advice, or your message, to anyone going through a similar experience? Maybe someone at the start of it?

Emmy: Just that… It does get easier. Better isn't quite the right word, but easier, yes. The pain does… settle, if that makes sense. You never forget, not ever, but it becomes something you can… sort of… carry with you, instead of being buried by. And you can share your grief with other people, that's important. Not to keep it inside, but to talk to the people you trust about how you're feeling. And, also, I think it's important to allow yourself to focus on what you had, as well as what you lost. For a while, I found it difficult to think about what a huge part of my life Beth was, in every way — Lizzie, sorry — because it was a direct contrast to what a… well, a huge gaping void that she left, really. But as time went on, I could think about that as something good; like her legacy, in a way. Not the fame, but just her.

I wouldn't be who I was if I hadn't had her as my older sister, and that's a really special thing. An amazing thing. I was so, so lucky to be her sister, and that doesn't stop being true because we lost her too early. *[pause] [laughing]* Sorry, you just asked for one thing, didn't you?

Yasmine: Oh, don't apologize! That was lovely. You're also carrying on that legacy, you know. Is that something you feel aware of?

Emmy: You mean, being the second Beck?

Yasmine: Yes.

Emmy: I hadn't really thought about it in quite that way, but yeah, that's quite nice, isn't it? I hope I'm making her proud.

THINGS I AM NOT

a superstar

wild

rich

Beth

THINGS I AM

older
wiser
happy
Emmy

ACKNOWLEDGEMENTS

First and foremost, thanks to Non Pratt, my wonderful editor, for seeing what this book could be long before it got there, and for championing both Emmy and me every step of the way.

Thank you to the whole team at Walker Books for the lovely welcome and for making this book what it is, with a particular shout out to Jamie Hammond for the absolutely gorgeous cover and Rebecca J Hall, who deserves some kind of typesetting medal for this work of literal art.

Claire Wilson and the team at RCW, the agent and agency dreams are made of.

Lorna Fraser at the Samaritans' Media Advisory Service. I'm so grateful for your time, patience and invaluable advice.

Yasmin Rahman, for being exactly what this book needed in its early days. I don't know what magic you pulled to get me to show you such an early draft, but I'm so glad you did.

Nick Lloyd, for the hardest lesson I ever learned and everything good that came before it, and to those who were there to share umbrellas during the worst storm imaginable. I hope there is some truth of that experience in the pages of this book.

My sister Anna, who is the reason all my fictional big sisters are so idolised by their fictional little sisters. I couldn't imagine it any other way.

The rest of my family – the Barnards, the Phillipses, the Patels, the Tomczaks, the Mays, the Curls. Rw'yn dy garu di.

My friends, with a special glass raised to Tracy, Holly, Tanya and Rosemary; lights, shoulders, sounding boards, bearers of wisdom and a damn good time, all at once.

Lora, for everything, but especially for the penguins.

Tom. Thank you for being there through every page.

And thank you to the Samaritans. You wonderful, wonderful people.

Thank you.

RESOURCES

SAMARITANS
www.samaritans.org

116 123

A free helpline available 24 hours a day, seven days a week, for anyone struggling with emotional distress in the UK and Ireland. They can also be reached via email: jo@samaritans.org

CRUSE
www.cruse.org.uk

Cruse provides bereavement support within the UK. Their free helpline number is 0808 808 1677. They also have a chat function on their website.

PAPYRUS
www.papyrus-uk.org

PAPYRUS UK is a charity for the prevention of young suicide (under 35) in the UK. They operate HOPELINEUK, which provides confidential suicide prevention advice. They are open 9am–midnight every day: 0800 068 4141.

SHOUT

www.giveusashout.org

Shout offers free, 24/7 text messaging support for young people in the UK. If you need someone to talk to about how you're feeling, text YM to 85258.

WINSTON'S WISH

www.winstonswish.org

Winston's Wish charity supports bereaved children, young people, families and professionals. Their freephone helpline 08088 020 021 is available 8am-8pm Monday to Friday.

Sara Barnard is a bestselling author of six novels for young adults. Her debut *Beautiful Broken Things* was a Zoella Bookclub pick and she went on to win the YA Book Prize with her third novel, *Goodbye, Perfect*. *Where the Light Goes* is her first novel with Walker Books.

Enjoyed *Where the Light Goes*?

We'd love to hear your thoughts.

🐦 @saramegan
@WalkerBooksYA

📷 @saramegan87
@WalkerBooksYA